D1809278

The author came to live in South West France in 2005. Discovering the history of the local region rekindled her interest in alternative theories of human spiritual evolution and resulted in writing this book as a way to formulate her ideas.

This book is dedicated to Mary Jean Wood

Helen Frindle

THE SENTIENT SHIELD

AUSTIN MACAULEY PUBLISHERS™

LONDON • CAMBRIDGE • NEW YORK • SHARJAH

A CIP catalogue record for this title is available from the British Library.

ISBN 9781788786270 (Paperback)
ISBN 9781788786287 (Hardback)
ISBN 9781788786294 (E-Book)

www.austinmacauley.com

First Published (2018)
Austin Macauley Publishers Ltd
25 Canada Square
Canary Wharf
London
E14 5LQ

I would like to thank the following people:

Gill Doward for her faith in me as a writer and for rescuing my 'hanging particples' and 'split infinitives'.

Polly Fairweather for introducing me to fascinating locations in South West France for inspiration.

David Monks for 'listening' to my 'ramblings'!

My husband, Roger Evans, for all the love, support and encouragement he has given me over many years.

Lastly, to Austin Macauley Publishers for actually reading my manuscript and giving me this chance to publish.

The Sentient Seal

The Sentient Seal rests deep beneath the earth, buried in a remote part of south west France. The leaves, rustling in the autumn sunshine float and flutter to the ground on the surface above. A golden light, an army of sun rays with golden heads, waits, glowing across the surrounding valleys.

The Seal has remained in its hiding place since the 13th Century. It was given into the guardianship of a group of women who had gathered together in a small community for survival. Either cast off by their men or waiting for them to return from the wars, they tended their gardens and fed and healed the poor in the surrounding countryside.

There was no leader as they lived in mutual support and love of each other. All decisions on the management and maintenance of the garden, the source of their life, were made together. The garden was tended day by day, year in year out. It talked to the women and together they evolved.

In the course of the life of the community, a small chapel with a cemetery was built. The women lived in huts, shacks, small cubicles for individual privacy and owned few possessions.

From today's perspective, their life looks harsh, but in its simplicity it held a key to eternity, not material but spiritual.

The Seal was carried to this community by a specially selected soldier who searched for a resting place where it would be protected. He had been instructed to move it from its original resting place because its whereabouts had become known.

There was another group of men, warriors of mixed race and species in pursuit of the Seal.

The Seal was placed with this particular community because it did not attract attention to itself. It was not a church or a sacred site, nor did it carry mythical legends. It was just a small *community in a remote rural setting which would be passed by. The trees surrounding the community completely concealed its existence from travellers on the tracks in the region.*

After the Seal was buried, guardian orbs were positioned high above the Earth to the East and West of the site to act as watchtowers, until the time came when it would be retrieved, activated and would provide the information it was destined to do along with the other seals.

Twelve Seals, the Sentient Shield, were hidden across the surface of the planet, waiting.

Preface

The storyline through this book concerns a journey towards an event called the Alignment; a specific time in the evolution of Earth's history where Earth plays a pivotal part in the overall process of evolution of the Universe. At the point of Alignment, Earth—and the Universe of which it is part—is enabled to ascend to a higher dimension. From a three-dimensional existence, 3D, it reaches through 4D to 5D, ascension being a higher level of spiritual and emotional development. A great deal depends on Earth, and importantly, the spiritual awareness of its population at that time as to whether ascension can be achieved.

Maddy, the central character, represents that which is present in us all and is symbolic of the awakening of spiritual consciousness.

This is a fiction in which I have brought together some threads of highly speculative sources, most of which have been challenged by the scientific community since the 1950s.

I must also point out that I am not a historian, archaeologist, physicist or an expert in the multifarious scientific professions that may be referred to in this book. I repeat: it is a work of fiction. However, I have given some references below in order to clarify some of the terms used to describe events and states of existence in order to give the reader the opportunity to pursue suppositions of his or her own interest, should he/she feel moved to do so.

Visitors from Outer Space

Since the 1950s, according to the writing of certain authors such as Erich von Däniken and Zecharia Sitchin, Earth has been visited by extra-terrestrial beings whose technological capabilities are far beyond even those we have today.

These visitors may have been responsible for the construction of monuments, such as the Pyramids in Egypt; monolithic structures, such as Stonehenge; and inexplicable phenomena, such as those which can only be viewed from the air, that of the Nazca Lines in Peru. For example, "The thirty seven mile long by one mile wide, Nazca Lines are criss-crossed by geometrically-arranged lines according to astronomical plans," writes Erich von Däniken and he questions, "what purpose would they serve other than as a landing guide for aircraft." [1]

"Classical archaeology does not admit that the pre-Inca people could have had a perfect surveying technique. And the theory that aircraft could have existed in antiquity is sheer humbug to them."

The Anunnaki and the Planet Nibiru

Zecharia Sitchin was versed in Hebrew, Semitic and European languages, the Bible, history and archaeology of the near east, and was also able to read and understand Sumerian. He wrote many books based on his translations of the cuneiform images that can be found on ancient monuments. Many of them depict what could be interpreted as a plan of our solar system indicating nine planets. He proposed an explanation for our human origins that involves ancient astronauts. [2]

"…(he) attributed the creation of the ancient Sumerian culture to the Anunnaki which he stated was a race of extra-terrestrials from a planet beyond Neptune called Nibiru. He believed this hypothetical planet of Nibiru to be in an elongated, elliptical orbit in the Earth's own Solar System, asserting that Sumerian mythology reflects this."

[1]Chariots of the Gods, Erik von Däniken
[2]The 12th Planet, Zecharia Sitchin

Although he sold millions of copies of his books worldwide his ideas have been rejected by scientists and academics…

"(his) ideas have been rejected by … (those) who dismiss his work as pseudo-science and pseudo-history. His work had been criticised for flawed methodology and mistranslations of ancient texts as well as for incorrect astronomical and scientific claims…"

However recent discoveries are now beginning to tie in with his theories…[3]

"…Researchers have found evidence suggesting there may be a 'Planet X' deep in the Solar System. This hypothetical Neptune-sized planet orbits our sun in a highly elongated orbit far beyond Pluto. The object, which the researchers have nicknamed 'Planet Nine', could have a mass about 10 times that of Earth and orbit about 20 times farther from the sun on average than Neptune. It may take between 10,000 and 20,000 Earth years to make one full orbit around the sun."

"The possibility of a new planet is certainly an exciting one for me as a planetary scientist and for all of us," said Jim Green, director of NASA's Planetary Science Division. "This is not, however, the detection or discovery of a new planet. It's too early to say with certainty there's a so-called Planet X. What we're seeing is an early prediction based on modelling from limited observations. It's the start of a process that could lead to an exciting result."

According to Zitchin's translations of the Sumerian cuneiform texts, which date back to approximately 6000 years, Nibiru takes 3,600 years to complete one orbital journey. It can be imagined that the gravitational effects caused by the size of this planet could create huge problems for the orbits of other planets when it moves closer to the inner solar system. Recent speculation suggests that this planet is moving towards the inner solar system and will approach the vicinity of Earth relatively soon.

---

[3]Wikipedia, NASA

Zitchin further relates that about 450,000 years ago, a deposed ruler of the Anunnaki on Nibiru found refuge on Earth. Discovering that the Earth had an abundance of gold, he and his followers began to mine for it. They needed gold to repair Nibiru's deteriorating atmosphere.

Due to the difficulties that the Anunnaki experienced working in the Earth's atmosphere, they decided to genetically engineer the indigenous population of Earth, combining its DNA with their own, thus creating a race of beings to do the mining for them. This genetically engineered race was homo sapiens—us. Zitchin correlates this with the stories of the first books of the Bible and other histories of ancient cultures.[4]

To speculate, if in the foreseeable future the existence of another planet is confirmed, might this give rise to a complete review of our planet's origins and the evolution of ourselves; the rewriting of our history books and the basis of religions?

Pleiadians

That the Anunnaki may not have been the only extra-terrestrial visitors to Earth and contributed to the creation of our species is also addressed in other literature, raising questions as to the inheritance of our DNA and the possibility that the Anunnaki may also be descendants of other visitors.

The Pleiadians, it is alleged, were our ancestors[5]; they came to Earth after exploring star systems, searching for planets which they could colonise; their own planet, Lyra, was dying. They colonised Earth for a time and have come and gone throughout our planet's history.

Others colonised the Pleiades, which is located in the constellation of Taurus. Alcyon is the central star of the Pleiades. Our solar system, along with others, orbits Alcyon on a wider orbit.

The technology possessed by the Pleiadians has made it possible for them to travel anywhere in our universe. They share many similarities with us but are more emotionally and spiritually evolved.

---

[4]Babylonian, Assyrian, Egyptian, Greek, Roman
[5]Pleiadian Perspectives on Human Evolution, Amorah Quan Yin

Photon Belt

In 1961, a photon belt encircling the Pleiades was discovered. Our sun orbits the Pleiades once every 25,860 years and reaches the midpoint of the belt every 12,500 years and takes approximately 2000 years to cross it. This particular cycle is nestled within a number of greater cycles. In 1962, we entered the sphere of influence of this photon belt.

The energy of the photon belt that Earth is passing through is of a spiritual nature, not physical. The 10,500 years of darkness, between the 2000 year periods of light, afford opportunities for human spiritual evolution.

Precession of the Equinoxes

One orbit of the Earth takes 365 days (366 in a leap year) which gives us one year and our seasons. The Earth itself rotates which gives us 24 hours—one day.

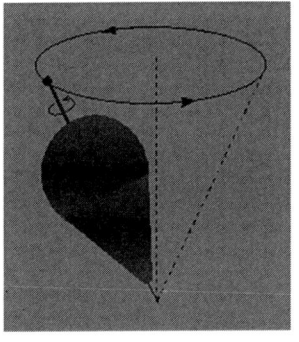

- The Earth's axis rotates (precesses) just as a spinning top does. The period of precession is about 26,000 years.
- Therefore, the North Celestial Pole will not always be pointing towards the same star field.
- Precession is caused by the gravitational pull of the Sun and the Moon on the Earth.[6]

Hence for example references in non-scientific literature to the coming of the 'Age of Aquarius'. Current precession indicates that the Earth is moving from the constellation of Pisces to the view of the constellation of Aquarius. This gradual movement into the new precessional cycle is said to have begun around the millenium.

---

[6]Wikipedia, Precession

In this book, I have speculated that completion of the precessional cycle and moving into a new cycle; entry into the Photon belt, and the approach of Nibiru are all happening at this time; hence why I have referred to it all as the Alignment.

Quantum mechanics (also known as quantum physics or theory):

…is a branch of physics; a theory of nature at subatomic level. Classical physics deals with atoms that can be perceived physically. So at quantum level, sub atomic, the physical is divided into particle and waves and can be described as energies. The precise measurement of these energies is expressed by 'probabilities' of position and viewed as unpredictable as to eventual outcome. Thus the nature of reality comes into question and suppositions that there are multiple dimensions; that there might be multiple versions of the Earth and of ourselves, evolving in differing potential probabilities.

It could also be suggested that quantum theory can be applied to explain many biological and physical phenomena that may be related to bodily function but cannot be proven.

The Nature of the Physical Body (DNA and Cellular Structure)

If existence is fundamentally not physical but a matter of particles and waves, energies, we as beings consisting of billions of particles are subject to the subtleties of the energies and frequencies in which we exist.

According to Russian researchers[7], western scientific research is interested in only the 10% of our DNA that is used for building our bodies; the other 90%, they have designated 'junk' DNA. The Russian researchers, however, convinced that nature was not wasteful, joined linguists and geneticists in a venture to explore the so called 'junk DNA'.

Their research explains phenomena such as clairvoyance, intuition, spontaneous and remote acts of healing, self-healing, affirmation techniques, unusual light/auras around people, the

---

[7]Scientists Prove DNA Can Be Reprogrammed by Words and Frequencies, Grazyna Fosar and Franz Bludorf

mind's influence on weather patterns and much more. They found that the genetic code follows the same rules as all human languages. They compared the rules of syntax, semantics and the basic rules of grammar and found that the alkalines of our DNA follow a regular grammar and have set rules just like our languages. The vibrational behaviour of DNA was also explored and experiment proved that living tissue reacted to words and sentences of human language, if the proper frequencies are being used, proving what esoteric and spiritual teachers have always known: that our body is programmable by language, words and thought.

The Russian scientists further discuss the process of hyper communication between entirely different areas in the universe, information transmitted outside space and time, and how this is most effective in a state of relaxation. Remote healing, telepathy or 'remote sensing' (intuition) could thus be explained.

I have used the above references to Quantum Mechanics and DNA to allow my characters to appear and disappear in different time lines and dimensions.

Religion

Religion has always been based on unquestioning belief and in all religions there is an understanding of reincarnation and an afterlife.

Individually, we all have our beliefs about the nature of our existence and its limitations. The only certainty we have is that we are going to die; we shed our mortal, physical existence. It could be suggested that we create a belief system in order to comfort ourselves that there is some purpose to our existence.

In the past centuries Science, in its quest for proof—answers to everything—has dominated western thought and in doing so, questioned our belief systems; we have been displaced from the nature of our emotional and spiritual existence. How does one prove that God exists?

Now with scientific explanations as to the nature of our existence, with the difficulties of measuring this with precision, perhaps it opens a new and refreshing debate as to the nature of belief systems.

Part I

Sudden Light

I have been here before,
But when or how I cannot tell:
I know the grass beyond the door,
The sweet keen smell,
The sighing sound, the lights around the shore.
You have been mine before,
How long ago I may not know:
But just when at that swallow's soar
Your neck turned so,
Some veil did fall – I knew it all of yore.
Has this been thus before?
And shall not thus time's eddying flight
Still with our lives our love restore
In death's despite,
And day and night yield one delight once more?

– Dante Gabriel Rossetti

Chapter 1
The Return
(France, 21st Century)

Maddy stepped out onto the balcony and the landscape fell away before her, it was breathtaking. The heat from the late afternoon sun shimmered over the patchwork of vineyards and woodland, covering the curves of the valleys.

Her friend Helen was equally taken by the view.

"It's stunning! I can understand why Colin wanted you to come and see it for yourself. Is he looking at it as a holiday home because it's very different from where you usually go?"

"You're right. South of Spain or France—sun, sea and sand up until now—mainly while the children were growing up. It is strange, something obviously struck him about this place."

"How did he find it?"

"An old friend, a colleague he had worked with, Chris, got caught up in some venture since he retired. It seems there were a number of people involved who had bought it between them, Chris included. Unfortunately, they all fell out, almost immediately after they had bought the place and it had to be put up for sale. Colin came out with Chris for a weekend to help him do some minor repairs and tidy the garden up at the time it was put on the market."

"So, are you thinking of buying it?"

"Well, that's why I am here. I wasn't keen when he put it to me. After all, we have only just moved out to the country after he retired, and that took a lot of effort. The thought of setting up another house, especially in a foreign country, did not exactly set me alight with enthusiasm. But something captured Colin's imagination. Looking around, it was probably the garden and the setting even though it looks pretty wild. It is fantastic, the view, the air—incredible. Anyway, he said he wasn't going to influence me, and that I should come out by myself and see what I thought."

"So…?"

"Well, it's absolutely beautiful, everything; the house, the whole region."

Turning to Helen she said,

"I know you are going to think what I am about to say is strange, but it's as if I have been here before."

***

Maddy Jameson and her husband, Colin, lived in a small village in Hertfordshire, not far from Bishop's Stortford. In fact, it was the village where they had both grown up and where both sets of parents still lived. Until fairly recently, they had been living and working in a suburb of London. Maddy was a primary school teacher in one of the city schools, and Colin a commodity trader on the stock exchange. Maddy, now 56 years old, had decided to take early retirement a couple of years ago as Colin, then 65, had retired. With three children now married, they were grandparents to four lovely grandchildren.

Both were enjoying their retirement, Colin following all the rugby and football matches and playing golf on a weekly basis. Maddy was not interested in sports other than an annual keenness for tennis when Wimbledon came round. She had developed a love for gardening and was enjoying planning and working in the small garden that went with the country house they had bought. Neither she nor Colin had had the opportunity to garden before as the house they had lived in in London had a small patch of concrete at the back, a patio surrounded by small beds in which they had put some bushes and flowers.

Recently a sort of lassitude had come over Maddy. She put it down to having settled into retirement. After two years, the initial excitement of freedom from the routine of work had worn off. It was as if she needed a challenge to add some adrenalin to her life.

At 56 she was active. Of medium height, she had light brown hair which developed blonde streaks on holidays in the sun. In figure, she was rather plump now which she blamed on the fact of having had three children. She had found it difficult to shift the extra weight gained during pregnancy and it had built up further over the years. Her father always referred to her as mousy but she was not unattractive and having been told that when she smiled her face lit up, it followed that she smiled probably more often than events required. Her most striking feature was her eyes, which were a bright blue, the colour of lapis lazuli.

Maddy and Colin had been married for 35 years. They first met when Colin's parents had moved to the village when he was in his teens. In the 1960s, everybody knew everybody else in small villages and it was not long before Colin got to know all the other teenagers. Attending the monthly village dance, he met Maddy and they struck up a friendship which had eventually resulted in their marrying when she was 21 and he 22. Both sets of parents were delighted; Maddy's parents, Madeleine and Tom Gill, had settled in the village after the war not far from her grandparents, whose family had been inhabitants of the village for centuries. Tom's father, Jack, had been very proud of his long ancestral history.

Maddy thought that her life was average and uneventful compared to some friends but then would reason with herself that that could be said about anyone's life. Recently, her father had died and she was surprised at the tremendous sense of loss she had felt at the time. It was this tragedy which had, perhaps, contributed to her feelings of lethargy that had developed over the past few weeks.

It was just a few weeks ago that Colin had returned from playing golf with an old friend of his, Chris, and had told her about the house on the border between France and Spain in the Pyrenees. Subsequently, he had disappeared for a long weekend with Chris to help him tidy up that house and garden as it was going to be sold. At the time she had not thought much about it other than realising how much she enjoyed the time on her own whilst he was away.

On his return from Spain, however, Colin had talked incessantly about the house eulogising about the scenery and idyllic feel about the place to the point where she had felt herself getting increasingly irritated, mainly because he began talking about possibly buying it. It was not because they could not afford it;

they were very comfortable, both had good pensions and considerable savings. Maddy had also inherited a substantial sum from her father's estate. However she was very aware, even more so than Colin, having moved house relatively recently, of the effort required to set up another new house. Considering buying a house in another country made her envision the struggle of dealing with people in another language. Neither she nor Colin was fluent in Spanish or French.

Eventually Colin had persuaded her to go out to Spain with a friend and to have a short holiday and look at the place. Hence, Maddy got in touch with Helen who was a school friend whom she had first met when they were eleven years old. They had kept in touch with each other all this time.

Maddy and Helen were opposites in all things. Where Maddy was academic, Helen, being dyslexic, had struggled through school but had excelled at sport and had always been an avid tennis player. She was currently the chairperson of her local tennis club. Helen was also very down to earth, had nine grandchildren and was totally immersed in the domesticity of her family life, babysitting and cooking vast lunches each Sunday for them all. Although Maddy loved her children and grandchildren, she, however, was not caught up in the same kind of life. She saw her family regularly but not necessarily each week; in fact it was more the opposite, her children would go weeks, sometimes months without seeing her. However, they would all get together at Christmas and Easter and these were special occasions.

Despite their differences, Maddy and Helen had remained firm friends over the years and had marvelled many times at the closeness they felt with each other. Neither had sisters, only brothers, and their friendship had filled this role for each other.

***

It was early in May and Maddy and Helen had spent the first few days of their trip in Barcelona touring the city and art galleries. Both were very interested in art and architecture and had loved the Gaudi influence in the city, especially La Sagrada Familiale and its fascinating gargoyles, making it look like an over iced wedding cake. They also took a journey to Figueres to see the Salvador Dali museum. Maddy was determined to make the most of her weekend away and not waste it entirely on Colin's enthusiasm for the house in the mountains.

On the day of the house visitation, they hired a car for a couple of days, a blue Peugeot, and drove up through the valleys, higher and higher, until they reached the town nearest to the village where the house was located. They had booked rooms in the town's largest hotel for a couple of nights, in order to have a chance to drive around the surrounding countryside. Having booked into the hotel, they unpacked and had a light lunch in the Hotel's restaurant. They met the local estate agent and, together, as directed by her, they drove up to the property.

The house 'La Borda', the local estate agent had informed her, had been renovated some few years ago. The builders had done a good job restoring the original features of a mountain chalet. There were a great many beams that had been resurrected from the barns that surrounded it and used in the renovation to give the building an ambience of permanence.

The entrance to the ground floor was on the side of the building through wood-framed, double-glazed doors. She thought of the winters in the mountains which were bound to be icy and probably with deep snow. The doorway led to a large room, obviously the living area, with the kitchen on the right hand side. The kitchen was outfitted with very modern kitchen units, the colour of sage, with a free standing island dividing the kitchen from a sitting area. In the corner, there was a wood burner; Maddy noticed a log pile on the left of the entrance as she came in.

Through into the interior, there was a small toilet on the left and a beautiful wooden staircase leading up to the roof space which was completely open from one end to the other. It had a wooden planked floor and Maddy thought of how useful it would be to store things; it also offered the possibility of putting a settee or sofa bed up there making it into a cosy alternative sitting room.

Somebody around here must be a master carpenter, thought Maddy to herself as the joinery of the whole house struck her as having been carefully crafted. Down the stairs and to the right, an archway led to a small lobby with a door to a large double bedroom on the right and a good-sized spare room on the left. There was a bathroom between the bedrooms.

Where there were plaster walls, everywhere had been given a wash of a very pale blush paint which with the sun shining through the windows gave the interior a warm glow. To Maddy it felt as if she was wrapped in a soft blanket, the whole place seeped through her whole being.

Returning to the entrance and standing shielded from the sun under the covered terrace, Helen asked her what she wanted to do now. They had been round the inside of the house quite thoroughly, both exclaiming at the quality of the workmanship. Maddy was casting her eyes over the surrounding garden and out to the valleys which stretched deeply down in front of her.

"Let's take a walk around the garden and see how far the boundaries extend."

The estate agent was sitting on the terrace and, turning to them, she pointed out where the boundaries were marked by white boulders. She told them that the easiest way down was by the swimming pool which sat on the first terrace.

Helen and Maddy crossed the gravel in front of the house and went down the steps to the pool which was enclosed behind a high wall with a building on one side which housed the machinery for the pool, a changing room, shower and sauna.

The pool looked very inviting despite the fact that it was early May. The sun was shining down hotly and Maddy took off her cardigan and rolled up her blouse sleeves.

"It's a pity we don't have swimming costumes with us," Helen said, "it's really hot! I wonder how warm the water is."

"Not very," replied Helen as she knelt down and swished her hand around in the water.

They walked around the pool and out through the gate on the other side and found themselves looking down on some terraces. There were some very old trees, straggled above the terraces which were completely overgrown with weeds and brambles. They continued down the side of the terraces and found themselves on a low stretch of meadow, down the sides of which were some fig and olive trees. The fig trees were full of the first signs of fruit.

They saw the white boulders that marked the boundary and as they walked along it and were about to turn up the side of the property, they noticed a foot path that ran parallel to it. As they turned, a man appeared; obviously a seasoned rambler with his rucksack and walking stick. He had a straw hat to shield his face from the sun.

"*Buena dia…*"

"Oh…*Buena dia*," chorused Maddy and Helen, hesitantly.

"Ah, you are English or…" he said.

"English, I suppose it is fairly obvious…" replied Maddy.

"Are you looking at the house? I thought it had been sold some time ago?"

Maddy wondered how much she should say to this stranger. "Do you live around here?"

"Not any more, though I come and go frequently. I have friends who live in the area. I come here to walk through the valleys. It a favourite place of mine."

"What's it like around here? The people and the villages, I mean," asked Maddy.

"On the whole friendly, although there are some who are not very keen on strangers coming to live in the area. Many of the houses and small villages have been revived owing to the influx of foreigners moving in as the local youth have moved away to the cities. It's very rural and quiet here, not much social life for younger families."

"Oh, well that sounds encouraging in a way. Do you know anything about the history of this house? It looks quite old."

"Only, that it has been renovated. Before that it had been derelict for centuries, by all accounts, but in the ownership of a family that had moved towards the coast. The Old Man of the family returned shortly before the Second World War and began renovating the place. He tried to get his family to take some interest in it but it did not work out. He died shortly after the war. A couple of years ago a local builder bought it off the family and renovated it."

"Interesting," murmured Helen, "they certainly have done a good job on the renovation."

"Anyway, I might see you again if you decide to take it, as I pass here from time to time. I had better be on my way as the sun is going down and I have quite a walk in front of me and want to get back before it gets dark. You can easily get lost around here. Good day."

Although he spoke English, he had a distinguished accent. Both Maddy and Helen discussed between themselves that it was difficult to place where he might have been from originally. The encounter left her with an odd feeling.

As she and Helen walked up to the house, the early evening sun made her feel very mellow and she realised that she had made up her mind. Having done so, it seemed as if a weight had lifted off her.

***

Looking back across the valley, Malachi paused and watched as the blue Peugeot wound its way up the track towards the main road that led back into the village. Turning he smiled to himself knowing that the task of the moment had been fulfilled.

***

Chapter 2
The Escape
(Region Comtes de Foix, Pyrenees, 13th Century)

Tomas Lamberte had been sent to collect his niece, Magdalena, or Malena as the family knew her, his brother's only child, and told to take her to a remote village in the Pyrenees within a region ruled over by the Comtes de Foix. He was to hide her away out of the reach of certain political and religious factions which were wiping out what they considered heretical movements.

Tomas had been a Knight Templar of the '*Ordre du Temple*' or 'The Poor Fellow-Soldiers of Christ and of the Temple of Solomon' as it was more formally known. Originally the Order had been formed by the Church as a Christian military order to provide warriors for the Crusades. However their interests developed beyond fighting into banking, commercial activities and to the acquisition of lands.

King Philip IV of France became nervous of the Knights Templar because he was greatly in debt to them and, more so, because they had their eyes on the Languedoc which was a province of the Kingdom of France. Seeing that the Knights and soldiers returning from the Holy Land were becoming a threatening mercenary force fighting for whoever paid the highest price, he initiated a campaign against them accusing them of heresy which eventually resulted in the destruction of the Order and its members being burned at the stake.

When the Church and the King turned against the Order, Tomas Lamberte, disillusioned, turned to working as a mercenary soldier for the noble landowners in their fight against the King and Church's drive to acquire more and more land. Moving from place to place in disguise, he had succeeded so far in escaping imprisonment, torture and the stake.

However, there was an even more sinister plot underlying the King and Church's action; in particular that of the Church's. It was because of this that Tomas had to remove his niece as quickly as possible to a place of safety.

Tomas was also a member of an obscure Order called '*the Cloister*'. *The Cloister* was an ancient order Tomas knew very little about, other than the fact that as the eldest son he had been initiated into it by his father when he was 14 years old. He had been taken to a temple beneath a Chateau at Perpignan and had sworn allegiance to its mysteries. It had been impressed on him that he held a mission in his life that superseded any orders issued by any other organisation and that he might be called on to act for the Order should the need arise.

It was the Steward of the Order who had told him that his younger brother Raymond, Malena's father, had been imprisoned in Toulouse and was being interrogated by the Inquisition. He had ordered Tomas to collect Malena and take her to the designated hiding place in the Pyrenees, which unlike the neighbouring province of Languedoc, was an independent fiefdom and not under the control of the Kingdom of France.

Tomas and Raymond were *Ecuyer*, i.e. untitled nobles, of the House of Toulouse which had been destroyed by a Papal Crusade against Catharism, a Christian sect considered heretical, that had grown in popularity and had posed a threat to the King and the established Church. The House of Toulouse was sympathetic to the Cathars and after the campaign the land belonging to the House of Toulouse was confiscated and annexed to France. The family had scattered but a few had retreated to Saint Gilles, the birthplace of their ancestor Count Raymond VI (1156–1222), where Tomas and Raymond were later born and where he thought he would find Malena.

Even though the Cathars had been successfully destroyed, King Philip along with the Pope, still nervous, continued their relentless persecution of all groups they considered heretical. It had become known to the local populace that Tomas and Raymond's family, the Lambertes de St Gilles, was disposed towards the Cathars. Tomas suspected that someone had betrayed his family in order to save themselves from the terrors of the Inquisition.

The Steward had told him that his brother and family had disappeared and been taken by an army employed by King Philip. Talking to the locals Tomas discovered that the army were distinctive by their clothing; tabards of black and white with a red cross. A young peasant girl, Helene, had approached him apprehensively and told him that Malena had been taken by the girl's family and hidden in their hut on the outskirts of the village.

When Tomas found Malena, she was distraught due to the separation from her father. They prepared to leave the village as soon as they could. The family who had been hiding Malena asked if they could accompany them because they feared for their lives as it was sure to be discovered that they had helped Malena escape. They told him that their daughter, Helene, had been taken in by the Chateau as a playmate for Malena. Later Helene had become her maid and the family had treated the girl well. It was her loyalty to them that had made Helene take Malena into her parents' house in hiding. The parents, Luc and Faustine, were elderly and there was a brother Jean who, Tomas judged, was in his late teens.

Tomas decided to take them along, as he felt that as a larger group they would attract less attention and provide more protection. Jean's strength as a young man would undoubtedly be of assistance as they travelled. The parents were not going to find it easy as they had a long journey across difficult terrain into the mountains, where they would be using ancient shepherds' trails completely away from the tracks used by locals or travellers.

Malena was the last female of their branch of the House of Toulouse. She carried a noble bloodline that dated back many centuries, in fact many centuries BC, and it was the mission of the Order to protect what was associated with it. It had been guarded for some 8500 years. Tomas had been told to believe that her future husband was predestined for her to meet, to carry the bloodline on. He found this difficult to comprehend and had not questioned it at the time. He was intent on just carrying out the order to rescue her. His job, as he saw it, had been drummed into him by the Order.

It had taken several months for the party to reach their destination. The Steward had told him that a Guide would appear from time to time to direct them to their destination. The man had appeared and disappeared, mysteriously, several times on their journey and eventually, Tomas and the party arrived at a commune of women situated on the outskirts of a small village in a remote mountainous area. It was a place known to the Order as a Sanctuary.

***

Malena was sitting on the stone step of the well dwelling on the changes she had had to endure in the past year. It was early morning on a sunny day in early spring. The first flowers were forcing their way up from their winter sleep. Clusters of snow-drops, celandine and violets lit up the slumbering shadows beneath the hedges. The trees were gently moving in the breeze, throwing a kaleidoscope of shade and light on the grass and the shingle of the pathway leading to the commune's meeting house glistened like the most costly jewels.

Musing, she recalled how her uncle had brought her to the commune. It had been a long and arduous journey; first along the coastal plain on the pilgrims' routes from St. Gilles and then climbing for a long time through and over the mountains to this remote village, in the depth of a valley, below the highest peaks. They had travelled for many days and nights, stopping often and taking refuge wherever they could. Luckily, the locals on route had been used to pilgrims and had offered them broth and hard bread. The people were poor but always hospitable and the fare given to them though so basic had sustained them after travelling all day.

The mercenary military life Tomas had recently been forced into, had made him aware of the paths of the Pyrenees hidden in the foothills and mountains. They had travelled most of their journey on tracks and paths hidden to even the most remote pop-ulations they had passed on their route.

Overnight, they had slept wherever they found shelter; in barns, haystacks and in '*les capitelles*', shelters for shepherds, dome like structures constructed of piled up stones on tracks that shepherds had followed for centuries. The shepherd's seasonal migration of their flocks of sheep to the milder climate of Catalonia had woven a maze of pathways throughout the mountain range.

The group had passed through a town and then a village to arrive at the commune. It had been a twenty minute walk from the village, in the centre of which stood a church. Malena had noticed a communal oven and several women passing in and out and sitting on the bench outside obviously waiting for their bread to bake.

The town was much further away and had a large market place with vendors selling a variety of basic items: spices, vegetables, chickens and cheese, and implements and tools for working the land.

When they arrived at the commune, they had been met by an old lady who greeted Tomas warmly. A group of about eight women had also gathered around them, varying in age, apart from one very small girl. While Tomas spoke to the old lady, Malena had stood behind him taking in her surroundings.

When they arrived, they entered a courtyard and stood in the middle of it. Malena saw two rows of small shacks; five on each side of a pathway and at the far end, a larger hut facing her. She later found out that this was the commune's meeting house providing shelter for their work activities which covered a wide range of crafts such as weaving, making clothes, preserves and drying herbs.

To the far side of the courtyard, stood a well with a single step on which she was now sitting. The well had a handle and wheel on the end of a cross bar held between two posts. She supposed this was to lower and raise the bucket of water and was right about this as, since then, she found this was to be her task; collecting water for their daily needs.

On either side of the courtyard were single storey sheds which were used for storing provisions and to house the chickens and geese which were roaming the yard pecking at the earth.

Another wooden building had been built into the surrounding trees nearby. It looked as if it was growing out of the shrubbery. This was the Chapel.

The old lady, Juana, who greeted them, was a Beguine. Malena had thought this a peculiar word. Juana had become the elderly patroness of the commune, which she called the

31

Beguinage, when the previous leader, Brunhilde, had died some months previously. Brunhilde had migrated down to the region from the North of France and carried the concept of the Beguinage with her. Interested, Malena had questioned the women in the community and discovered that a Beguinage was a group of women who devoted themselves to prayer and good works. They were not in holy orders like nuns, as they did not take vows. They lived on the fringes of towns and villages and looked after the poor. They could return to the wider community and marry, but whilst in the Beguinage each had their own dwelling shack which accounted for the small cubicle like structures running down each side of the main pathway. Malena had been allocated one of these for herself. The women all wore robes of the same rough wool dyed brown material with capes around their shoulders. Their hair was tied back and concealed under lighter wool wraps.

Tomas had told Juana and the women a brief story to satisfy their curiosity. He knew that they accepted whatever explanation was offered without question from those who turned up in these circumstances. He had taken his leave of the women reassured by them that Malena would be looked after and kept safe.

He had then taken Malena aside and told her that she had to stay with the women in the commune, that they were good and would look after her. He impressed on her that she should live quietly, do what they told her and that they would protect her from evil people searching for her. These same evil people would be looking for him and it was important that she was safe and he did not want to lead them to her. For her safety he had to leave possibly for a long time. If she needed to get a message to him she was to give it to the elderly woman, Juana, who knew how to contact him.

Delving into the folds of his clothes Tomas had then produced a locket which hung from a silver chain. It was delicate and decorated with a petal pattern. Kissing her on her forehead, he had said

"It belonged to my mother, your grandmother. Keep it safe. See, it has the same marking as that on my ring." He turned his hand so that she could see the signet ring on his little finger.

"It is for you so that you remember who you are and the family you belong to."

With that he had turned and left, not looking back.

**

Malena started, looked up and glanced around. Something had jolted her out of her daydreaming and she spotted the robin sitting on a branch at the entrance of the Chapel. The Chapel was the building growing out of the shrubbery that she had noticed when she first arrived at the Beguinage. It was where the women congregated every day for prayers and singing. They sang a great deal.

The robin was her friend amongst other birds that populated the trees and shrubberies surrounding the domain; he was her favourite. She assumed he was a male and noticed that there was another nearby that could be his mate. Her robin seemed to barely tolerate the other one though.

Her life was very different now. Before coming to the commune she had lived with her father in a castle. Her mother had died shortly after her birth after a long and arduous labour. She had no siblings. Her father had been her closest companion, spending long hours with her and taking her with him when he went out on his estate to see his tenant farmers. An only child in a privileged position, she was indulged with many maidservants attending to her every need. One in particular, Helene, grew up with her. Slightly older than Malena she had been her main playmate from when she was a toddler. Helene, her brother Jean and their elderly parents now lived close by in the village.

Remembering how the soldiers had taken her father away, she shuddered. At the time she had not understood why they had come for him and all she had done was to scream, 'I don't understand, I don't understand'. They had to hold her back and she had lost consciousness.

The castle she had lived in was large and draughty. The living quarters of her father and herself had been behind the Great Hall. It was very warm inside; heavily curtained and carpeted with fabrics brought from the Middle East by the Crusaders and their entourages passing through. Soldiers, like her Uncle Tomas, had often spent the night at St. Gilles on their journeys to the northern cities as it was the port from which the crusade ships departed. She and her father were happy to pass time listening to

33

the tales of the passing crusaders about the crusades and legendary stories of the old Queen Eleanor and her husband Henry. Malena used to sit, hugging herself in the warmth of the fire, listening to these stories and the scandalous escapades of the daring Queen.

Malena was 17 years old now and had become aware that she was beautiful. Her long, red-blonde hair was caught back with plaits tied into a central larger plait. Her eyes were unusually bright; so blue that at times they appeared a deep violet colour. Against a very translucent clear skin and small refined features it was difficult not to be struck by her looks. She emanated an uncanny presence and people had often said that she must be of royal blood. Uncomfortable at people's attention and acknowledging that she seemed to unsettle people, she always wore her head covering so that it completely covered her hair and a great deal of her face.

But now, look at me, thought Malena, wrapped in an unbecoming wool chemise and over garment, the colour of mud. Her uncle had brought her to this place deep in the countryside and she saw in front of her a drab existence of labour, day by day. Over the past year, since her Uncle had left, she had been sinking gradually into a mindless oblivion not helped by the weather which had been icy cold with snow and wind relentlessly battering and even blowing away some of the weaker structures that made up the Beguinage. There was always the wind, sometimes howling and whistling as if some dark entities were out scouting for unguarded souls.

Sitting in the sunshine this morning, however, she had felt her spirits lift a little. She had been sent to draw water and then fell to daydreaming. Thinking of her father in particular and the life she had been used to she wiped a tear away remembering, feeling lonely and wondering about her future. The robin hopped nearer to her, as if sensing her despair.

A cloud passed over and when the sun came out again a shadow fell alongside her. She turned and saw a man standing a few yards away. Malena had not heard him approach and she did not recognise him as one of the local men that came to the settlement. The commune had visitors on a regular basis, poor people seeking food or herbs for cures and odd job men who came to repair tools or work with the animals. But this man was not one of the locals that she was acquainted with. However, there was something familiar about him.

"I'm sorry, I didn't mean to startle you. I am passing through the neighbourhood. I stayed in the village last night and they directed me to this place. I have been looking for you as I have a message from your Uncle, Tomas Lamberte."

He handed her a small parchment package sealed with wax and she immediately recognised the seal was identical to that on the locket that hung around her neck.

Opening the note she read:

My dear Malena,

The man who gives this note to you is a trusted friend. As he was passing through the region, I asked him to find you and see that you were faring well. I was concerned for you when I left in such a hurry. Offer him hospitality and send a message by him to reassure me that you have settled into your new life.

Always remember that you can get a message to me by Juana. Your Uncle Tomas

Turning to the man, she said, "What's your name?"
"Michael."

Malena looked directly into his eyes which were a deep blue. His skin was pale and clear and he looked quite young. He was dressed in a cream wool garment that completely covered his body. His head was under a hood that came forward over his brow, so she could not see the colour of his hair. He wore heavy leather sandals not pattens which were the usual footwear of the locals. Unusual, though, was the fact that they were not muddy from having to walk from the village on what was at the time a very muddy path. Whether it was his light coloured clothing or the sunny atmosphere, she felt peaceful warmth pass over her.

In the letter, her Uncle had asked her to offer this stranger hospitality so she told him to follow her and they walked off, down the central pathway, towards the meeting house. There was nobody in the house apart from Danielle, the youngest inhabitant, who was moving buckets of vegetables towards a pail of water in which she was going to clean them. It was her turn to help cook the midday meal.

"Would you like something to eat? I can offer you some bread and cheese and a cup of wine."

"That would be very kind, thank you."

Malena told Danielle to fetch a cup of hippocras while she took a small loaf of the bread baked that morning and started cutting it into thick slices. Then untying the rope that held the muslin holding the cheeses she let it down and took out two of the small rounds of goat's cheese. Placing the bread and the cheese on a wooden platter she put it on the central table and fetched some of the apple chutney she had made herself last autumn.

"Oh, you need a knife." With that realisation, she was about to go and find one when Michael said,

"Don't worry, I have my own," and he took out a knife from the belt under his robe. It was an unusual knife and its design intrigued Malena.

While he was eating Malena busied herself; tidying the implements on the side table and talking to Danielle about the evening meal they were going to share. She was aware of the visitor's eyes following her and found herself colouring slightly. When he had finished, Michael stood up and went and stood in the doorway. She went to stand beside him assuming that he was about to take his leave.

"This is a very remote domain; do you get a great number of travellers dropping in?"

"No, rarely. All I have seen since I have been here are the local people and a man who travels through the region sharpening knives and who comes once each year. The village is at the end of the valley and does not lead anywhere so unless people come to visit relatives or to see the priest they have no reason to choose this route."

"Before I go, it would please me if you would show me round. I can then tell your uncle about your life here."

Telling him to follow her, Malena led the way around the back of the house and stood in a small herb garden that had steps leading up to the main track. On the back of the communal house, there was a small shed-like structure opening out onto the herb garden. This was where the poultry, game or meat, if they were lucky enough to get any, was prepared for cooking. There were also wooden buckets and other vessels for emptying the leftovers from their meals, which went to feeding the poultry and the two pigs kept on the lower garden.

Giving him time to look around and explaining her daily tasks to him, Malena then continued down some steps to a rectangular meadow. Emerging from the winter's snow, the grass was short with few wild flowers. To one side, directly beneath the house on the upper terrace, was a circle enclosed by cherry trees and laurel bushes. Pruned back by one of the local lads from the village they looked like a ring of primeval animals, dancing around the circle casting eerie shadows in the brilliant sunshine. Inside the circle there was a central stand made of carved stone and on the top, a sun dial. Some turf seats had been made around the circle, too. People came down here to sit and pray or in the summer, when it was very hot, to cool off in the shade of the trees.

Leaving the ring by its lower entrance, Malena took Michael down to the vegetable garden and physic garden. Most of the elderly women were well versed with herbal remedies to cure all kinds of ailments and they tended the gardens between them. They walked together down the pebble path between the planked beds of vegetables and herbs and out through an archway that led to a steep bank with stone steps wedged into it; making it a stairway to the cemetery which was small and catered only for the women who had lived in the commune.

They circled the property, returning near to the well where they had first met. The only place left was the Chapel, so Malena took him across to it and through the archway door that led into its interior. It was an unusual place for worship. Its roof had been woven with the thinner branches of the laurel bushes, which had been allowed to grow out wildly. When woven, the branches had been pliable, but now, dried out, they held the tree growth back and the domed roof looked smooth; like the upside-down interior of a wicker basket. The lower walls of the chapel were made of stone boulders that had been chiselled and fitted together and formed a more or less perfect surface that was about two metres high. The stone wall held back the growth of the trees outside.

At the far end, there was a square window, about a metre square, within which was a symbol similar to the one on her locket. This window faced east and caught the sun as it rose in the morning. There were no seats as the women prayed and sang, standing. Beneath the window there was a large long flat stone resting on two more stones, waist high. On this, there was a wooden carved chalice. Malena noticed Michael taking in the atmosphere of the chapel and wondered if he was a priest or pilgrim on his way to *Santiago de Compestela.*

"Would you mind if I stayed here for a few minutes on my own?"

She left him in the Chapel, saying she would fetch some water; she was thirsty and thought he would be too. Something had made her curious, so before going for the water she hid around the corner out of sight. Peering through a crack in the door she saw him standing thoughtfully and then glancing around. At one point she thought he was going to come out, but then he hesitated. He had his back to her and she saw him reach into his robes and bring out something but could not see clearly what it was.

With his back still towards her she saw him raise his arms above his head and she caught sight of what looked like a sphere. He began to chant and the next thing she saw was a faint light, gradually beginning to brighten then fill the chapel until it was so bright that it was blinding and there was a crack like thunder and she was thrown back onto the ground. When she picked herself up and went back to the spy-hole, the light was no longer there and she had to quickly run across to the well and start drawing water.

Michael came out of the chapel and crossed the yard towards her. By this time she had filled two wooden cups with water and as he approached, offered him one. As he took the cup of water, he said:

"Thank you for your kindness in showing me around. I can see that you have settled here very well and I will pass this on to your Uncle. Is there anything you would like me to tell him?"

Hesitantly, trying to think of something, she replied:

"No, I don't think so."

Giving her some moments to reflect, Michael then said.

"Now, I must take my leave."

He looked directly into her eyes, smiling, his deep blue eyes holding her gaze, mesmerising her. He turned and walked away.

Michael disappeared as quickly as he had appeared. Malena had turned from him and then back and he was gone. She looked around and could see no sign of him. She sensed that she had been looking at his back as it receded and then felt a sudden weakness come over her. She went and sat down again by the well. It felt strange, she knew he had been there but she could not quite remember what had happened other than showing him around the domain.

Later on, in the day towards eventide the sky became cloudy. The commune was high up in the mountains on the side of a valley. When the sun went down, it turned cold very quickly. The cloud cover lowered and completely obliterated the surroundings. Malena could hardly see the communal house at the other end of the yard.

***

Late in the evening of the same day, a party of soldiers arrived in the village. Heavily armed and dressed in black and helmeted, they rode into the centre. As it was dark the houses had been shuttered up by their occupants, however there was one lone figure, the priest, making his way back to the church.

Father Bernard Amaury was cold and hungry. He had been out to see one of the villagers who was passing over. He felt emotionally drained too, as the man had refused to make a confession and the priest had noticed that he was starving himself to death. He felt the tug of the muscles around his heart, signalling to him to have a light supper and get to his bed as quickly as possible and rest.

The soldiers rode up out of the dark at the priest, frightening him. He put his arms up to shield himself. Seeing the priest cowering, one of the soldiers shouted to the others to back off. After the horses and riders settled, the soldier who had taken command approached Father Amaury and asked him if he had seen a traveller pass through the village. He was able to answer truthfully that he had not seen anyone other than the usual villagers going about their affairs during the day.

Unnoticed by the priest and soldiers, a young man had just emerged from a narrow alley opening onto the square. He had shrunk back into the shadows when he saw what was going on. He could hear most of what they were saying and he was alarmed. Jean had seen the traveller and knew that he had gone to the women's commune. What for he did not know, but he had felt that it was something important and urgent. It was he who had directed the traveller to them, in fact shown him the way, as he went there daily to help the women.

He wondered now what it was about. The group of soldiers looked haggard as if they had been riding for a long time. He recognised the insignia of the French King on their chests, the striking red cross against the black and white tunic. To have come so far from the Court in their pursuit of a traveller meant, he realised, something was definitely not right.

The soldiers let the priest go and circled in the square, obviously trying to decide what they should do as it was now getting dark. He reasoned that the priest had pointed them to the cottage and barns on the outskirts of the village, where he, Jean, and his family lived. His family often gave overnight shelter and food to travellers passing through in exchange for a few coins. It was the family's way of earning some extra means to support themselves as life was hard. He saw that he had assessed the situation correctly and that the Priest had directed the soldiers to his own family as they led off down the street towards his home.

Jean did not know what to do, whether he should go and warn the women or not. He decided against it as night had drawn in and there was also a thick mist descending. From previous experience, he did not want to be out on the side of the valley in these circumstances. It was easy to get lost, even if you knew the area as well as he did. He decided to wait until morning but to keep an eye on the soldiers.

He made his way home, skirting the village and approaching the house at the rear and saw his sister Helene emptying a pail of water onto the kitchen garden outside. He put his finger to his lips to signal her to say nothing and they entered the kitchen. Whispering, he told her and their parents what had happened. His parents busied themselves gathering water and food for the soldiers who had demanded to be fed. His father Luc had shown the soldiers where to stable their horses in the neighbouring barns.

Jean knew that the soldiers would be sleeping in the lofts above the stable so he decided to keep out of sight until they settled down for the night. They were not to know that the family had a son as well as a daughter, as he sensed their visit was not going to be a lengthy one; just the one night, so he doubted whether they would talk to anyone long enough to find out. He would find somewhere to hide where he would be alerted should any of them decide to do anything unpredictable.

Helene, along with some neighbours who had been called in to help, was putting up trestle tables immediately outside the house on which to put the food. The soldiers were milling around outside the barns drinking the local rough red wine, stamping their feet impatient for the meal. The neighbours called in were serving them with downcast eyes and avoiding talking to them. The villagers were always wary of strangers especially soldiers who they knew at the slightest provocation could get angry and violent. Soldiers such as these were to beware of; roaming through the countryside, often on their way back from the Crusades and leaving trails of devastation, looting, raping and razing whole villages to the ground. However, these seemed to have a specific purpose; fed and sated, they very quickly disappeared to the barns. After a few hours had passed, Jean crept out and listened. He heard the soldiers snoring, nothing stirring, not even the stray dogs and, satisfied, he returned to his post and managed to doze.

As dawn began to lighten the sky, Jean rose and positioned himself outside the barns around the corner by the log pile, and waited for the soldiers to emerge. They came out, saddled their horses and mounted. In a group they circled, the horses were restless. It was cold and the mist that had fallen last night had not lifted. The horses stamped and snorted out clouds of mist. Eventually, a cry went up and calling one to the other the soldiers dispersed in different directions out of the village.

Jean saw two soldiers taking the track that led out to the commune and satisfied that the others had taken the other routes out of the village he wrapped his cloak firmly around him, covered his head and ran off down the lane leading to the Beguinage. A few yards out of the village, he took a short cut that led across the valley to the settlement. Very few people knew of this path and it cut a good twenty minutes off the walk from the village and he knew he would get to the women before the soldiers.

However, the soldiers never reached their destination. The mist had become so dense that it completely obscured the Beguinage along with the paths and tracks leading to it in the surrounding countryside. The soldiers had followed what they thought was a main track but had eventually ended up deep in a valley in thick woodland. The path disappeared. Frozen, they desperately sought a way back but only succeeded in losing themselves further in a forest. Miles from the village and on tracks leading them deeper into the mountains, as the day passed they realised they were lost and abandoned hope of finding their way back to the village.

Jean stayed at the Beguinage throughout the day, rewarded with a large bowl of their vegetable soup and a great hunk of rough bread. By evening, he felt confident that they were no longer in danger and returned to the village. He discovered that the soldiers had not returned. Several men of the village had also been following them. As the mist had been so dense it was assumed that they got lost. However, everyone was on alert in case they returned.

***

Malachi stood on a promontory high above the valleys surrounding the village. He was able to see the village and the Beguinage and for many miles around, including a full 360 degree sweep of the Pyrenees. Satisfied that all was well, he lifted his arms slowly and as he did so the mist in the valley which had covered the village and the surrounding countryside dispersed.

***

Over time Malena's memory of Michael's visit gradually faded altogether. At times, she had one dream that kept coming back; it was of her standing in the garden holding something in her hands. She knew it was precious but could never actually remember what the object was after waking up.

***

Chapter 3
Tomas
(France and England, 13th Century)

After leaving Malena with the sisters at the Beguinage, Tomas did not return to St. Gilles but went directly to Perpignan and the place where he had been initiated into the Cloister, the Temple at Canet. He had arranged to meet the Steward there after he had been given the order to rescue Malena. The time and day had been fixed before he had gone to St. Gilles.

His journey down from the mountains had been uneventful; there were not many towns or hamlets. He had taken the tracks leading around these, stopping only at one of the remote farm holdings that had no neighbours. The family had been very welcoming. They fed him and gave him shelter overnight. Riding alone, it had taken just two days as he travelled faster on his own. With Malena and the party it had been slow going.

Approaching Castle Roussillon, he felt his skin tingle aware that there were lookouts posted on the battlements of the building. As far as he knew, few people knew that there was a Temple built into the footings of the castle. Tomas had no idea when the Temple had been built there, only that the Cloister had used it for their meetings for centuries according to his father.

Tomas approached the flat surface of the side of a boulder. The boulder itself was immense, its mass deeply embedded into the rocky landscape surrounding the foundations of the castle. He scanned the surface and located the symbols he was looking for. These had been cleverly concealed in a fissure in the stone where the casual observer would not see them. They had been etched into the stone and contained in a vertical rectangle. The symbols were in smaller squares within the rectangle. For each of the symbols in turn, he intoned a sound he had been taught at his initiation. What happened next was always a mystery to Tomas and awe-inspiring. As if by magic, a doorway appeared in the boulder and he was able to walk through it into a tunnel.

The Steward was waiting just inside the tunnel and they proceeded down it and into a chamber to the left of the passage. Beyond it, laid the Temple where he had been initiated many years before as a young adult. They were not alone; other members of the Order were present along with a stranger whom the Steward introduced as Michael.

They sat down on benches at a large table in the centre of the chamber. There were no other pieces of furniture or ornament in the room. In the passage way, immediately outside, there was a dresser which contained the vessels for ceremonies. These in themselves were very simple, but each carried designs of ancient symbols around its rim. These symbols had mysterious powers that were activated by the incantations of the temple servers.

"How was Malena when you left her?" the stranger Michael asked.

"Distressed, it was a long and hard journey after her ordeal at St. Gilles. We were not troubled as the route we took had many pilgrims going to Santiago de Compestela. Then when we turned towards the mountains it was very desolate. The armies usually keep to the main routes. I knew if I kept on the tracks that we would not be noticed. There were hamlets whose inhabitants I knew would be sympathetic to the cause and they gave us food and shelter. It took many days to reach Bourg Madame. Everybody was tired and anxious."

Tomas's voice petered out, fatigue was beginning to overwhelm him.

"What about the peasant family of her maidservant?"

"That was easy. The inhabitants of the village near the Beguinage were very accommodating. Juana explained the situation to them and they took them into their houses for the time being. I have asked the family to stay and keep a watch out for Malena. I thought if they were in the village they would notice any strangers coming into the village. If they thought there was some danger, I told them to let Juana know and she would get a message to the contact in Canet who would pass it on to the Order.

They were happy to stay as I think they realised the danger they were in too."

"And the sisters at the commune?"

"Good women, who have been there for a long time and supported by the village people who go to them for healing and medicines. They will look after Malena and I think she will settle down to the life there. Obviously it's very different from what she is used to but she knows now that she had to get away. She is still very upset about what happened to her father; they were very close, as he lost his wife when she was born and there were no brothers or sisters."

Tomas knew that he had to broach the subject of what he should do next as he knew that he would now be sought by the King and Church. Word had reached him that they were searching for him.

"I know what you are thinking."

Michael said, looking directly into Tomas' eyes. Tomas found Michael's attention disturbing as his eyes seemed to penetrate his being, almost hypnotically. He found it difficult to cover up anything he was thinking and it was making him bluster and redden up.

"I know the Church and King are searching for me, they want me to lead them to Malena and any other people or groups connected to her. They are intent on wiping out all traces of the Faith. Our family have already suffered and I know of several others that have been troubled. The Inquisition they formed has grown and nobody is safe. I have heard that you only have to glance at a bible or say something in a joke and it gives them an excuse to lock you up and interrogate you."

Tomas ran out of words, beginning to feel desperate.

"I have escaped so far but I need to get away, far away."

"I agree, you have done well and completed your task here. That is all the Order asked of you. I am going to tell you about a particular religious group and then you can make up your mind about what you want to do. But I think you will understand that they can be of help."

Michael then proceeded to tell him about the Blue Friars, so called because of the colour of their robes.

"They have houses in Saragossa and Valenciennes, but recently due to the Inquisition they have had to abandon these and have been moving about trying to avoid persecution. Their faith has similarities to other groups that the Inquisitors consider heretical. Recently some of them, realising that they were not going to escape the Inquisition as it swept through the countryside, have been making their way to England and have already established a settlement near a small village in the south-east of that country. They have been lucky as they had papers from the Pope which gave them security as they travelled.

Others of their brethren are now on their way to join them. If you wish, you could make contact with one of the groups of Friars going to England and travel with them. Once there you could decide what you want to do, but the advantage is that it would remove you from the search that is going on here for you. If you decide to go, I am sure that you could stay with their settlement, even be taken into their Order.

I must also tell you that you could call on the protection of a more noble source should you have any anxiety over persecution."

Tomas was surprised, "I am not aware of any family in England?"

Michael continued, "You know that your full name is Tomas Lambertes de St. Gilles?" Tomas nodded.

"The Lambertes de St. Gilles are one of the families that form part of the Raimondine dynasty, a dynasty that has a long history. The Raimondines are the extended family of the Counts of Toulouse and in the past they provided some of the most enlightened rulers in Europe. However, along with other groups considered heretical they suffered persecution by the Church and gradually lost their lands and the noble house disintegrated. It is still there but scattered throughout Europe.

Early this century, at the time of the outbreak of the Crusade against the Cathars, the ruler of Toulouse was Count Raymond VI. His fourth wife was Jeanne of England, the daughter of Henry II and Eleanor of Aquitaine.

Raymond fought against Simon de Montfort, the most violent enemy of the Cathars, but was forced to leave his lands and to go into exile to England taking with him some nobles and family that fought alongside him. One of these nobles was Ramon Lambertes St. Gilles; a distant cousin of the Count and loyal supporter. This man was your grandfather.

After some years the Pope eventually allowed the Count to regain his land around Toulouse. Unfortunately, however, his son Count Raymond VII later lost the land. However, whilst exiled in England, he and your grandfather made connections with the members of the Royal Household.

Although Ramon, your grandfather, returned with Count Raymond, he left behind some of the family in England. The family name there still remains St. Gilles. When in noble company, should you come across the name before approaching them make sure of their beliefs. Not all of the family were supporters of the faith."

Tomas had been listening intently to Michael while he was speaking. His knowledge of his family history was scrappy and he found it difficult to bring the pieces together. A great deal of what Michael was telling him, he knew already but there were things which had puzzled him. For example, why had his family dropped the name St. Gilles and just called themselves Lamberte. It was clear now that it was due to the past persecution and the need to be as discreet as possible. It all made sense now, as did the pressure his family had put on him to keep their beliefs a secret.

Now at 45 years of age, listening to Michael and dwelling on the events of the last few months, he began to feel weary wondering when it was going to end. The thought of being on the run, hiding, seeking shelter from strangers and the general poverty of the situation sent a stabbing contraction into his chest. The lure of going somewhere far away and setting up a new identity began to grow in him like a sunrise creeping above the horizon.

"With whom do I make contact if I want to go with the Blue Friars?"

"I know they will be passing through here on their journey from Spain. They will be resting at a small hostel in Canet on the outskirts of the village. Many monks and holy men stop there on their travels making their way north, picking up on the pilgrim routes, going to and from Santiago de Compostela. If you wait near the hostel, you will see them when they arrive and you can approach them. Be careful what you say at first as they are wary of revealing their identity. However, give them this and it will act as a password for them and they will know that it is safe to speak to you."

Michael wrote a few words on a slip of parchment, folded it and handed it to Tomas and then rose.

"We are finished here and I must go. I have work to do yet with Malena before she is fully settled with the Sisters."

He placed a piece of parchment on the table in front of Tomas and told him to write a note of introduction for him to give to Malena to set her at ease. Tomas was not used to writing; pausing, he tried to find the necessary words. He knew that he probably would never see her again and he did not want to convey this in any way to her. Michael put his hand on his shoulder, sensing his distress, and somehow the words came to him. Michael brought over some wax which he had melted down. He told Tomas to seal the letter with his signet ring so that Malena would know it had come directly from him.

Passing back through the entrance of the Temple with the Steward, Michael turned to Tomas and clasped him tightly.

"All will be well now, things will go more easily with you day by day and you have a good life in front of you. Do not worry about Malena! We will make sure she is safe and well cared for. We have many contacts. Now, go in peace."

**

Tomas watched as Michael turned and disappeared swiftly down the track, the trees and bushes of which almost immediately closed around him giving his departure a ghostly feel. It was as if the spirits had carried him off.

Tomas bade farewell to the Steward and turned down a track towards the coast and made his way to Canet. He found the hostel easily and the following day the Blue Friars arrived. He handed them the note from Michael and they immediately seemed to recognise his plight and quickly took him into their group. They shared a meagre supper and the next morning continued on their journey with Tomas following.

Tomas had been given a hooded habit of rough blue wool which covered him completely and he was swallowed up by the line of travellers and pilgrims as they wound their way on the old Roman road, the Via Domitia, to Narbonne and then northwards towards Toulouse.

Months later, and after a hazardous sea crossing, they arrived on the south coast of England. Struggling through the crashing waves onto the shingle beach, Tomas lost his balance several times and ended up having to be dragged out of the churning water by the other friars. Eventually he saw, towering over him, the garrison of Dover Castle which he had been told about by the sailors on the ship. It was everything they told him and now ominous in the dying light of the day. Black clouds and drizzle added a further chill to his already rigid bones and muscles. He told himself that he had arrived.

After spending the night in a hostel in the village below the castle, next day they set off on their journey toward the north east in pouring rain. Although it was spring, and the days were beginning to draw out, the overcast sky and chilling rain did not make their progress easy and it was some weeks before they arrived at the small village that was their destination. Tomas was beginning to wonder whether he could get used to this grey and sombre landscape.

On the morning they arrived, watery sun was breaking through the storm clouds and Tomas thought what a difference it made to the landscape. In the incessant rain on their journey he had noticed the tracks closed in with undergrowth, hedges and huge old oak trees covering the way. However, with the sun shining down he remarked on the many wild flowers beginning to appear, but with closed blooms as if they were protecting themselves until they were assured the sun held true to its promise.

They had passed through a wooden gate and made their way down a lane towards some buildings with thatched roofs and smoke coming out of their chimneys. As the sun broke through the canopy of trees, everything seemed to take on a sparkle. Rain drops glistened as they dropped from leaf to leaf to the ground. Time seemed to be holding back and the world became animated, moving and dancing in slow motion around him.

They arrived at a large courtyard, surrounded by barns and outbuildings. A pathway led out towards some further buildings that looked like dwelling houses. One of the friars, the one who seemed to have some authority amongst the group of Friars, Father Guillaume, walked across the courtyard and took the track between some small thatched cottages. The other friars and Tomas followed and, as they came out of the lane, a large stone building appeared before them. It was considerably larger than the churches the friars had pointed out to him on the way. He later found out that it was the foundations of an Abbey that was being built gradually by the monks and friars who lived on the site.

Father Guillaume entered the main entrance and within a few minutes emerged with a priest. The priest said that they had been expected for some time and that accommodation had been prepared. The priest went back into the building and emerged with a couple of young monks who came over to the group. The monks took the party to a refectory at one end of the Abbey and gave them soup and bread. On their journey, food had been irregular and hard to come by. Consuming the simple meal partly relieved their weariness.

Afterwards, they were taken back to the dwelling houses on the lane and the friars were allocated houses to share. Tomas found that he had a small room to himself in one of the cottages. Looking around he found a peace settling over him. In past years it had been a long time travelling, being on the run and then the escape with Malena into the mountains. Though he was a relatively young man, he realised the toll this had taken on him.

Over the next days and weeks he settled into the life of the monastery, enjoying the strict routine of prayer and work that occupied the community. The day started early with Vigil and call to prayer and then carried through the day with observance of the Hours. Everybody had a job to do; gardening, cooking, gathering herbs, building. Tomas was initially given jobs in the garden and found this suited him well and later he helped with the animals. The grounds of the Abbey contained its own small farm.

He also came to realise that some of the inhabitants of the settlement were not monks, holy men, priests or friars. It also seemed to be a place for refugees of, mainly, religious or political persecution. It seemed England was more tolerant as long as you did not draw attention to yourself. There were women and young children about, as the community also supported families.

After some years at the Abbey, Tomas married one of the young women in the family community. Happily married, they produced nine healthy children. Tomas died in his early sixties, having enjoyed a contented family life in his last years. For their married name, Tomas had decided to use the one that Michael had recommended would be the most favourably looked upon, St. Gilles, should he ever be in the presence of noble company. As the centuries passed after Tomas' demise, the family name passed down was shortened even further to Gill. However, by the 20th Century family descendants, interested in ancestry research, discovered the origins of the name and started to call themselves Lambert St. Gill, retaining the Lambert as a son's middle name.

***

Having left Tomas, Malachi made his way to a high point overlooking the castle and the surrounding area. He could see the tracks and paths leading down to Canet and the sea from where he was standing. He saw Tomas walking steadily down the track. Light was fading, the sun setting behind the mountains beyond throwing a burning glow into the sky and casting deep purple shadows in the valleys below the peaks.

He waited until he was satisfied that Tomas had arrived in Canet and then turned to leave, saying to himself, "Now to Malena…"

***

Chapter 4
Reunion
(Somewhere, No Time No Space)

Malachi had left Malena safely in the hands of the women of the Beguinage (Earth Time 13th Century), set Tomas on the path to safety and been to check on Maddy (Earth Time 21st Century). He then stepped up from Level 3 through the frequencies to Level 7.

Malachi always found it difficult stepping up and down, especially down to Level 3. At that level, he felt the density of his physical body to be heavy and uncomfortable. Many attributes of bodily functions, at that level, seemed to him disagreeable; especially, the odours that emanated from him and the humans he came into contact with. When going down, sometimes it was difficult getting his arms and legs moving in a co-ordinated fashion and he had to give himself some Earth hours to adjust.

To add to the discomfort of frequency readjustment, having just returned from Level 3 he had been summoned to a reunion on Level 10, which meant a further stepping up. Stepping up to Level 10 was not impossible for him, but it meant raising his vibrational frequency appropriately which took some effort. However, going up and not down was at least going in an easier direction for him.

Malachi had been expecting the summons as it was time to liaise with the Overseer regarding the contract he had undertaken and the events which were happening within his spectrum. Entering the Chamber of Reunion, Malachi noted that there were many *Fraterne* and *Marechal* stirring restlessly filling the space.

Fraterne were beings from the highest dimensions; ascended masters able to travel by thought anywhere in the Universe.

Marechal were such as him, appointed by the *Fraterne* to be guardians of sectors of the Universe and operable in the lower dimensions, not yet fully ascended. As part of their individual ascension process, they had been appointed as sector guardians within the Harmonic Universe of which Earth was part. Although they were able to take on the physical appearance of humans, their original forms were various as they were drawn from diverse locations throughout the innumerable Harmonic Universes that comprised the Source; the Creator of All.

Malachi was appointed directly overseeing the sector that contained Earth, the Solar System and Galaxy of which it was part. The matter he was dealing with imminently and which was giving concern was contained within the time spectrum: Earth time, 8,500 BC to 2050 AD, and which commenced in the region on Earth that was known as Sumer.

The 'Chamber of Reunion' was a special place located out of space and time. In the centre was a swirling pool that resembled a huge bowl of viscous indigo liquid. It looked like a whirlpool but was not water. Malachi knew this to be the portal to a passageway that would take you to the entrance of the Infinite Void. It was like looking down into the centre of a well. He knew also not to get too close to the edge as it could draw you into it. Unlike the beings such as the Fraterne, he knew that he would not be able to withstand the frequencies that he would be subjected to during transportation through the passage. He also knew that it would send a shock wave through the dimensions he existed in and destabilise the section.

All present had averted their attention towards Overseer Fraterne, Nammu, who had assumed the features and dress of an Egyptian Pharaoh. The gathering was gravitating towards Nammu, adjusting their cellular sound and light frequency codes in order that they could share the telepathic language. An initial thought was sent out by Nammu.

"Urgent invocations have been received from the planet 'Ki-Gi-Kia' (Earth) guiding us here to this sector at a spectrum of 2000 years of the planet's terrestrial linear time within three dimensions. The invocations have increased during the latter part of this time line."

Nammu paused, his thought directed towards Malachi.

"Malachi you were appointed Marechal of this sector and guardian of the soul group that is sending these invocations. Can you continue?"

Malachi inclined his head slightly in response.

"Invocations came to me as Marechal of this sector. You rightly assumed that it lies within a sub-section of my guardianship. They have been coming from a tribe now living in the northern hemisphere of the planet.

Initially the invocations came at the beginning of the time line mentioned. As you know, this planet is of interest due to its pivotal position in the coming Alignment. The effect on this Harmonic Universe and its evolution has been closely observed. Its evolution has been interrupted many times; the planet has experienced destruction and regeneration in order to resume its natural evolution.

Some millennia, prior to the timeline we are concerned with, the ruling family of the civilisations on Earth at that time were Visitors from another planet who were mining the resources of Earth for their own purposes. Prescient of the devastation that would occur to Earth due to the dangerously close proximity of their home planet in its orbit around the Sun, they abandoned Earth which was swept by giant tsunamis.

Not all of the population of the planet perished at that time. The survivors of the flood are the current species on the planet and are their descendants.

Since that time, the planet has been left alone and the human population have shown that they are evolving back to source naturally. They have been open to several threats from the visiting ex-terrestrials over the last 5,000 years. However most of these have been purely observational.

However, things have changed. Currently the planet in its timeline is experiencing precession, moving into the constellation of Aquarius. Its star, the Sun, is also moving into a two thousand year orbit within the galaxy and will experience, along with its planets, a higher frequency which will aid ascension. The Earth will be in a rare position that will not occur again for millions of Earth years. This will mean for the species seeing beyond their individuality. It will be able to return to group consciousness governed by Universal Law.

In the coming Alignment, the Time Portal Systems (TPS) and Dimensional Lock Systems (DLS) will open allowing travel through time and dimensions in this universe. These are all things on the positive side where technical advice and assistance will be given to the planet and it inhabitants when needed by the Fraterne and Ancestor Guardians.

However, there is a negative side. The population of the planet in the last 200 years has been increasing at a rate so fast that it is now overpopulated for its size. Along with this, due to industrial and technological development, humans have caused pollution to the planet and it is under stress due to severe climate changes and plate movement below the surface causing earthquakes, volcanoes and tsunamis. Many humans are dying due to this.

There is a threat that is even more alarming, coming from a species in a desperate situation. The Halqu are a renegade race who have been roaming this Universe, causing a great deal of trouble. This group is dangerous as it wants to possess the Earth and it is due to them that we have been receiving the invocations.

The Halqu want control of the planet at this time as they want access to the time and space travel portals available at the Alignment. Earth is beneficial to them as it is within the same frequency dimension as their own planet.

Their planet had evolved to a high level of spirituality and technological development involving genetic engineering. However they abused the basic principles of genetic manipulation which resulted in their race beginning to die out. Seeing what had happened and having the ability to travel in time, and inter-dimensionally, they sent out a research team to seek a way to return to their planet at a time when they began their programme of genetic engineering to reverse the mutations.

Though they had experimented quite successfully with time travel and inter-dimensional travel, it was not enough as after leaving their planet the research team found themselves unable to return. They could travel back in time but could not enter the portals to their planet as they were not open at an earlier time. Therefore they had locked themselves out of their own system.

In their search, they learned about the coming Alignment when the portals would be open. As the development of their planet correlates to that of Earth, they realised that it would give them a way back. They have been present and waiting for this event to use it to access their own planet. As the time of Alignment has drawn nearer, they have increased their efforts to take control of Earth and its inhabitants so they would have the greatest advantage.

However, in their attempt to take possession they placed a 'net' around the planet and this has been causing the problems that have given rise to the invocations. The 'net' throws out holograms from time to time, casting amnesia over the population of Earth; creating wars, plagues and disasters which have averted the humans' attention away from their original purpose of evolution and ascension. The energy created by these diversionary tactics fuel the Halqu's powers of control and debilitates human individuals *en masse*.

Despite this, the resilience of a certain percentage of humans has been spectacular in many ways and they have succeeded at the present time in raising their frequency. They have begun to approach a resonance by which the majority will be able to ascend at the time of the Alignment.

As you know, we, the Marechal, Fraterne and Overseers, have been watching the Halqu, checking their intentions. The Ancestor Guardians have tried to reach agreement with them as sharing the same origins of all Source material, their goal is return by ascension. But to no avail, they continue with their destructive objectives. Accordingly, at the time of the Great Flood it was necessary to take a precautionary step against intervention by ex-terrestrial objectives and the Ancestor Guardians placed a shield on the planet's grid unknown to the Halqu. At the time of Alignment, the shield will counter the effect of the 'net' placed by the Halqu, blocking their access, and allow the ascension to proceed.

The Shield is made up of twelve Seals, placed with twelve clans on specific grid points. In each clan one female is designated each generation, along with a male counterpart who becomes her protector. The cellular coding within the DNA of the female triggers the activation of the Seal at each specific location. The location of the Seal has been kept hidden from the female and her protector.

I was appointed the Marechal, guarding the locations of the families and Seals. At the appointed time the female and the Seal will be united triggering the activation, this will happen simultaneously with all twelve Seals placed in the twelve locations. The net placed by the Halqu will fold down and dissipate and the planet and its inhabitants will ascend to the Fifth Dimension in this Harmonic Universe. A wave will go out enabling the Universe to ascend itself and trigger ascension throughout all Universes. We can all understand the profound significance of this event and the possibilities it offers.

I think you can now guess what I have to say next. At the time the invocations began, knowledge of the grid was betrayed to the Halqu by a member of the family holding one of the Seals. I was made immediately aware of this and relocated the Seal and the family to a new hiding place. Since that time, the Halqu have been desperately seeking its location. So far they have been unsuccessful.

At this moment all of the Seals and families are secure, safe from Halqu intervention. I have visited all of the incarnates and the Seals through time and they are all secure as of now. As Alignment is approaching, I have notified the Orders and the initiated males. The next objective is to remind the females of their soul contract. All of this is in process.

However, one family is particularly vulnerable; the same family who suffered betrayal by one of their relatives initially. The Halqu came close to finding the family but I was able to remove the designated female and male to a safe location. It is they who have been sending the invocations. It is my task to guard the safety of this family. I am working with the male initiate of the family to wake up the female and will be shadowing her through to the actual point of Alignment."

Malachi, then, made his mind void of thought as he felt it was enough. He knew that those present, already knew much of what he had reported but knew, at the same time, that they needed to be alerted in case difficulties arose and he needed to call them in.

Nammu took over to close the reunion, agreeing that vigilance of the Shield be a priority. All were to attend to the invocations they received. He also assigned specific Marechal, whose specialities were protection, to assist Malachi with regard to the family under threat. He closed by sending out to them the message

"All time, all things are now and complete."

Nammu's image gradually faded in the space as did those of the other Fraterne and Marechal.

Malachi remained behind dwelling on the moment, grateful for the assistance he was going to be given. He wondered who the other Marechal would be and where and when they would appear. Travelling between different time zones and dimensions checking on the incarnates was not easy but whilst away from them, individually it would be reassuring to know that he could leave protection.

Leaving, he stepped down to Level 7 to rest and to regain his strength, for the preceding events had taken a toll on his resonant energy.

***

The Legend
The Song and the Stone
(From time indeterminate)

The centuries following the occupation of 'La Borda' by the Beguinage saw the property gradually fall derelict. The occupants, the women, were either growing old and dying or marrying into the neighbourhood if they were young.

Malena married Jean, the brother of her friend and servant Helene. Jean, a freeman, was able to set himself up as a farmer; growing enough to support his expanding family. He and Malena had several children. He also began gathering a herd of sheep. When his flock became large enough, he joined other sheep farmers in the area and took his turn taking the large herds of sheep over the Pyrenees into Arago to pass the winter months grazing on the lowlands where it was warmer.

Eventually, Malena and Jean died but their family grew and spread out over the surrounding region from the Pyrenees to the Mediterranean coast. They became shepherds, farmers, herdsmen, carpenters, bakers, farriers. Their talents were vast but they always lived in the country.

The family carried a story, a history which was passed down through the centuries, and became a Legend in the region.

The Legend told of a Princess who carried a precious stone who was brought secretly to the mountains by a Knight. They had fled from a band of evil renegades who wanted to possess the Princess and the stone.

The Princess carried within her a song and the stone was the accompanying instrument. They were connected by a magical golden thread that held them in an eternal bond—they were the

Seal. The Seal, of which the Princess and stone were part and whole, was one of twelve Seals which had been hidden in special places on the Earth; the Shield.

The Knight placed the stone in a secret hiding place in the earth near the Princess.

The Knight wore a neck chain that possessed magical powers. Having completed his task, he used it to transform the Princess into a common maidservant and at the same time made her forget what she had experienced.

The Princess, though now changed to a lowly servant, remembered deep in her soul that her task was to pass on her secret, her Song. Without any memory of her encounter with the Knight, she met and married a herdsman living nearby and gave birth to several children; all boys except for one girl she called Magdalena. From that time on there would always be a girl-child called Magdelena within the family and there would always be a son of the family appointed as Protector of the Seal until the appointed time.

A day would come when the twelve Seals would unlock the gates of heaven and fly the Earth and its peoples to heaven. All of 'goodly heart and will' would pass through the gates of memory to live in the gardens of Eden. Until that time, the Seals would remain secretly waiting.

***

Chapter 5
El Zagel de la Frontera
(Early 20th Century)

The *Zagel,* or '*el zagelese*' as they were known, were a large family that populated an area stretching from the high Pyrenees across the Catalan/French/Spanish border down to the Mediterranean. A descendant could be found within the vicinity of any town or village in the region.

Knowledge of the family's origins stretched far back over the centuries. A story that was regularly told to strangers was that the family originated in the 13th Century from a small border village high in the mountains. It was said that the Patriarch of the family had been a shepherd herding flocks back and forth across the Pyrenees. However, there came a time when, tired of his nomadic lifestyle, he had settled in the village with a wife and spent the rest of his life there. He became a carpenter and kept a small holding with livestock. When he died, he left a large family whose descendants gravitated away from the mountains and scattered across the Languedoc Roussillon and into Catalan.

After the First World War and before the Spanish Civil War, one family of his descendants moved back to the village and repossessed a derelict property that was reputed to have been their ancestral home. This family, without realising, had turned it into a small-holding much as their original ancestors had; keeping goats, some sheep and cows, chickens. The family name Zagel remained and had followed the descendants down through the centuries.

Jorge Zagel was the Patriarch of this family. He and his wife Raymonde had three children. They had lived in the centre of Perpignan but had found the comings and goings of refugees and other migrants unsettling and had decided that they would move away and live a rural life. He remembered his family history and had taken an excursion out to the mountains and rediscovered the site of his family's property.

When Jorge reclaimed '*la petite ferme*', it had been semi-derelict with no more than a couple of rooms and an attic. A talented carpenter, he constructed a wooden staircase to the attic giving the family bedrooms. On the ground floor, they made their living quarters and installed a range for cooking and heating. There was also a rough outhouse which Jorge had repaired and turned into a wash house and storage space.

Just after they resettled on the outskirts of the village Jorge had an affair with Raymonde's friend. Raymonde threw Jorge out of the house and they divorced. Jorge was angry about this, as he felt she should have understood that the passion would have passed and he would have eventually returned. But instead she had flown into a rage which had not abated over time and Raymonde and the children became very hostile to him. Retrospectively, he had had to admit to himself that he had treated them very unfairly, leaving her without any money or transport. Raymonde and the children had had a terrible struggle to survive in the wake of his affair and departure.

Jorge had returned to the city and left the family at 'la petite ferme'. The children had stayed close to home, supporting Raymonde as much as possible.

Their eldest boy, Pierre, married and worked locally as a joiner and builder and had a hard time supporting his mother and his own family. Pierre had a son, Simon, by his first wife and two girls, Emeline and Marthe, by his second wife. Jorge's two daughters were also married; Michelle had twins by her first husband, Daniel and Esther and Madeleine by her second. The youngest daughter, Constance, had only one child, Beatrice.

Now well into his 70s, Jorge felt it was time to make peace with his family. He was restless, uncomfortable with his feelings and he knew he had to do something before he got much older. It had to do with something that had been given to him as a young man.

It was a rather strange looking Collar with an emblem hanging from it. On one side of the emblem was what Jorge described as a circular leaf pattern, very simple in its design, and on the other side another circular pattern, intricately engraved with tiny symbols and images. The provenance of the Collar had not been made clear to him other than that it was a part of the mysterious story that circulated about the origins of his family.

***

The Collar had been given to him by the Steward of an Order into which Jorge had been initiated as a very young man. The organisation was called the 'Order of the Cloister of Lilith' and into which a male in each generation of Jorge's family was initiated at an early age. When initiated into the Order, Jorge had been told a history which dated back many thousands of years. This came as a shock to him, as it recounted the lineage of his ancestors going way back before the Egyptian dynasties. The Order had been formed to guard the descendants of his family, until a specific time in the future.

Jorge was not a particularly religious person, though well read in philosophy and theology. He had come to realise that although the Order had certain rituals and religious connotations, it was not as such a religious order in the sense of it being affiliated to any particular religion or philosophy.

The Order met informally once a year in a back street room in Perpignan, though when he was initiated he had been taken to a temple beneath a chateau near Canet. There were only a few members but he had been told that long ago there had been a greater number.

When initiated, Jorge had been told that it was his duty to keep a discreet watch over a designated female within his family as she would play an important part in an event in the future. However she was unaware of her role or of the existence of the Order. The female designated to Jorge was his cousin Madeleine who lived near Toulouse. It had been easy to keep in touch with her as their families had grown up together and he got on very well with them. He had met her recently and she, like him, felt it was time to hand on some of her belongings especially her jewellery. She had given Jorge a locket and asked him to give it to her namesake Madeleine, one of Jorge's grand-daughters.

Part of the initiation drilled into him was the importance of his role and that at some time in the future he would be contacted by the Steward of the Order at which time he would be instructed to pass on his guardianship. At the last meeting of the Order, the Steward had told the congregation that a significant event would occur early in the 21st Century bringing great changes to the planet and all of its inhabitants. He referred to it as the 'Alignment'. He gave specific instructions as to the role the Order would play at that time and told Jorge it was time to pass his guardianship on and to pass the Collar to the next designated female, Madeleine.

He had subsequently mused over the coincidence of his cousin giving him the locket to pass on to Madeleine. He had casually examined the locket before putting it away and noted that the symbols on both sides of it were the same as that on the Collar that the Steward had given him.

**

At the moment this child was troubling him. Though he referred to her as a child, Madeleine was eighteen years old. Raymonde, his ex-wife had died several years ago and since then Madeleine had been going through a difficult time. She was the only child of Michelle, from Raymonde's and Jorge's eldest daughter's second marriage, and had become particularly close to Raymonde prior to her death.

Raymonde had sensed something was not right with her grand-daughter and her parents and had kept a watchful eye on her. There was some kind of feud between Michelle and her first husband which had made family relations difficult. Unfortunately, Madeleine's parents had noticed the closeness between Madeleine and Raymonde and they had stopped Madeleine from seeing her. Because she knew she had not much time left, the enforced estrangement between her and her granddaughter had upset Raymonde greatly and she had contacted Jorge and told him what was troubling her. More importantly, she wanted to be sure that someone would be looking out for Madeleine in the future.

Jorge had met Michelle's second husband and had disliked him on sight when he attended their wedding. It had been the first time he had seen his whole family together for many years. He had to admit, he felt like a stranger amongst them. On meeting his daughter's husband there was an instant recognition between them that they were not going to get along and following this, family ties had become even more strained. Since then, he had not had much contact with his daughter or Madeleine as she grew up.

Over recent years due to Raymonde's death, he had become closer to Madeleine. Jorge, now elderly, had many infirmities and needed care on a daily basis. His son Pierre, taking pity on his father, had constructed a small chalet in the grounds of '*la petite ferme*' for Jorge. His family were taking turns looking after him and he had a nurse visiting him once a week to see to his medication.

***

Visiting her cousins, Pierre's daughters Marthe and Emeline, Madeleine had met her grandfather and gradually began to spend time with him. Since her grandmother's death she had matured from a gawky teenager to a very attractive young woman. She seemed to enjoy his company and in particular the stories he told her of their family history.

Madeleine had heard of the Legend and dismissed it as a fairy tale, but as she had listened to the family history she began to understand how certain stories transformed into myths.

Her life had not been easy. As an only child of her mother's second marriage, she felt suffocated by her mother and especially by her father. Although she got on very well with her half brother and sister, Daniel and Esther, there was always an undercurrent of tension between her mother and their father, her mother's first husband, which had split the family, most taking sides against her mother in favour of her first husband.

This had particularly hurt her as she had a special relation-ship with her grandmother and visiting her on a weekly basis had been an escape for her. They had spent special time together, playing the piano and singing. Her grandmother had a wonderful voice and had taught her a great deal, musically.

After her grandmother's death, Madeleine's visits to the farm had ceased. Her grandmother had lived near to her Uncle Pierre and his family. At her grandmother's funeral she met her Grand-father properly for the first time. To her, he had always been a shadowy figure in the background of the family. All she knew about him was what her grandmother had told her; how upset she had been when they had divorced some 20 years ago.

In the last year, when visiting her uncle, she had learned that her Grandfather had returned to the farm because he was old and his health was failing. On one of her visits, he had been at the supper table sitting beside her and they had gotten into a conversation. Madeleine found him charming and intelligent and discovered that he had been an artist in his youth.

She remembered the painting over the fireplace in her Grandmother's house of Vesta, the Roman Goddess of the Hearth. Her grandmother had told her that her grandfather had painted it in gouache straight on to the wall. The painting had always fascinated her. It seemed to rise, hovering over the mantelpiece, vibrant in primary colours, quite primitive in the way it had been painted. As a small child she had spent most of the time at family gatherings with her head in her grandmother's lap staring at the painting. In the firelight, her grandmother stroking her hair and she sucking her thumb, her world would transform into a flickering lantern slide of indeterminate shapes amongst the hum and chatter of the party going on around her.

Over the last year she had visited her grandfather regularly, enjoying his company. On her more recent visits his talk had turned to a more sombre note and he had started talking about his age and health and mortality. On her last visit, he said he had decided that the time was right for him to pass on some of his belongings to his grandchildren.

***

Chapter 6
Madeleine
(France, 20th Century)

Walking into his chalet, on this visit, Madeleine noticed straight away that her grandfather was looking slightly dishevelled and out-of-breath probably because he had been over-exerting himself. She also noticed papers and cardboard boxes that had been turned upside down, as if he had been searching for something.

After greeting him, she went over to the kettle and turned it on to make a pot of coffee. This was their normal ritual and having laid out a tray with cups and saucers, she carried it to the kitchen table and sat down with him.

"So, what's going on…?" she asked.

"Oh, I have just been having a sort out, getting rid of all the junk that has accumulated over the years. I told you that I was going to pass on some things which at the moment are mouldering away in the cupboards. I have had a sort through. Some things may be valuable and others only of sentimental interest you know, family history. There is one item, however, that is both valuable and sentimental and I would like you to have it."

Jorge had been searching through some boxes as he was talking to Madeleine and peered up at her from under his eyebrows to gauge her reaction. He went to a small cupboard fixed to the wall and reaching up, took down an old and battered rusty tin box. He brought it over to the table, where they had been sitting drinking their coffee. He prised off the lid and lifted out a package wrapped in a tattered piece of dark blue wool cloth. Unfolding the cloth carefully, he revealed a blue velvet box which contained a folded Collar. Unravelled, it was a heavy looking emblem suspended from a thick woven ribbon. Jorge turned it over in his hands thoughtfully and then passed it to Madeleine

"This Collar is part of the Legend you may have heard about from the family."

"But I thought that was a fairy tale," said Madeleine.

"Well, let's call it a story about your family that needed to be passed down through the ages to ensure the original truth wasn't forgotten; the Collar is part of it. It does not feature in the story, as it probably would have instigated some zealous individuals to set out with a search party to find it. Nobody knows that it exists, other than me and a small band of people formed to look after it."

Jorge began to feel uncomfortable as he was not sure how much of what he knew he should pass on to Madeleine. The Order had told him to pass the Collar on to her but had not told him what he should or should not tell her.

From time to time, he had wondered whether the Order and its Members had just enjoyed the rituals and secret meetings as male bonding sessions. Now they seemed more serious and he felt at a lost as to how to deal with the instructions he had been given.

"It dates back for many centuries, probably at least to the 13th Century.

Normally it is passed down to a male in the family who is initiated into the Society but this time I was told to pass it on to you. However, one of your cousins will be initiated into the Society just as I was and he will act as a guardian to you. I have yet to choose one of my grandsons for the job."

"Why are you calling him my guardian as if I am going to need protection of some kind?"

Madeleine took the Collar and turned it over, peering closely at its design. It certainly looked very old and she was not sure what it was made of. It certainly was not gold and although silver in colour, it did not have any black areas in its crevices that would have accumulated if it was as old as her Grandfather said.

Madeleine looked up and caught her Grandfather staring intently at her.

"It is quite extraordinary and its design suggests it may have some purpose. I don't suppose you know what that might be? It does all seem very strange." She looked quizzically at her Grandfather.

"No, I can't help you there. I dismissed the stories myself, particularly the Legend. However there is a group of us who have always been aware of its existence and of the time when it should be passed on. Apart from a meeting once a year, nothing has happened of interest until now.

I was going to suggest you could wear it from time to time but it is extraordinary and it would probably cause comment from your friends. It might be valuable, so I think you need to find somewhere safe to keep it and then forget about it as I have done until now.

Oh and by the way, your Aunt Madeleine asked me to pass this locket on to you. Coincidentally it seems, she felt the need to divest herself of some of her possessions as I am doing. This is something you can wear."

He handed her the locket.

Jorge knew from the meetings that there had been no threat to the Collar's existence for many centuries and in many ways the Order had become complacent. The associates had met, exchanged pleasantries over the small ritual that took place annually and parted not seeing each other until the following year.

Still dwelling on the purpose of the Collar and all that her Grandfather had told her, Madeleine did not respond immediately to his instruction to keep it safe. Turning it over again in her hands, she knew that it was not something she could wear without causing comment. She also noted that the locket had similar markings to those of the emblem. The locket presented no problem as she would be very happy to wear it, but the Collar would be noticeable and where to keep it safe was a cause for concern.

Although not living with her parents she and her mother were close and had no secrets between them, but her father was another matter. She knew that her mother passed on everything to him. There was a great deal of bitterness in the family between her mother's first husband and her second husband. Her father had a quick temper and she felt she could not trust him, should he become aware of any secret such as this.

Jorge asked Madeleine how she felt, "You look troubled."

"I am thinking about where I can keep the Collar safe. It is not something I can wear. The locket is lovely and I can wear it all the time. I will have to give it some thought.

Anyway, thank you Grandfather. These are the first pieces of jewellery that I possess so they already have a special sentimental value to me."

Madeleine folded the Collar with its ribbon and emblem carefully and replaced it in the box and wrapped the blue cloth around it. She tucked it into her bag. The locket she put on immediately.

"Shall I make us another cup of coffee?"

"Lovely! Then you can tell me about what you have been up to last week."

She spent the rest of the time with her grandfather answering his questions about her day to day life, where she was living, what she was studying, if she had friends, if she had a boyfriend!

***

Her grandfather's last question about a boyfriend softened her as she told him about Thomas, or Tom as she and their friends called him. Tom, Thomas Gill, was English and had been travelling through the towns of the South of France on a sabbatical from his University Studies in England. They had met at a mutual friend's party six months ago. She had found out that he was studying history, and that he had a particular interest in the middle ages and the genealogy of the Royal Families of Europe.

Leaving her grandfather, she biked back to the small apartment where she was living in the back streets of Bourg Madame. She lived alone after moving away from her parents to escape the family arguments.

Madeleine had been lucky to get the accommodation; her mother's friend owned the house which had easily split off into the few rooms that constituted her living space. She had found a job in a bakery nearby and was able to get by.

She was exceptionally bright and also musically gifted but, as was normal for most girls of her background, she had left school early. From an early age she was able to play the piano by ear. Her mother's friend had had a piano in the house which she had willingly moved into Madeleine's rooms and enjoyed hearing the music that drifted through the house on a daily basis.

It was March, just before Easter and as she cycled back she began day dreaming about her friendship with Tom which had developed out of an instant rapport.

Her thoughts turned back again to the Collar and what to do with it. It was obviously valuable and she was beginning to feel tense about having to look after it. Initially, she had felt overwhelmed that her Grandfather had thought her special enough to own it. Although her rooms were comfortable, the house was in a rather seedy area of the town and recently there had been several break-ins and warnings from the local police to be on guard against thieves. She supposed she could leave it with her mother but things between them were not better, in fact they were worse as her father had told her to stay away. She had not seen her mother for some months. For the time being, she decided to keep it close to her all the time and decide later on what to do with it. She also wondered whether to confide in Tom. It was a family secret and although she was beginning to have deep feelings for him, it was early in their relationship.

Madeleine was very conservative about her appearance; aiming at neatness rather than fashion. Her mannish dress, however, accentuated her looks. She had beautiful blonde curly hair that, when caught in the rain, crinkled into ringlets and formed a halo around her head. With a clear translucent complexion and brilliant blue eyes she looked like an angel. This was what struck Tom speechless when he was first introduced to her and time had not diminished this feeling.

When she arrived at her rooms, she was delighted to find that there was a fire burning and the smell of something cooking; some kind of stew by its aroma. Tom was a great cook and he had introduced Madeleine to some of the traditional dishes of England. He shouted from the kitchen and she went through to greet him. He was comforting and kissed and held her for a few minutes before telling her to go and put her things down and freshen up as dinner would be ready in a few minutes.

It was a mutton stew, neck of mutton cooked slowly for several hours with onions, carrots, pearl barley and some local herbs, dished up with baked potatoes. It was just what she needed because she was cold and tired. They drank a *Corbiere* wine with the stew and took their time at the dinner table. Tom had placed candles on the dinner table and around the room. The warmth of the softly lit room crept into her and she began to feel quite drowsy. Seeing that she was very tired, Tom said he would return first thing in the morning to do the washing up. Gratefully agreeing Madeleine saw him to the door, kissed him goodbye and then went to bed.

Madeleine forgot about the Collar and the conversation she had had with her grandfather and fell almost immediately into a deep sleep.

Dreaming... *I was visiting a village where a large group of people were producing a spectacle. They were all busily involved in the production, making costumes and painting the scenery. I peeped through the door of the theatre; the stage was full of people standing in rows. It felt odd, as if they were going to perform naked, but peering closer I saw they were all wearing flesh coloured garments. I passed on to where I was going to stay and walked up a small rise and stood in front of a large building with blue doors. The doors opened, I hesitated to enter...*

***

Chapter 7
Simon
(France, 20th Century)

Jorge watched as Madeleine cycled down the track leading from 'la petite ferme'. He stirred the logs in the fireplace, poured himself a glass of wine and sat in front of the fire.

Jorge had always understood that at some point, the Collar would be passed on to the designated female and it seemed the time for this change had arrived. He now had to choose one of the males in the family to carry on the protective role that accompanied the guardianship of the Collar. He also felt cheated as he realised he had been denied the truth of what it was about. Obviously something very important, possibly dangerous, in view of the secrecy in which the passing down of the Collar had been hidden.

***

The Order had been created a long time ago to protect the family, the female lineage and the Collar and to make sure that the knowledge was passed on at the appropriate time to the next generation.

Through the centuries, the appointed members had no idea of the special powers that were held within its symbolism. They had scant knowledge of the underlying purpose behind the Cloister. Messages were received by the Steward but no questions were ever asked by the other members as to how these messages were received or who delivered them. It was accepted as part of the tenets and rituals of the Order that no questions should be asked.

Jorge now had to appoint the next guardian. *Who should he choose*, he wondered, running their names through his mind.

His son Pierre had been married twice. By his first marriage he had a son Simon. Simon had, up until recently, reacted badly to his father remarrying and having more children. He had ended up living on the streets in Perpignan, jobless and destitute, but had now returned to his father and was living in one of the shacks not far from where Jorge was living now.

Pierre had tolerated his son's behaviour and allowed him back into the family to work alongside him. Pierre was a carpenter and craftsman and recently Simon had been working for him and shown signs of developing into a craftsman himself. Pierre had two girls, Emeline and Marthe, by his second wife.

Jorge's youngest daughter Constance married only once and had an only child, a girl, Beatrice.

His grandson Daniel, the son of his eldest daughter Michelle, had a sister Esther and they were the product of Michelle's first marriage. Madeleine was their half-sister by her mother's second marriage. Daniel worked for an engineering company in Barcelona. Jorge knew that Daniel, along with his sister Esther, liked the good life and socialised at the weekends. Whenever there was a family gathering at weekends, they were always late to arrive having slept in late and looking decidedly bleary eyed and hung over.

So he mused; his choice it seemed was between his son Pierre, Daniel or Simon. He very quickly dismissed his son Pierre as he lacked imagination; his perspective on life was very black and white and Jorge felt he would laugh at the story and the connections with the Order.

Out of the two, Daniel and Simon, he favoured Simon. He liked Simon who had developed into a thoughtful caring adult. He had a good sense of humour and always relieved tense moments in family reunions with light remarks that made people laugh. He recalled a scene when his extrovert ex-wife had been singing and became increasingly red in the face with her efforts. Simon had made some amusing remarks about her performance and had made the whole family and Raymonde laugh. He had a way with people that endeared him to them.

So, that was it. When Simon would call next, he decided, he would gauge his reaction to the possibility of introducing him to the Order.

***

Totally unexpectedly, Simon turned up the very next day with a tractor load of logs that he was delivering to his father's chalet and Jorge marvelled at this; almost as if the thought had gone out and magically triggered Simon's visit.

Although it was March and the spring weather was warm, it was still chilly in the evenings needing the fire to be lit for comfort. Simon unloaded the logs by the side of Jorge's chalet and entered, asking his grandfather to make him a cup of coffee while he started to stack the logs immediately outside the kitchen door.

As it was warm and sunny, Jorge ventured out onto the terrace in front of his chalet and set the coffee down on the wrought iron table. Simon sat down with him and they lapsed into a comfortable companionship that did not require either of them to enter into immediate conversation.

Simon was grateful for a few minutes' respite from his 'daily grind', as he termed it. It involved getting up at 6.00 a.m. every day, including most Sundays. His father was an exacting employer. Simon often thought it had something to do with the fact that Pierre and his mother were still not on good terms and that he was a daily reminder of this sad fact.

Jorge asked Simon if he had seen anything of the family since Christmas, as he had not. Simon said that it appeared everybody was well and working or otherwise occupied with their education. However, it seemed that there had been some trouble with his Aunt Michelle's family. Because of the unhappiness, Madeleine had moved out of the family house and was now living in a friend's house in Bourg Madame. Simon thought it was also due to the fact that her father did not approve of her boyfriend, an English man. Jorge, having heard Madeleine's side of the story, could now understand fully what had happened.

Eventually, Jorge turned the conversation towards the family's history and asked Simon whether he knew of the family legend. Simon laughed and said that whenever he told anybody his name, wherever he went in the area, mainly bars, he was always teased about it.

Jorge continued.

"I have to tell you something concerning the legend which is important to me and to your family. The legend developed out of a story that our ancestors created many centuries ago. It had a purpose, mainly to keep alive some knowledge that had to be kept secret until the time came when it would be needed.

Within each generation a male is selected from our family to become initiated into an Order called 'the Cloister of Lilith'. The Order is organised by a Steward and made up of a number of men. In the past they were called 'Ecuyer', which was the term given to untitled gentlemen of noble families. I was made a member just before my uncle died; he was your great-uncle. Part of the Cloister's teaching is that whoever holds custody of the knowledge has to pass it on when he is nearing the end of his lifetime. At that time, the Steward instructs the members and the family member what should happen."

Jorge paused to see how Simon was taking in what he had to say.

"So what is this knowledge that our family has been secretly guarding for centuries?"

Simon asked with slight amusement in his voice. He was trying to conceal suspicions that his Grandfather was having some kind of elderly memory lapse.

"It is very simple actually," Jorge continued, "if you remember the legend it refers to a Princess; well the Princess is what the Order call the 'designated female' of each generation and she carries the bloodline of our family. It is she who has to be protected along with a Collar that has been passed down.

The meetings of the Order are held annually and some on special dates. Usually they are brief, with only a short ritual reminding us of our purpose.

At the recent meeting a stranger appeared and took part in the proceedings. It was him and the Steward who told me that the time had come when the knowledge and the Collar had to be passed to the designated female of our family, as the time was approaching when she would need to become aware of the role she would be playing in future events. The Order still requires a male relative to continue his protective role.

I have already handed over the Collar to your cousin Madeleine, and she has taken its care seriously. I know I have not been closely involved with the family over the years, but I have watched you all grow up. Of all our family I saw Madeleine and you as the two in the family that might take this seriously. I may be wrong?"

At this, Jorge paused again and looked at Simon closely. Simon felt himself reddening and coughed.

"I know that you may think this is all a bit bizarre and that, probably, I am having a moment's senility but it does have to be taken seriously. I can't believe purely because it has gone on for centuries, all very quietly hidden away, that there is not something very important attached to it. How this eventually evolves, I have no idea only that deep inside me I know that something important is going to happen and that it has been our family's lot to carry it down over the centuries.

I am not giving you a choice as I want you to be my successor in this. It will be your task to keep an eye on Madeleine throughout your life as I have with your great-aunt Madeleine, who up until now has been the designated female."

All the while his grandfather had been speaking Simon had felt himself sinking further into his chair. His mind had drifted off and he was startled out of his day dreaming by his Grandfather peering closely into his eyes.

"Are you all right boy? You look dazed. Probably, it all seems crazy to you as it did to me when my uncle told me about it. However, I have told you and now you are the holder of the knowledge and there is something we have to do together."

Simon stirred into action.

"Wait a minute, you say Madeleine has the Collar and is keeping it somewhere? Do you know where?"

"No idea. That is the point, nobody should know."

"And, now, I have to be her protector."

"Yes, but at a distance. She knows that one of her cousins is involved but very little about the Order itself. By keeping her unaware, the Steward and the Messenger, the stranger who turned up, safeguard the knowledge. It has been a protective measure that has been placed on us. There is a force watching over us, you will understand it when you take part in the ritual."

Simon recoiled somewhat at the thought of being 'watched'. Up to now, his life had been quite difficult. He knew it was his own fault; he had withdrawn from the family when things between his mother and father had become difficult and he had disappeared to Toulouse. Eventually they had divorced and both parents remarried. During this period, he had progressively lost job after job and his sense of direction. All the time he blamed his father. It was when he was absolutely destitute and living on the streets of Toulouse, he had, by chance, encountered Madeleine. At first she had not recognised him and it was then that he realised how glad he was to see someone he knew from the family. He had followed her down the street until she realised who he was. She was horrified at how he looked and had taken him in. He had slept on the floor of her tiny apartment and she had fed him and got him new clothes. It was because of her encouragement that he had come back and made peace with his father and started working for him.

The other thing he had begun to enjoy was socialising with his family and his grandfather had obviously noticed that he had a particularly close bond with Madeleine. As he had grown up with her, he had realised that they both shared the same kind of attitude from their parents. It was not necessarily neglect but dismissal and over-harsh criticism. He saw that they had both withdrawn but in different ways. He saw that Madeleine's way had been to go into herself, into her music, cutting herself off by playing and studying intensely. He saw it now as an escape in just the same way as he had frequented the bars and lost himself by drinking too much, and the amusement of his acquaintances.

The idea of being her protector was not unpleasant. Even more so because of her friend Tom, who had also become his friend. The three of them had spent some pleasant evenings together. He noticed that his grandfather had been giving him time to think and not pressuring him for a response. Having had the time to take in the story, he decided that he would go along with whatever it was his Grandfather wanted him to do. If it turned out to be just a story, well, that was not so bad; it was interesting. If there was something in it, then as Madeleine's protector he would be able to help her if something bad should happen. Of all his family, she was the one person who really mattered to him.

"What are you doing next Wednesday evening?" his grand-father's words broke into his thoughts.

"Er… I will have to check with father about work, but I haven't any other plans."

"Good! Then I have a week to set up a meeting with the Cloister and I will take you along to meet everyone and enrol you. I'll ring you later in the week to confirm everything. I must ask you and insist, however, that you say nothing of what we have talked about to anyone else, ever. Do you understand? Not even your father, who has no idea of my involvement or that of any of his great uncles going back in time."

"That's fine with me. I don't see many people other than my father and his immediate family."

Jorge put his arm around Simon as they got up and walked towards Simon's car.

"Go now, and, as I said, I will ring you. The meeting will be in Perpignan. Will you pick me up and take us together?"

"Of course, no problem! Just let me know."

Simon drove off in his battered Citroen. It was bouncing around and a cloud of smoke was coming out of the exhaust. Jorge shuddered at the thought of the long journey down to Perpignan. The roads were winding and precipitous with great drops on the edges of the gorges. He thought to himself that 'They', whoever They were, had better be looking after them.

***

Chapter 8
The Order – The Cloister of Lilith
(Chateau near Perpignan, France, 20th Century)

As he had promised his grandfather, Simon collected him at 6.30 p.m. the following Wednesday evening. He was allowing plenty of time. Jorge had told him that the meeting would not start until 9.00 p.m. and the journey from Bourg Madame to Perpignan took about two hours.

The journey was not particularly difficult, but the roads were cut into the side of the mountains with very few barriers guarding drivers from the edges which fell away with dangerously steep drops. Concentration was the key to navigating down the winding roads. One advantage was that there was usually very little traffic at that time of day. Simon drove around Perpignan and headed for the coast. His grandfather had told him that the meeting place was at Canet about twelve kilometres further on.

Canet is the seaside resort near Perpignan and Simon, although he had lived with some relatives in Perpignan during his schooldays, had only visited it a few times. He did remember that it was a small fishing village and that there were some very imposing ruins on the road approaching it. He also remembered being told that an old Roman road, the Via Domitia, ran along the coast.

He remembered from a history lesson that the Romans had built the road to join Spain to Italy passing through southern France. He had learned more about this from Madeleine's friend Tom, who was interested in the history of the region and they had spent time comparing the route of the Roman road with that of the pilgrim routes to Santiago de Compestela in Spain.

Following his grandfather's instructions, they did not reach Canet but turned towards the ruins; the remains of a 12th century chateau. They arrived at the foot of a circular tower and Simon was told to follow a rough track. He wondered if his car would stand it. The Citroen was an old car and although it was generally reliable, he was not keen to push it to its limits. The track, however, was passable and as they circled the base of the tower he was told to take another turning. They drove round a thickly hedged bend and came to the red bricks of the tower. His grandfather told him to pull up and he stopped the car. As he did so, he noticed that there were other cars under the trees nearby which concealed them from the view of the roads above.

They got out and walked towards the base of the tower. Simon could not make out where they were going as all he could see were large boulders that formed the foundations of the castle. The air was very still and there was no sign of life, human or animal. His grandfather paused and turned facing one of the boulders. He raised his right hand and made a series of signs, while chanting at the same time. Miraculously, an opening appeared and his grandfather beckoned him to follow.

Beyond the entrance they came to a very old wooden panelled door with iron studs and a huge iron circular door handle. His grandfather rapped the door using the door ring. After a minute or two the door was unlocked, and swung open heavily with a thud, revealing a passage way leading under the tower.

The man who opened the door was wearing a white woollen robe, similar to a monk's habit with a hood which was pulled down; Simon could not see the man's face. They were led down the passage way for a good five-minute walk. Luckily, thought Simon, there were no other passageways leading off so should he need to escape he would have a straight run for the door. He did not know why he was thinking of escape, perhaps because the atmosphere was beginning to get extremely claustrophobic. There was no electric lighting. The man who had met them was holding a torch which was the only light in the passage.

They arrived at another heavy door and the man knocked on it and it opened to reveal a long rectangular room. Inside, there were several men wearing hooded white robes. The room was well lit and Jorge was greeted warmly by the gathering.

While his grandfather talked to the group, Simon glanced around taking in his surroundings. The room was narrow and lined completely in what he took to be pink marble. It glowed warmly in the light of the lanterns that were placed in small niches down the sides of the room. At the other end of the room there was a large alcove in the wall which contained a plaque with a relief etched on it. He could not make out the imagery depicted on it from where he was standing. On each side of the alcove was a column in Greek classical form and in front a small table, again, made out of marble. A faint recollection came to him of a visit he had made to the Abbey at Caunes Minervois where some of the architecture had been made of the local marble which was the same colour.

On each side of the room there were raised platforms with an aisle between. There were quite large niches, or alcoves in the walls behind the platforms. Simon thought they looked like the headboards of beds as if at one time people might have slept there. There were four on each side. The central aisle leading to the alcove was laid out with seven large stone paving slabs, each depicting a different scene; some had birds and animals and there were also soldiers and athletes. Each had an astrological sign too.

His grandfather was still engaged talking to the group. Simon noted that from time to time they had glanced over in his direction as if talking about him. His thoughts went to Madeleine and a wave of emotion came over him about his decision to be her guardian. However, the formality of the surroundings and the people in it were beginning to unnerve him.

Another person had joined the group though he had not been aware of when he had entered the room, he had not seen anybody leave to fetch him. The group had drawn back from the newcomer who was talking to his grandfather who turned and walked over to Simon.

As they approached him, Simon noticed an impressive medallion fixed onto a wide plaited leather support that was placed around the man's neck resting high on his chest. They were introduced; the man's name was Michael.

Michael took Simon's hand and looking directly into his eyes asked him if his grandfather had explained why he was here, and what his duty would be in the future. Simon said that he was unclear as to what his duties would be, but looking around, was now realising the gravity of the commitment he was about to make.

Michael said, "Yes, it seems you have grasped the situation."

"Yes."

Michael glanced around at the other Members and motioned them to come closer so they could hear what he was going to say as well.

"In the next fifty or so years, into the beginning of the next century, there is going to be a great change happening to the Earth and for all the people living on the planet. These changes will become very evident at the beginning of the new millennium 2000. Jorge, at a certain time during the following period the designated female of your family will be called upon to perform certain duties."

He turned to Jorge.

"You have passed the Collar to Madeleine?"

"Yes, and told her to keep it safe. I also explained a little about the Order and that somebody would be in the background looking out for her. She accepted this and there did not seem to be a need to tell her more as I thought it might have troubled her."

"You think she is aware of its importance and can be trusted?"

"Absolutely, she is a good girl. The troubles she has had with her parents and family have made her mature much more quickly than her contemporaries and I have no doubts about her trustworthiness."

Michael turned back to Simon and continued.

"The change that is going to occur is going to be of great benefit to the planet and everybody. It is a significant point in the evolution of human beings."

Michael paused as Simon's face had been changing and his skin had taken on an ashen tone. Michael wondered if Jorge had made the right choice from his family.

"I understand that you may feel rather daunted and that it may also make you question your upbringing and education. However, I must have your understanding that this is serious. The Cloister has been in existence for thousands of years for this purpose and not for amusement."

Simon felt embarrassed as that is exactly what he had been thinking. He was also disconcerted, as he felt strongly that this

Michael seemed to be able to read his mind. However, in response he said that he was finding it difficult to take in.

"I can follow what you are saying though, as I said, I am not sure I understand fully."

"Your role does not at the moment require any more from you. You will be contacted when the time comes for you to do anything and that is some time in the future. Now, we must initiate you into the Order."

Michael led the group down the aisle and the Members took up positions in front of him forming a semi-circle. Michael and Jorge stood Simon in front of them. What followed seemed to Simon like a church service, there were various chants, perhaps in Latin, though it seemed rather a strange language with many guttural sounds. Jorge handed Michael the ring from the little finger of his right hand. Funny, Simon thought, he had never noticed his Grandfather wearing it before. Michael took the ring and gave it to Simon indicating that he should put it on the little finger of his right hand. Michael removed the medallion from around his neck and held it in front of Simon, and asked him to place his right hand on it.

"Take this ring as a symbol to remind you of your allegiance to the Cloister. Wear it at all times and pass it on only to the next designated member of your family. All present ask you now to affirm your allegiance to this Order of the Cloister of Lilith and to carry out the duties required of you, now and in the future."

Simon glanced around at everyone present and nodding said, "I do."

Michael closed the ceremony by chanting a short verse and the group moved away.

Talking to Simon and Jorge, Michael said that time was running out and that there was going to be a war in Europe. Jorge nodded as he had heard murmurings of this in the local bars. Continuing, he told them that Madeleine would be leaving to go to England soon. Simon was shocked. He had seen her recently and enjoyed their usual closeness, yet she had not mentioned this.

Michael reassured him and said that soon it would be extremely difficult to travel and life was going to change radically for everybody. He also added that it was necessary for him to follow his cousin to England. Simon was even more stunned at the possibility of travelling anywhere, least of all to England, which seemed impossible on his limited means. Michael reassured him that all would be made possible for him.

"When you next see your cousin she will tell you that she is engaged and going to England with her fiancé."

"But she is not even in a serious relationship with her friend Tom," protested Simon.

Leaving the chateau and driving back to Bourg Madame, Simon was very quiet.

"Wondering what you have let yourself in for I suspect?" his grandfather offered as a way of breaking the silence.

"It all seems a bit unbelievable to me, but it is about Madeleine and if half of what has happened tonight is about her safety then I am not going to question anything. All I can do now is trust."

Taking his eyes off the road for a moment he looked at Jorge searching for a response.

"It is all you can do, as I trusted your great uncle when he handed me the ring," replied Jorge.

***

Leaving the Chateau, Malachi was satisfied that all was well for the time being. In the coming months and years on Earth there was going to be trouble.

As always when he experienced material existence at the lower levels, it disturbed his vibration and though he could if he wanted to go straight to the next stage he decided to step up to Level 7 and re-energise.

***

Chapter 9
Between Past and Present
(Europe, 1930 – 1950)

After returning from the visit to their grandfather, and all that ensued, life changed dramatically for Madeleine, Tom and Simon and for the rest of France.

It was early in 1939 and there had been talk of war for some time. Tom's parents, Jack and Evelyn Gill, were very concerned for him and had been writing to him weekly urging him to return to England. Because of his feelings for Madeleine he had put off responding to them and doing as they suggested. He had been spending more and more time with her and had almost moved into her tiny apartment in the centre of the town.

In the local cafes and bars they heard increasing talk of war between England and Germany. Tom and Madeleine were aware of the frequent political meetings in the region since the outbreak of the Spanish Civil war in 1936.

People were restless and the expatriates from all over Europe living in the south of France were nervous, continually debating whether they should return to their home country or stay and trust that that part of France might escape the conflict. There were many people feeling threatened, especially artists, writers and philosophers who would all be in danger of persecution.

In August, Tom's parents arrived. Frustrated by his non-response to their letters, they had taken a rash decision to go to France and convince him that he must return to England. They had come by boat across the channel and then train down to Perpignan. It had not been an easy trip as they had to change trains frequently.

Tom was their only child and very much loved. His mother had over-protected him as a child and this had made Tom break away in his teenage years. He had been lucky enough to get into Oxford University and the freedom he enjoyed there and his interests in politics, history and philosophy had led him to take the decision after his graduation to travel to France. At the time he met Madeleine, he had not yet decided on a career choice and had worked his way down to the South doing odd jobs; mainly helping in the vineyards.

Having made their way up to Bourg Madame, his parents were relieved to find their son well and they settled into a local pension and arranged to meet him and Madeleine later. Tom chose a local bar that served evening meals and he introduced Madeleine and brought them up to date on what he had been doing on his travels.

His parents then took over the conversation. Trying not to sound too dramatic his parents related to the couple the situation that was developing in Europe with the rise of the Nazi Government in Germany and the threat of war. They told Tom that a limited form of conscription had been introduced in April that year, with the Military Training Act being passed the following month; only single men 20 to 22 years old were liable to be called up. However, they told Tom that should war be declared, there was the possibility that all men between 18 to 41 years old would be called up to fight and this would include him on his return to England. They discussed with him the alternative, should he remain in France.

Tom and Madeleine had not really taken in the immensity of the problems that Europe would be facing in the coming months. They also found themselves in an even more difficult situation realising that should Tom go back to England, it would mean indefinite separation. A sense of desperation fell over the pair.

Jack and Evelyn decided to leave Tom and Madeleine in the café as they realised that they needed time to talk things over. They went back to their lodgings and agreed to meet them at breakfast in the same café the next morning. As they left, they pressed home the fact that they would need to leave as soon as possible. Madeleine felt as if someone had shot an arrow through her heart and a sense of loneliness struck her to the core.

"What are you thinking…" Tom eventually asked Madeleine.

"I am feeling a bit overwhelmed, there's so much to take in. I suppose we have been so happy that we have ignored the situation. What about you?"

"Yes, the same. Even more so, I hadn't thought about returning to England. If I went back, what would it mean? I would have to go into one of the armed forces almost immediately. But for you, I can't imagine what might happen here. There are already refugee camps on the beaches, but if the Germans came through it would drive people the other way into Spain. It just seems like it could be a complete muddle and potentially dangerous."

Madeleine thought for a moment.

"I probably will stay here in the mountains, out of the way as much as possible. Supporting my family is the only thing I can think of at the moment, though even that is a bit of a farce as most of them really pay little attention to me, or know me for that matter, except my grandfather."

Thinking of her grandfather reminded her of the Collar that he had given her and also the importance he had emphasised to her of keeping it safe. She wondered whether this was the time to tell Tom about it.

"Hey, you seemed to have left me... Are you okay?" Tom asked.

"Yes, sorry. I was just thinking about my grandfather."

Tom also had been thinking and took her hand across the table.

"You must know how I feel about you. There is a way of resolving things. What I am saying is that you can come back with me to England. We can marry when we reach England. Oh hell! I am doing this the wrong way."

Tom ran out of words. At the suddenness of Tom's awkward proposal, Madeleine felt her eyes filling up with tears.

"Oh God, I did not mean to upset you! I am sorry. I know that it would be too much to expect you to leave here. I was only thinking of myself, selfish really, as I could not bear to think of leaving you. I just know that I have to go back to England and that I must take part in defending my country."

Madeleine reached out to Tom and took his hands. He moved around to her side and held her in his arms comforting her and waited for her to calm down, his throat dry, in anticipation of what she might have to say.

"Everything seemed so empty until you came into my life and the thought of never seeing you again frightens me. I am scared because I can't speak English and I will be a foreigner in a country that will be at war. I have no idea what the future of France will be. All I know is that I will be with you. Yes, I will come with you."

A flood of relief rushed through Tom and for them both, it seemed a weight was lifted off them.

***

After making their decision Tom and Madeleine told his parents. Jack and Evelyn were rather taken aback but tried not to show their reaction. They decided to make the necessary arrangements to travel back together. Within a few days they had arranged transport to take them to Perpignan where they could pick up a train which would set them on the journey back to England.

In the meantime, Madeleine went to see her parents and tell them the news. This was met with utter disbelief and them trying to persuade her against marrying Tom and leaving France. Madeleine was at a loss to understand their reaction. What was it they thought they were losing if she went? They certainly had made no steps before to keep her close or ever show any affection towards her.

With them following her around, she packed the few possessions she had at the family home and left on what she felt were bad terms. It was a sad state of affairs to leave like that.

Madeleine also decided to go up to her grandfather's chalet and tell him the news. At her grandfather's chalet she was pleased to see that Simon was there too. They embraced, pleased to see each other. As usual she made a tray of coffee and took it over to them. They were lounging on chairs on the veranda as the sun was hot with a breeze rustling the leaves on the trees nearby. It was a sight she would keep in her memory for later and she stood for a minute or two taking it all in. It was very relaxed as it always was between the three of them.

Placing the tray on the small table she drew up a chair to join them.

"I have some news, you may be surprised."

Her grandfather and Simon exchanged knowing looks.

"Tom's parents arrived the other day and have persuaded him to go back to England as they feel that war is imminent."

Her grandfather nodded sagely.

"Yes, I can understand that, there has been a discussion about the situation down in the cafes of the town."

"Well, here is the surprise, I am going with them. Tom wants us to get married. We have become very close. And you get on with him very well don't you Simon?"

Simon had been struck speechless remembering what Michael had said at the Temple recently. He stared at his grandfather. How could Michael have known of this turn of events? He was also thinking that he would have to prepare himself to go to England to follow Madeleine.

"Well, aren't you going to say something…?"

"Of course, it's a surprise! I did not know you were so involved with Tom. I like him, but to uproot yourself from here and go to a strange country seems rather sudden. Are you sure you are doing the right thing?"

Simon turned to his grandfather silently pleading with him to say something.

"You are rather young to be thinking of getting married aren't you? You are only nineteen, how old is Tom?"

Her grandfather asked.

"He is twenty-two and I feel as if I have known him all my life and in view of my parents' attitude towards me, he feels more like family than they do."

Simon and Jorge resisted persuading her to stay. They kissed her and gave her their blessing. Later, after she had left, Jorge helped Simon with his plans to follow Madeleine. They decided his best course of action would be to start travelling north. Jorge thought he was bound to be involved in the conflict in some way if the war began but did not share this with Simon, as he thought he had a difficult enough task without being given any discouragement.

***

The family's journey back to England was not easy. *En route*, stopping at various towns, everything seemed very quiet with the local police more evident. From the train windows they saw convoys of trucks full of soldiers weaving their way along the roads, running parallel to the railway tracks. Madeleine wondered where they were going. They all looked so young. She felt sympathy for them, leaving her own family behind and setting off into an unknown future.

Luckily Tom's mother Evelyn spoke very good French. On the journey she chatted to Madeleine about their family, jokingly referring to her husband's passion to preserve his family's history.

Evelyn told Madeleine about an ancestor who had travelled to England from France in the 13th Century disguised as a Friar and came to a monastery near where the Gills lived. Eventually, he had left the Order and married and it was from him that her husband had descended.

Our family name is 'Gill' but Jack discovered going back that our full name is 'Lamberte St. Gilles', you can see that it has been shortened over the centuries. We also know that it originates from a town in southern France, St. Gilles, do you know of it?

Madeleine nodded.

"Yes, St. Gilles is in the Camargue. It is one of the points on the pilgrim route to Santiago de Compestela in Northern Spain. We often see pilgrims making their way there from different routes via Bourg Madame."

"Lamberte St Gilles. It has a nice ring to it," said Madeleine.

"Jack is researching further speculation about the family's connection with the Counts of Toulouse around the time of the genocide of the Cathars in Southern France. You may know something of that as it all happened in the Languedoc not far from where you come from?"

She turned to Madeleine looking for a response.

"Yes, I have heard of the Cathars, mainly from the history lessons in school. They don't like to talk about it very much, as there are still people who consider they are Cathars and it is a bit of a sore point with the Church."

"I can imagine," replied Evelyn.

Twisting the locket that her Aunt had given her, Madeleine felt a slight sense of loss. She had no knowledge of her own family's history. When her grandfather had handed over the Collar and told her how old it was and that it had been handed down through the generations, it had come as quite a revelation to her.

Apart from knowing her immediate family, she had no knowledge of her family history. There had never been any interest shown in her family of their history.

Evelyn was still talking and Madeleine tuned in to what she was saying.

"Jack has a very old ring which was passed down to him. I have seen it but it is kept in a Bank vault in London, as it is obviously a quite valuable heirloom. It looks like a seal that would have been used to seal letters with wax."

Madeleine thought that was interesting and her thoughts went, immediately, to the Collar she had in her possession. She had wrapped it and hidden it deep within her luggage. She would ask them to put it in the bank vault with the ring.

***

Arriving in England, Madeleine settled to living with her prospective in-laws. Tom's parents lived in a large family house in a small village, Denton, near to the site of the monastery that Evelyn had told her about.

The decision as to whether to marry was made for Tom and Madeleine. Tom was called up and they thought it would be better for Madeleine if they married so she could continue to live with his parents.

Soon after their marriage, Tom was enlisted into the Intelligence Service of the Ministry of Defence due to his Oxford background. He was sent on a rigorous and secret training and Maddy had no idea where he was for months at a time. The War years passed with them hardly seeing each other.

Madeleine, with the help of Evelyn, became an auxiliary nurse at the local hospital and came to love her work. The Gills were very good to her and, like them, she longed for the War to be over and Tom to return.

Life was difficult, as it was, for the entire population during the War.

***

Madeleine's cousin, Simon, with the mission to keep an eye on Madeleine and to protect her, had travelled north when she left with Tom and his family. He had reached Northern France but had been unable to cross the channel. Due to pressure put on him by groups of young men such as himself, he had enlisted in the army.

During the war he later became part of the French Resistance, staying mainly in the sections of Northern France and working with the English Intelligence Service which sent spies.

Neither he nor Tom realised they were in the same line of work trying to get people in and out of France secretly, even though their paths crossed several times.

***

Part II
The Alignment
(France 2000 – 2012)

A dot, a spark, was struck in the universal forge of darkness. It magnified and its light became a living energy. Suspended in 'being' the living energy waited. Time, as perceived by humankind, was not known. Other 'beings' came and added their light to the energy and a 'knowing' emerged as to how it would become. The contract was sealed.

Overseer Fraterne Nammu and Malachi stepped down their frequency to draw close to the birthing of the human child. They saw the soul as 'the being' slipped into the baby's body. The midwife overseeing the birth drew the baby away from the mother and wrapped it in a muslin towel. She gently flicked the baby's foot and the infant's mouth opened and gave a gasp and then a healthy cry. Seeing the successful birth, the Guardians withdrew. Earth time had now to pass to the appointed time and the maturing of the soul in its incarnation.

From another dimension, another group of beings had stepped into the time/space continuum of the exact moment of the birth and were also observing. They had been searching through aeons and located their focus to this place. They too had to wait for the appointed time.

Chapter 10
The Gills
(England Post-War, 1948)

The mother was overwhelmed, tears running down her cheeks, as she clasped the new-born to her breast. A little girl; perfect in every way. Her name was to be the same as hers and she would carry her grandmother's name too. Madeleine Raymonde Zagel Gill had entered the world.

It was May 1948 and in the days when fathers were not welcome in the delivery room. Madeleine Gill, the midwife and her doctor were very happy following the birth. Dr Sharp who had been the family doctor for many years stood back viewing the scene. He was relieved it had been an easy birth not like Madeleine's first baby, a boy, who had been born some eighteen months previously.

"I think Tom is waiting outside, I will go and tell him the news and then send him in. Well done, she is a beautiful baby."

Madeleine's first born, Charles George, Charlie for short, was being looked after by her husband Tom and his parents. She too was relieved at how easy the birth had been and lay back against the pillow and bathed in the glow emanating from the creation of this little being.

Tom entered the room with a huge bunch of flowers and a tiny teddy bear that his mother had sent along. He kissed Madeleine and, sitting on the edge of the bed, put his hand out to cup his daughter's head which was covered with a fine down of fair hair.

"Beautiful just like her mother."

He bent and kissed Madeleine and then the baby's forehead.

***

In the days and weeks following her birth, Madeleine sensed this child seemed different in some way. Maddy, her name had been quickly shortened, seemed a contented baby rarely crying and sleeping well. She was no trouble, unlike her brother who, it seemed to his mother, had cried and screamed non-stop since his birth in October 1946.

Madeleine, the little boy Charlie, and Tom had to endure one of the worst winters in 1947 so Charlie had not been outside at all since his birth until the late spring of 1947. At the time they were living in a small cottage on the outskirts of the village of Denton, in the grounds of what was once part of Ashbridge Priory.

Since the war, Tom had found it difficult to settle down and had taken a job as chauffeur to a family who owned one of the largest houses in the district; Asherton House. He needed to be earning to support his family while he sorted out what he wanted to do with his future. It was to this cottage that Maddy was taken after her birth.

At the time Asherton House was one of the few large houses in the small village, approximately twenty five miles outside of London. It sat on the edge of the village green. Tom and Madeleine's tiny cottage was in the grounds of the house.

Tom had lived in the village of Denton all his life, apart from when he had gone to University and then taken a sabbatical in France which is where he had met Madeleine. He had brought her back to England with him just before War was declared.

The War had occupied the first six years of their married life. Tom had been in the army and had spent most of the time in France. Languages and a career in the Civil Service had been his potential future before the War. In the first year after it broke out and through his father's connections (his father had worked as a Civil Servant in the Ministry of Defence), he had been recruited into the Intelligence Service and spent most of the War travelling through France helping the British and French Resistance. He felt lucky to have survived as so many of his comrades had not. He had been 22 when he went into service; the majority of services recruits had been around the same age, some younger. It had been a time of rapid growing up. Now at 29, with a wife and young family to support, life had become serious.

His father had retired after the war and it was through his connections with the local aristocracy and ex-colleagues at the Ministry of Defence that Tom had been given the job as chauffeur while searching for a position that was more suited to his education and experience during the war.

Madeleine, being French and arriving in England at the outbreak of war, had a more difficult time. However, with Tom's mother's help coaching her in English and her contacts with the local war effort, Madeleine had found herself training to be an Auxiliary Nurse.

She discovered that it suited her very well. With her gentle manner and ability to communicate well with people in general, she found the various aspects of medical knowledge she had to acquire interesting and easy to learn. She turned into a very competent nurse respected by her colleagues.

After the end of the War, the arrival of Charlie first and then Maddy had delighted them both. Even though the country was still recovering from the war and rationing was part of their lives, the babies seemed a perfect reward for having survived.

Charlie and Maddy, because there was only eighteen months between them, grew up very close together. They were very different. Charlie veered towards the sciences in school and eventually University graduating with a Physics degree.

Maddy's inclinations led her to an interest in the arts. Very creative as a child, she eventually trained as a teacher. She married a local boy Colin Jameson in 1969. They met when they were teenagers when he moved with his family to the village. Colin eventually became a trader in the City of London and they moved to the suburbs of the City and Maddy took a teaching job in a local school. With Maddy's income, they managed to have a very comfortable life enabling them to do very much as they pleased. Within the course of time, happily married, they produced three children; two boys and a girl. Maddy's parents, Madeleine and Tom proved to be doting grandparents.

Apart from the usual trials of life, births and deaths for Maddy and Colin, life together was good although the odd unusual things did occur from time to time.

***

One such occasion arose on Maddy's twenty-first birthday; six months before her wedding to Colin. Her mother took her out for the day as a birthday treat and during the course of their lunch gave her what she called a very special present.

"I am going to give you, or rather pass on to you, something that was given to me when I was about the same age as you. It was at the time that I met your father when he came to France before the war. At the time I was not very happy living with my parents."

"Is that why you have never spoken very much about them?" asked Maddy.

"Yes, I suppose so. I was very close to my grandmother, your great grandmother, her name was Raymonde and you are named after her. I barely knew my grandfather, as he and my grandmother had divorced before I was born. Things were very acrimonious between them and he had been ostracised from the family. In fact it caused a great deal of disharmony in the relationships between their children, one of whom was my mother, Michelle. However when Raymonde died I met my grandfather at the funeral. He became ill and moved to a small chalet at my Uncle Pierre's farm in the Pyrenees. Because of my unhappiness, I used to escape frequently to the farm. He and I became close. Shortly before he died, he gave me this."

Madeleine took out a blue velvet box and pushed it across the table to Maddy. She nodded at Maddy and said, "It's yours now."

Intrigued, Maddy took the box and opened it and took out what she first thought was a necklace. However, as she unravelled it, she saw that there was a heavy emblem attached to it.

"What is it? It is rather unusual."

"All I know is that it is very old and that it has been passed down through my family for centuries. As you are now the same age as I was when it was passed to me, I thought you should have it now. Grandfather told me that there is a legend attached to it that dates back to the Thirteenth Century.

I do remember there was a legend attached to the family, we all knew of it, and so did everybody in the region. However, I can't remember much about it now other than it was about a princess and that she carried a 'song' and that at a particular time she would be called upon to carry out a task.

I was also told by him that I had to look after it, his words were 'Guard it,' and not let it leave my possession and then pass it on at an appropriate time to my daughter, or if I did not have a daughter than to a close female relative.

I was told that somebody would come and tell me to pass it on, but no-one has turned up. It only came to mind because, out of the blue, I had a letter from my cousin Simon. It was a bit rambling, remembering our childhood and all that went on, and also about grandfather. He mentioned this necklace or rather the Collar is how he described it. I was surprised that he knew about it."

"You've never spoken about a cousin Simon."

"Well, actually you have quite a few uncles, aunts and cousins in France. Simon would be your second cousin not your uncle, though if you ever met him you would probably call him Uncle as he is of the same generation as me.

That's all I can tell you really as I have lost touch completely with my family in France. Grandfather did tell me that someone in the family would look after me and although I have had no contact with him, Simon did come to live in England after the war so it may be him. We don't see much of him as he is a bit of a recluse; living up in Cumbria in some kind of derelict house near Lake Windermere."

Maddy turned the Collar over in her hands trying to take in this information.

"It is not something I could wear so what shall I do with it?"

"I agree. I had the same thoughts when I was given it. I think it is valuable, it's not gold or silver; I can't identify the metal at all, but the symbols look very unusual too. It is not something wearable for social occasions. It does need to be kept somewhere safe.

Your grandfather Jack is very interested in history and when I came to England I was told all about his family going back centuries. At the time I was told he had a ring that belonged to the family and which was valuable because it was very old. He kept it in a safe box in a Bank in London. So, not knowing what to do with the Collar I asked him if he could put it in the box with the ring to keep it safe.

I told him it was a family heirloom and when he saw it he was really interested in its history of which, of course, I could tell him very little. Anyway he took it and until this week I had not seen it since then."

"So what about the ring?"

"Well, I expect it will eventually be passed down to your brother, Charlie, just to be fair, as you have the Collar."

Maddy had been listening intently to her mother; realising that she had been given something very special, but she also felt ambivalent about the responsibility of looking after it. The fact that it was so old also intrigued her as she had no idea until this moment that her family did have such a history.

"Well, I think if Granddad agrees it should be left in the Bank, don't you. You have gone to the trouble of taking it out to hand it over to me, but surely the best thing is to keep it safe."

"Yes, I suppose so. I think the handing over to you was the important point. Oh, it all seems a bit mysterious to me, all this handing over and passing down, I can't put my finger on whether or not there is some purpose to it."

Maddy nodded, "Yes I agree, it does seem a bit strange, are you sure you can't remember any more?"

"Not a thing, it's almost as if I have been kept in the dark about something for a particular reason."

As she finished the sentence, Madeleine felt a chill run through her and she drew her jacket closer around her shoulders. It was a warm day and all of a sudden clouds had brewed up and passed over the sun casting a dark shroud over everything outside the restaurant window.

"It looks as though there could be a storm coming, perhaps we should make a move and get back."

Having enjoyed their mother-daughter bonding they kissed and parted; Madeleine carrying away the Collar to replace it safely in the bank. At the same time she felt a sense of relief as if something had been lifted off her shoulders.

***

On the side of a moor in Cumbria, Simon sat outside his house overlooking the lake. Malachi sat across the table from him. Both were musing about the past. This was the second time in Simon's life that Michael, the name he knew him by, had appeared. The first, back before the war when his grandfather had taken him to the Cloister meeting and then two weeks ago he had just appeared out of the blue.

"Did you send the letter?"

"Yes, but I have not had any reply yet."

"Don't worry. I received a message that the Collar has been passed on to Maddy, Madeleine's daughter. Are you going to pass your guardianship on to someone else?"

Simon thought for a few minutes.

"I can't think of anyone in the family as I have lost touch with them all. They are scattered all over the place, mainly in France. There is Charlie, of course, Maddy's brother, but I have never met him so have no idea how he has turned out."

While he was speaking, Simon was twisting the ring on the little finger of his right hand. He always wore the ring and remembered when his grandfather had passed it on to him.

"So you are going to have to continue with the overseeing. The Alignment is approaching soon, early in the first years of the new millennium, so probably there is no need to involve anybody else."

"You say soon; soon to you is a long time for me, thirty years or so. I am not sure I am going to make it to the year 2000 let alone beyond that. I will be 80 by then. Anyway I don't understand what you are saying, all this mystery."

"Courage my friend, you are healthy and live a simple life that will get you through. We are watching anyway so if there is any danger we will assist."

Exactly who was watching and who would assist seemed, as Simon said, a mystery to him. After a short while, Malachi got up and left. Simon watched as he walked away, always puzzled how at a certain distance he seemed to literally disappear into thin air.

Michael's sudden appearance a few weeks ago had shaken Simon somewhat. It was a long time since he had seen him and the conversations he had had with his grandfather and his initiation into the Cloister was a distant memory.

Although he had promised to keep an eye on Madeleine he had also forgotten about that too. He had found himself settling in England after the war and now that he thought about it, it was strange as he had a strong loyalty to his native country. He had had no contact with Madeleine since the last time he saw her in

France at their grandfather's house just before she left with Tom for England.

Michael's appearance and his request to him to write to Madeleine and ask about the location of the Collar had surprised him and awoken memories of his earlier life.

Like Tom, he had had problems settling down after the War. He was single and had many English contacts he had made during the course of his resistance work. He had travelled across the channel and went north. He had no idea what he was going to do and, like Tom, had taken odd jobs initially to tide himself over until he decided what he wanted to do.

He had been very quick to learn English and after a few years he had become a teacher of languages in one of the new secondary schools that were cropping up throughout the country. Content with his semi-reclusive life in the glorious surroundings of the Lake District, he became increasingly introspective and began researching and writing about ancient civilisations.

***

Chapter 11
The Croft
(Pyrenees, France/Spain border, 2005)

Maddy was tired, normally she enjoyed the flight from London, especially, due to the descent into Perpignan airport when she could see the Pyrenees in the distance.

It had been an early flight and Colin had dropped her off at the airport at 5:00 a.m. for her flight departure at 7:10 a.m. It was perfect timing and easy checking in. They had booked that flight as it pre-empted the families going on holiday for the Easter break. The children had not broken up yet from school.

Maddy was going to the Croft; the property that she and Colin had decided to buy eighteen months earlier, to be exact, in the autumn of 2003 after her visit in the spring of that year with her friend Helen.

Before agreeing to buy the place, Maddy had wrestled with her feelings having, at that time, only recently moved to the country from London. She had been enjoying the first six months of their retirement and it had seemed to her that she was taking on a burden that she was not sure she necessarily wanted.

However, they had bought it and two subsequent weekend breaks and a fortnight's holiday, the previous summer, had changed her attitude completely; so much so that she and Colin had decided to spend the whole summer at the Croft this year.

One of the things that had finally changed Maddy's mind was the prospect of the garden there. Since retiring, Maddy had rediscovered a love of nature and she had turned into an avid gardener. The potential of creating a wonderful terraced garden full of flowers and vegetables in what to her was an incredibly idyllic setting had rekindled a deep urge to create within her.

They had called the property The Croft because it seemed appropriate. Perched on the side of a mountain foothill, it looked like a shepherd's stopping place. It had previously been known as 'La Borda' or, by the very old locals, 'la petite ferme'.

It was now early in the second spring since they had bought the property and they had decided to come out and stay until the end of September, possibly October, depending how they felt and what the weather was like. It was going to be the first really long period that they had spent together at the Croft.

As it turned out, Colin had not flown out with Maddy. At the last minute he had discovered that his passport was out of date and therefore he would have to renew it before he went anywhere. Because Maddy was so cross with him about this, it had almost spoilt the family party that their daughter, Grace, had organised as a send-off, knowing that her parents would be away for some time.

Despite everything, once aboard the aircraft Maddy calmed down and enjoyed the flight which landed at Perpignan airport on time. Maddy picked up a hire car from the airport depot and set off for the mountains.

En route, she stopped at a small supermarket and bought some basics; milk, bread, cheese and olives and a carton of bouillabaisse to heat up for a light meal later on. When she would arrive at the Croft, it would be late afternoon and by the time she had unpacked she knew she would want something simple to eat before going to bed.

After crossing the flat coastal plain from the Mediterranean, the car began to climb up through the Tet valley, with its eroded sandstone cliffs on either side of the road, and Mount Canigou in the south.

The Croft was much higher up in the mountains, not far from a town right on the French Spanish border. It was rather unusual, or so Maddy thought, as it was sign-posted Bourg Madame on the French side and in the middle of the town you crossed into Spain and the signposts changed to Puigcerdà. However, the Croft was near a small village the turning for which was on the French side, Bourg Madame.

As predicted, by the time she arrived in the afternoon, the sun was beginning to sink down behind the mountain peaks and the heat was draining from the earth. Although it was lighter here in the evenings than in England, it was going to be dark within an hour or so.

It was overwhelming, the purity of the mountain air and the clarity of the landscape. Maddy always felt that she shared this with more than herself and always felt a tingle of excitement run through her. It energised her and she always felt disorientated at first as if the world was on hold. There seemed to be a timelessness about the region.

She had to remind herself, though, that there were days when mist and cloud descended, the temperature dropped and you were left feeling isolated, sitting like a bird in a nest on the edge of a craggy ledge.

Although it had been renovated, the original building of the Croft was very old. It was a stone building and the stones forming the walls had been piled up, one on the other, on a wide rocky ledge that formed the foundations. It was not a very large house and they had bought it at a reasonable price because of its fairly remote location and because the vendor, Colin's friend Chris, had wanted to sell the property as quickly as possible.

It stood alone; a twenty-minute walk from the nearest village which was quite small and only supported a Boulangerie and a Café. From their frequent visits to the Café, Colin and Maddy had learned some history of their purchase.

The story was that it was thought to have been part of a larger complex of dwellings, possibly a small hamlet of four or five cottages. In addition, they had been told that there was a well on the property but so far they had not been able to locate it, walking through what was a wilderness of a garden. In fact in the time they had spent there they had only had time to concentrate on furnishing the house. They had not yet ventured too far into the land that constituted the whole of the property.

There was quite a considerable acreage of land stretching down in front of the Croft and they were considering how to transform it into a terraced garden. Maddy was looking forward to preparing some plans and features for the garden over the summer. The house was on one level with a patio and pool on the terrace below. They had not had to do any work to the interior of the house as it had been renovated very well and fitted out with a modern kitchen and other amenities. In the time they had the property, they had furnished it simply and turned the attic space into a bedroom-cum-second-sitting-room for the family when they came for their holidays.

As Maddy opened the door, she heard something heavy beating in the air and turning she saw a large bird swoop from above the roof of the house and down, down into the valley. It must have been perched just above the Croft and as she watched it soar she thought it must be an eagle. The beauty of its size and glide mesmerised her for some minutes, as she watched it disappear into the depth of the valley.

As she entered the Croft, a damp and musty smell met her along with a sense of dust flying up from the floor. It was always that way, and she knew that it would take a couple of days to bring the house round to being cosy and lived in. She did not mind this, in fact enjoyed it. It always reminded her of when she was a child playing house in her father's shed in the family garden.

Maddy brought in her suitcase, flight bag and shopping items. Opening the windows throughout the place to catch the last warmth of the day, she unpacked her suitcase. The bed linen had been stored in waterproof bags, so they smelt fresh as she got them out. She quickly made up the bed and then went out to the living room.

When they had left the previous autumn, Colin had made up a fire ready to light when they arrived on their next visit. Maddy was able to put a match to this and soon the room began to feel warmer. Unpacking the groceries, she heated the soup and made up a simple tray for her supper and carried it to the armchair in front of the fire. There was also a bottle of wine in the cupboard, so opening this she poured herself a glass and settled down to enjoy her meal.

She woke up at 2:00 a.m. the next day, stiff in the armchair. Leaving everything, she went straight to the bedroom and climbed in between the lavender smelling sheets and fell back, drowsy, into a deep sleep.

Dreaming…

I am in a very old house. The house had many rooms, large and stacked from ceiling to floor with leather bound books embossed with gold. As I glided past, I ran my hand along the shelves as if to take out a volume. There were many huge china vases and oil paintings by Italian masters. In some rooms there were frescos on the walls and tapestries depicting pastoral scenes. The floors were covered in antique Persian carpets laid over marble floors. Chandeliers hung, heavy and deep, glittering as they moved in a gentle breeze that was coming from a window that opened onto a balcony. The balcony had marble balustrades, heavily sculptured, and looking down I saw that it was held by caryatids below. Looking out, I saw hills and valleys stretching out before me with mountains in the distance. It was vibrantly green and the sun shone brilliantly. There must have been a shower as the trees and grass near me glittered as if every leaf was hung with the most precious diamonds, glinting as they jostled hanging in their space. I was gasping for breath, the sight was overwhelming and I sighed deeply. I had returned.

Chapter 12
The Garden

Since arriving a week ago, Maddy had made great advances in settling in. The house was now feeling lived in and had acquired a more established look. She had made a couple of trips into Bourg Madame and had bought pots and pans and utensils for the kitchen and also some soft furnishings made by local needlewomen. It was all looking very comfortable and rustic.

Maddy had also ventured into the garden, deciding that she would deal with the wilderness nearest the house and work out and down from there. So far she had only managed to clear the area immediately in front of the house. Though it looked tidier it was quite bare and her thoughts were about how she was going to plant it. Mostly she felt with shrubs and flowers that would fill the space and reduce weeds and tending prospects. The less work it was, the better in view they might be coming and going rather than living here permanently.

One slight cloud on the horizon, however, was that Colin would not be coming down as soon as they had anticipated. His passport had arrived, but in the meantime his friend Chris had asked him to do a consultancy job which was going to be part time over the summer months. Maddy felt annoyed that he had accepted without asking her. She felt that they did not need the extra money but when Colin had announced that he was retiring, she had felt at the time that it was out of character for him. He was a workaholic and she had never thought that he would retire. So, annoyed but not surprised that he had jumped at the opportunity of some work, she had to come to terms with being alone in the months ahead.

Instead of waiting for him, she would go to the local nursery on her own and buy the plants and shrubs required. It looked as if the design of the garden would be her decision.

Let him arrive and grumble, she thought defiantly, *I am not sitting around waiting for him to come otherwise it will be just time wasted.*

After the disappointing phone call with Colin that morning, Maddy decided to start making a list and went inside the house to make a cup of tea and to find pen and paper. Coming out onto the terrace she sat with her eyes closed and enjoyed the warmth of the sun on her face. A slight breeze and rustling in the undergrowth drew her attention down onto the lower terraces.

Making her way down through the garden, she saw a large black cat on its stomach eyeing a bird on a nearby tree. All of a sudden it shot up the tree after it. However the bird flew off and the cat was left sitting precariously on a branch. Approaching the tree she saw that the cat had unusual markings, predominately black, and some ginger fur down the middle of its face that looked like a streak of lightning. It made it look very strange.

Standing down below in the garden, she looked around and realised how much work there was to do. It looked as if it had not been tended for centuries and there were some very old gnarled cork oak trees with vines and shrubs clogging their roots and growing to the top of the trees. Making her way through the undergrowth, she came across some areas that must have remained from the older settlement there. Pulling away weeds and dead branches, she revealed a sundial. Looking around, she sensed that she was in the centre of what had probably been a circle of trees, probably fruit, as some of the branches were carrying some white and pink blossom.

Continuing on the path, she noticed a structure that had not been apparent before as it was completely covered in vegetation, branches and shrubs. It was peculiar; the lower part appeared to be a stone wall. Like the foundations of the Croft, the stones were stacked one on the other. But the wall went up so far and the upper part seemed to be made of interwoven branches of the trees surrounding it. It blended so well with the undergrowth that it was almost completely concealed. Certainly looking down on it from the terraces above, you would not see it.

109

Intrigued, Maddy tried to find a way in. Struggling through the brambles she eventually came to what looked like the only entrance. It was completely blocked by the undergrowth but she was able to get a glimpse of the interior. Light flickered within the space and revealed what seemed to be an unusual ceiling. She had expected beams but instead it seemed to be made of something woven, in fact it looked like an upturned willow basket.

She decided that it would be well worthwhile clearing the area around the structure in the next day or so. It would make an interesting focal point in the garden and also perhaps a quiet area to sit to read. Turning, she was startled by the cat who had followed her curiously. It shot off up towards the house. Looking up the garden, she noticed somebody at the door of the Croft. She made her way up the path as quickly as possible but arriving at the door found nobody there. Walking around the house, it revealed no sign of anybody. It all seemed uncannily still and quiet. The cat seemed to have disappeared too.

Bemused she stood looking out across the valley. In the distance she could see some storm clouds mounting, scudding towards the valley. On her previous visits to the Croft, she had become used to the sudden changes in the weather, winds that whipped up and sudden downpours that occurred within minutes.

Taking her tea cup, Maddy went inside having decided that there was not much she could do in the garden as it looked as if the weather was deteriorating. The sky was moving dark grey and purple clouds over the mountains and in the distance she could see squalls of rain throwing white mists over the canopies of the forests below. The sun was lowering itself and would soon be behind the mountains.

Having guessed rightly what was going to happen, Maddy lit a fire and sat reading while the storm raged around her. The temperature had dropped quite rapidly and the wind was gusting outside in fury, throwing branches of the trees into a frenzy. Twigs and leaves were hitting the window making Maddy start. A branch had broken and was hanging tenuously, holding on as if with stretching fingers it did not want to let go of its life.

Tomorrow, she would walk into the village and find the nearest garden centre.

***

Malachi sat on a large rock on the side of the valley across from the Croft and sighed. The cat, Isolde, was telling him of her experience with Maddy. From what he gathered there seemed to be a veil surrounding her, holding her back.

There was something about her he could not fathom. This would hinder his getting to know her which he knew would be part of his job. It could be her dependency on her husband. Isolde had told him that the husband was not going to be around much and that this seemed to have clouded Maddy's aura when she found out that morning.

For the role she had to play in the unfolding drama, Maddy needed to be emotionally independent and not looking to her husband for personal fulfilment. Knowing her, he was therefore surprised that there seemed to be this block. He wondered what it was and decided to make a call on Nammu.

Time was closing in and if they needed to spend some time assisting Maddy's awakening, they needed to get started. Understanding that this had to be of her 'free choice, free will' in accordance with universal law, he thought they might have to call in extra help and somebody to release her.

He summoned Isolde who, at that moment, was teasing a vole that had stupidly poked its nose out of its home. He knew she was playing but the vole did not and he scolded her for frightening the creature.

Transforming into humanoid form, she stood by him inwardly smiling at the stern ticking off he had just given her. Together they stepped up through the levels to meet Nammu.

***

Chapter 13
The Block
(Somewhere, No time, No space)

Malachi entered the Chamber of Reunion on Level 7 and noted that alongside Nammu there were other Marechal awaiting him and Isolde. He thought Nammu looked rather ominous appearing on this occasion as a huge black panther. He felt Isolde twitching and edging herself behind him. Silence was stinging the Chamber and he began to feel on edge.

"Welcome Malachi," Nammu greeted him.

"We note that Earth, 'Ki-gi-Kia', has entered the ascension phase on the photon belt and that she is struggling with the changes in frequency. However, we have also noted that the frequency of the population has risen sufficiently to help her through it. It has to be maintained at that level, Earth time, for the coming years if she is to ascend. The period of precession has commenced and we have noted the rogue planet's orbit as it is approaching is affecting the gravity of the outer planets of this solar system and the effect this is going to have when it approaches Earth. One could say the situation is warming up."

With his last words, Malachi knew Nammu was throwing an ironic reference to his last trips into the Earth atmosphere.

Malachi acknowledged with a slight bow of his head.

"How goes it with your travels and the soul Lilith?"

Malachi sensed that he wanted him to continue.

Isolde stood beside Malachi, transformed from a cat into a beautiful young girl with long black hair that had an auburn streak. The auburn hair was plaited and wound through her hair and around her forehead. Dusky and wearing a long silver blue gown she seemed to hover in the space exuding a glittering aura.

"All has been well since Earth time 13th century. I have visited many times and also sent Isolde."

Isolde inclined her head in agreement.

"We have watched the female Maddy, the one whose family is vulnerable, and we see that she is now relocated to the place where her component disc is hidden. We have been there to observe her and her acclimatisation to the place.

However we are unsettled about her, she does not seem to have the attunement or awareness that we would have expected from her to have as one of the Ancients choosing her soul task. She does not seem to have any memory or connection with her previous lives or her destiny apart from a slight apprehension that she has noted of 'returning'. Indeed we are concerned. We feel there is a block around her that we cannot penetrate and which will prevent her from remembering her role. It seems more serious than the usual amnesiac experience the contracted have. We are asking you and those of ancient ascendancy…" Here Malachi swept a glance around the gathering. "Is there a reason for this? We cannot progress further with her at the moment due to this."

Nammu turned away pausing for reflection.

"You are right, of course, Malachi and your senses do you credit; there is a block on Maddy. In fact the guardians and I had to return to her pre-birth and place the block on her."

"How is it I did not know of this? It seems you have kept this from me, presumably for a good reason?"

Malachi felt his resonance depleting and realised that he was becoming angry. Aware of the effect this could have on him he took control and switched off the triggers.

"Yes we had to do something, otherwise we would have lost her and it would have meant all the measures we had put in place to assure ascendency would have been lost."

"So what happened?"

"When we last met, we talked of the Halqu and the net they placed around the planet and the intervention the guardians made to counteract this, the Shield. The Halqu had no knowledge of the Shield until a member of Maddy's soul family betrayed the secret. That was why, at that time, you moved her and the disc to a safe place. That's where you have just been."

Nammu had been prowling back and forth and at this point he stopped and faced Malachi searching deep into his being.

Malachi felt himself moving backwards with the force of Nammu's gaze, searching to read how Malachi had carried out his task. Nammu continued.

"Since that time, the Halqu have been following bloodlines and families with no success until recently.

Returning to the site where they lost the Seal, they tracked down a family who they suspected were the carriers. Having followed families down since the 13th century, they noticed some traits and histories that conformed to the kind of family that would have been the carriers. They located the family in England and were present at the birth of Maddy. Malachi, you and I were present but not aware that the Halqu were watching also.

As Maddy grew up in the Sector you have been watching; seemingly she has had a fairly smooth existence."

Malachi nodded to indicate his agreement.

"However, the Guardians became aware that she was being taken by the Halqu from her cradle to their laboratories and examined for her DNA. Unfortunately, it did not come to our notice until she was in puberty. As she was growing up they tried to steal her DNA. They abducted her several times in the attempt to remove some of her eggs which they were going to use for genetic engineering. This was part of their plan with Maddy as well as with other subjects.

They stopped abducting Maddy because the abduction process involved raising her cellular structure to a higher frequency to transport her to laboratories on their spaceship. Unfortunately for them, but fortunately for us, her body could not withstand the higher frequency and therefore they abandoned their attempts with her. However, at that time the damage they did to Maddy was great and irreparable. Their abduction process subjected her to chronic gynaecological problems and she was on the verge of dying.

As you know human beings have the right of free will, there was nothing we could do to help her without her requesting us. One day, the pain was so severe she collapsed and felt so desperately ill that she cried out for help and said that she wanted to die. She felt her life's course to that point had been so painful that she had decided, or rather her soul had decided, that she did not want to incarnate further.

It was from that moment, as Guardians within Universal Law we were able to intervene. Due to the severity of her deteriorating condition, she arrived in the consulting rooms of a specialist gynaecologist who was able to help her recover. Bearing in mind her wishes, we removed her to a parallel dimension in which to follow the course of life she set for herself. Because of what happened, we went back to before her birth and threw a protective blanket over her awareness and this left us with the Maddy in the dimension that you have been observing.

We can understand your puzzlement about the Maddy you are dealing with?"

Malachi assented as it did not seem to have any connection with the person he had observed.

Nammu continued.

"We needed Maddy's DNA and cellular structure to be in as optimal condition as it possibly could be to fulfil her soul contract. You are quite right, she has to become aware of her task and it does mean we have to remove the block. Again, quite rightly, it is something that you cannot do alone. We have sent an envoy to remove the blanket gradually. We have kept this process as pure as possible, which included not making you aware of the situation, mainly because, as you can appreciate, since we were not aware of being watched at Maddy's birth we cannot be sure that the Halqu have not found some way of infiltrating our security systems.

As you have seen under our guidance, she has been relocated back to the place where the disc is hidden, which is the start. Tell me, is it safe, has it remained concealed over the centuries?"

Malachi confirmed that it was. He had sent Isolde into the Chapel to verify this.

Nammu continued, "We have set in place a course of events that will help to awaken Maddy to her contract. You will continue as her guardian. You have Isolde to assist you to ensure Maddy's safety. There has been an increase in other species visiting the planet. Most have good intentions as they are aware of the coming Alignment which they see as beneficial to them. But we have to be on the alert for other intruder races. The Halqu are an example of having been very clever at developing their cloaking technology, it has been increasingly difficult to keep track of them.

Everything is going to plan but we have to stay alert. Malachi! Isolde! Return to Maddy now. And Malachi, that will mean you appearing in material form and living as a human nearby. You will need to stay close by and warn of any intruder interference."

Nammu concluded with his usual acknowledgement.

"All time, all things, are now and complete," and dissolved into space.

*****

Malachi bowed his head, turned and went to the frequency modulation area. He waited, indecisive as to where he should go. Part of him wanted to take a trip to the deactivation level and recharge his cells. His mounting anger and then its calming had taken a great deal of energy from him.

However, he decided to return to Maddy's time and place and settle into a house in the village and watch as a human being. As she got used to him being in her life he would be able to see, at first hand, if anything threatening appeared. He could also recharge himself though he did not find it appealing; because of the density of the planet it took a great deal of concentration to raise frequency. This led him on to thinking of how they were going to be able to raise Maddy's frequency to what was necessary.

He disliked being in human form. The uncleanliness of it all repulsed him. He knew he was going to struggle with acting as a human and that he needed to cultivate a particular persona to cover his true revulsion.

Isolde stood quietly by his side, her eyes large and questioning.

Malachi, taking her arm, guided her into the modulator and set the frequencies. Thinking the activation symbol, they looked into each other's eyes as they disappeared from the chamber.

*****

Chapter 14
Maddy Meets the Locals

This particular morning Maddy decided to take a break from gardening and to walk into the village. On previous trips with Colin to the village, they had been to a café in the centre with tables set outside. The weather had been sunny and there had been a few people sitting out under gaily coloured umbrellas. This morning, apart from buying some bread, her main aim was to go to the café and have some human contact.

After the previous day's storm, the wind and rain had dissipated overnight and as Maddy walked towards the village she felt the air fresh and cool on her face. The clouds were vaporising as the heat of the sun broke through. She realised it was going to be a glorious day with a clear blue sky. As she walked down the side of the valley, the air was full of the scent of thyme and other herbs and the small flowers of early spring, celandines and violets. Looking out across the valley she could see the village in the distance, the church tower and some of the roofs of the village houses standing out against the background of the trees in the valleys below. Beyond the woodlands she saw the mountains still with snow on their peaks. The view was quite stunning and she began to regain glimpses of the dream she had woken up to that morning. Her mind began to run over events of the previous day in the garden and the cat. She wondered who it belonged to, as there were no close neighbours.

As she continued her walk, she tried to grasp the rest of the dream but it eluded her and reaching the outskirts of the village she stopped wrestling with her memory. She decided to take a shortcut to the centre of the village on a lane that ran along the wall of the cemetery. It was only a small cemetery but had many tombs belonging to the local families, some very elaborate. Passing the cemetery she walked down the street towards the Church and then round the corner into the square. The café, Les Guingettes, sat in the opposite corner with its tables set outside in a courtyard.

She went to the Boulangerie first before crossing over to the café as she knew that the shops closed at 12:00 p.m. on the dot and she wanted to linger over her coffee and not feel like she had to rush off. Buying a baguette, Maddy lingered over the cakes and asked the shop girl for a '*Jesuit*', a large cake made of flaky pastry filled with crème patisserie.

The name of the cafe had intrigued her and she had looked up the word guingette and discovered that it was a term used for a 'waterside refreshment place in the open air' and that these places had originated in the outskirts of Paris in the 18th century. Maddy knew that the owners of the bar were from northern France and assumed that knowing something of their history had thought it a good name for a cafe.

Entering the café, she noticed that there were quite a few local men seated at the bar. Outside there was a large group of men and women, chatting loudly. She had only been to the bar a few times with Colin on their previous trips, so she was delighted when the barman, the owner, came round to her side of the bar and kissed her on both cheeks. His wife came out too and did the same as if they were all old friends. They asked her how she was and she told them in rather inadequate French, as they did not speak any English, that she was alone and that Colin would be joining her later.

Maddy ordered a large '*crème*', the local term for a large coffee with milk and went outside into the courtyard, choosing one of the empty tables adjacent to the large group. Putting her shopping on one of the spare chairs, she sat and turned her face to the sun.

At the same time a couple arrived and were greeted effusively by the large group. They began to look around for somewhere to sit but by this time all the tables were taken. They turned to Maddy and asked if they might share her table. Although they spoke in French she realised they were all English speaking. Moving herself and her shopping round the table to make room she, of course, agreed. They smiled at her and she smiled back as one of them got up and approached her.

"We can't help noticing that you are English?"

He was quite an attractive man with an educated voice.

Maddy laughed.

"...and there I was thinking I could bluff my way into the local community."

He responded laughing.

"Well, fortunately or unfortunately most of the local community around here are English, or Dutch, or German though there are obviously still some of the indigenous French left. Daniel, or rather Dan, I live in one of the old houses opposite the church in the village."

"Colin, that's my husband, and I have been over frequently. It's strange that we haven't come across each other before."

The group who had been listening to this exchange invited her to join them and they all started to move the tables closer, shaking hands with Maddy and introducing themselves. After the initial pleasantries, she discovered that they were all retired and had chosen to move to the region, most having visited the area on holidays during their earlier years. They all lived locally in the village or on the outskirts.

Conversation began to turn into a discussion about living in France, politics and the local Town Hall and difficulties with being an expat. They told her they met regularly and had formed a group studying the history, culture and language of *Occitan*. Maddy discovered much of what they were saying reminded her of a book she had read years before, *'The Holy Blood and the Holy Grail'*, which she realised was set in the region. The group also told her some of the history of the Cathars and she found herself intrigued.

They asked where she was living. She told them about the Croft and that she and Colin had renamed it and that previously it had been called 'la borda' or 'la petite ferme'. She was taken aback at their reaction. They all became animated and told her how it had always had magical associations. They did not elaborate further as some of the group wanted to go off for lunch. Their conversation turned towards discussing the date and time of the next meeting of the History Group, then they all parted inviting Maddy along if she felt she was interested.

The sun was well up in the sky by the time she walked back up the mountain. What an interesting morning and she had discovered something about the Croft. It almost seemed mysterious. The way they had reacted seemed puzzling. She was looking forward to the meeting. It could be fun and it would mean that she might make some friends.

Approaching the Croft, she noticed some birds in the distance; the huge bird and its partner soaring on the thermals. She had noticed that they only came out when there was a clear blue sky and it was very hot and still. She really must find out what kind of eagles they were.

***

Maddy spent the following morning working in the garden. Fascinated by the building she had found down in the lower terraces, she decided to work on that area. Pulling away the long grasses and dead wood she gradually made some start, revealing its structure. It was odd in a way, like a living form.

It reminded her of an artist she had read about, David Nash, who lived in a converted chapel in North Wales. His work concerned all aspects of wood from which he made sculptures; growing, carving and burning pieces of trees. Maddy had even taken a short holiday trip to the area to see one of his art works called the 'Ashdome'. Nash had planted a ring of ash trees in 1977 and as they grew over the years, he had pruned and guided them into a dome shape. Recently she had checked on the 'Ashdome' out of curiosity and watched a short video on its progress.

In common with the Ashdome laurel bushes, rather than ash trees, had grown all around the outside and up the sides of the building; the top branches reaching out to the sky some 15–20 feet. She saw that there were stones forming a shoulder high wall around the building. As she was 5ft. 3" she reckoned it was about 5ft. high. She also uncovered a semi-circle of large stones to one side of the building that enclosed a space in front of what must have been the entrance. Hacking away the branches of laurel, she revealed an entrance and managed to get inside.

She was staggered and gasped. In front of her was a space some 24ft by 16ft. Although there were branches which had grown into the space, on the whole the space was clear. The darkness inside it had obviously discouraged any growth. Looking up in front of her, she saw light coming in through what looked like an aperture made up of woven branches. Moving towards it, she saw that it was actually a window about a metre square within which there were bars in the shape of petals coming out of a central circle. Through the window a shaft of light was directed down onto the floor, obviously it would change its position during the day. Maddy began to think it was positioned to catch the rising sun as she began to think about north, west, east and south and which way the window captured the light. The design of the petals struck her, and she felt herself groping around in her memory for some connection.

The window threw light into the aperture of the roof and again she gasped as it confirmed her glimpse of it the other day. The branches of the laurel bushes had grown and were tightly woven into a smooth surface like a wicker basket, probably water tight as the interior did not feel damp at all. What a strange building and what was it used for?

Feeling quite exhausted by her efforts and realising it was midday she trudged back up the path to the house. Making a sandwich and getting a beer from the refrigerator, she took her lunch out onto the terrace and settled on the wicker lounger she had bought recently in Bourg Madame. Noting that the midday sun even in April could be very hot, she had placed the seat under the shade of the trees. The branches above her like graceful arms fanning a light breeze. Finishing her sandwich, she thought she would close her eyes for an hour or so as it was too hot to work. She could go down later to the… what should she call it now, not the building. She would have to think of something special and name it.

Dreaming…

I am sitting with the audience in a theatre looking at the scene before me, where there are actors in Greek or Roman dress. At the climax of the play, the leading actress walked up a steep flight of stairs. There was no rail, only the steps which were quite narrow and small. Reaching the summit she held up her arms to the sky. The play finished at that point. People leaving the theatre were talking about the principal actress. I got up and was half way out of the amphitheatre, looking down onto the stage, when a man came up from the lower seats. He seemed familiar and I struggled to remember who he was. He had a sheaf of papers under his arm and smiling he said, "You could do this." I felt disturbed and indecisive. I felt I could do it… But what was it…?

Maddy came to drowsily and felt something touching her legs. Looking down she saw the strange cat she had seen the other day brushing against her legs. It began to purr. She leant down and it let her stroke it, raising its head and brushing its ears across the back of her hand.

"I will have to give you a name if you keep turning up." Going inside she found a dish and filled it with water, took it outside and put it down by the door. The cat immediately went and took a drink from it.

Maddy remembered that she had meant to go back down to the building below to browse around. She had been up and down the garden several times and now there was a pathway which made it easier to descend. The cat followed her down. She could not help but wonder where it had come from and whether it belonged to someone nearby, though there were no dwellings that close as she had observed on her trips to the village.

In the afternoon sunshine, the building threw out some interesting shadows. The sunlight bounced off the shiny surface of the laurel leaves, their colour shimmering through silver to deep emerald green. Inside the air was cool and threw off a damp mossy odour that was not rank, but made the atmosphere very earthy. Emerging after a few minutes she realised the cat had disappeared but noticed that somebody was walking along the edge of the garden. As the building was near the boundary she realised that he would be passing close to her. From a distance she thought she recognised him but could not remember where from.

"Hello, so you decided to buy the place then?"

Maddy then remembered that he had passed here the day she had viewed the property. Helen had been with her.

"Yes. I remember now, you passed by when I came out to see the place about two years ago now. And yes, we decided to buy it and come out for holidays. I remember, you enjoy walking in the mountains."

"That's right. I have just moved back myself, actually, into the village. I knew that somebody had taken this place as I belong to a local history group and a friend told me that they met you at the bar the other day. I wasn't sure whether it was the same person though. What made you decide to buy?"

"I am not sure, at the time it was my husband's enthusiasm but I somehow fell in love with the place. I also had some strange feelings that I was meant to be here, it felt like returning to somewhere that I knew very well. Can't explain it really, not sure why I am sharing this with you. Anyway I am enjoying it. I am here for the summer now."

"Are you on your own?"

"Yes, a job came up; Colin is a workaholic and annoyingly work seems to be consuming more of his interest than being here at the moment."

Feeling that she was saying and telling this stranger too much, she stopped talking. *Why have I suddenly opened up to this man, this stranger? I have only met him once before.*

He must have sensed her reticence as he said.

"Sorry I did not mean to give you an inquisition! Rather insensitive of me as we have only just met. My name's Michael and you are?" He put out his hand to shake hers.

"Maddy Jameson."

"I am on my way back to the village. I am renting a small house there. Enjoy the rest of the day. I expect we will see each other at the meeting."

Remembering the meeting was in two days' time Maddy said, "Oh! How is the group run? What happens?"

"Usually somebody gives a talk. I am not sure what the next topic will be. Afterwards, there is usually a small buffet with drinks so that we can all discuss the subject and just generally socialise; quite an enjoyable evening, actually. They are a nice group of people."

"I am looking forward to it and it will be a way of learning about the area. I expect at some point I must brush up on my French and Spanish, but at the moment it seems mostly an English speaking group."

"Yes, it is always run in English."

"Well enjoy your walk, see you then, bye."

"Goodbye… a bientôt," and he disappeared down the track.

***

Maddy and Colin had got into the habit, since she had arrived at the Croft, of speaking daily; morning and evening. Speaking to him that evening Maddy told him about her discovery in the garden, the cat and the chance meeting with the passer-by and also about joining the local group.

Relieved that she was coping well without him, he teased her saying that it sounded as if she was staying there permanently; joining a group and doing all the work.

"I thought that this was going to be our holiday home."

"Well, I think it's good to do what I am doing as it means we can be part of the community when we come down and will know some people. Also, who knows we might end up spending a great deal of time here?"

***

Malachi, making his way back to the village, was feeling irritable.

Isolde remarked, "You turned up on cue, and was that you in her dream? Very theatrical," she sniggered. "What's the matter? You look, well, out of sorts."

"I just don't like being in this human form, it's so uncomfortable, the heat, the clothes, the vegetation and now I have to go back and probably am going to have to make conversation with whoever I am unfortunate enough to bump into. It's all very well, Nammu expects a lot."

"Oh stop grumbling! At least you don't have to change shape so radically. I am wearing this damn fur coat and believe me, there are some rather nasty animals lurking around in the bushes. I have already had quite a few scraps with some of the local population, from which they won't recover, I have to say. Very tedious."

"Mmmm… See what you mean," murmured Malachi seeing a large Pyrenean mountain dog approaching with its owner.

Isolde had disappeared swiftly up the closest tree and was quivering and mewing high up above him. The dog began to bark aggressively, its owners hanging on to its lead.

Malachi and its owner nodded at each other and passed on quickly.

"Come down, Isolde. Let's get back before anything else happens. Anyway, we have to make a visit to a relative of Maddy's in Scotland. He needs to come here and help us with Maddy."

***

Chapter 15
Meeting with the History Group

The following week Maddy was getting ready to go to the history group meeting when the phone rang. It was her daughter Grace who wanted a leisurely chat.

"Nothing wrong is there, with the children and David?"

"Everything is fine. I just wanted to see how you are getting on out there on your own. Dad came for lunch on Sunday and told us about your gardening exploits and that you seemed to be enjoying yourself. He seemed relieved as I think the job is taking far more time than he anticipated so I don't think he will be joining you that soon."

Maddy was pressed for time, being rather late in the afternoon to get ready; having spent all day in the garden again. She chatted for a few minutes more and then told her daughter she would ring her back the next day.

Having a very limited wardrobe, she was undecided what to wear. Packing back in early March, she had only put in a few pairs of jeans and blouses and a couple of thick jumpers and a fleece. She had not anticipated anything social which on reflection was a bit silly, because if Colin had been with her they would probably have gone out to restaurants to eat on a fairly regular basis. Maddy realised that she had hardly been out socially since arriving and also noted that her consumption of alcohol had reduced drastically accordingly. She wondered if that was why she was feeling much more alive and energetic than she had done for some years. She and Colin thought nothing of drinking a bottle of wine, perhaps two sometimes, in the evening when they were together.

She had thought that she would buy a few items during the course of her stay based on the weather. Recently it had been very warm, in fact quite hot, and she had thought she would have liked some lighter clothes and was thinking of going to the larger town nearby to do some shopping.

Now, however, she selected her most respectable pair of jeans, a white blouse and the blue fleece. Having put on some make up for the first time since she arrived, glancing at herself in the mirror she was pleased with what she saw. Her face had taken on a light tan and glowed healthily. The blue of the fleece was an exact match for her eyes and with her hair lightened in the sun and now carrying blonde streaks, she felt quite attractive.

Although it was only a twenty-minute walk into the village, she decided to take the car as it would be dark when she returned. She knew there were some wild boars wandering in the woods nearby and she did not want to risk an encounter when they came out at night.

Maddy had been told that the history group met in the room above the bar, Les Guingettes. When she arrived, she saw a couple she had met the previous week having a drink at the bar. They greeted her warmly and offered her a drink. They told her that some of the others had arrived and were already upstairs. Together they took their drinks and went up to join them.

The salon upstairs was a large room, with windows overlooking the square below. It was sparsely furnished with a few simple tables and chairs; the chairs were arranged in rows as if anticipating a large audience.

Dan, who had introduced himself to her at the bar the previous week, came over and greeted her with the French 'kiss, kiss' on both cheeks. He was a pleasant man and told her that he was the co-ordinator of the group's activities. As he was talking, she noted that he was very good looking for his age which she judged probably to be in his late 60's.

A small well-groomed woman came up beside him and introduced herself as his wife, Deirdre, and proceeded to take over the conversation. It seemed she and Maddy shared some common interests as she was an ex-teacher and art lover. Another couple approached, they knew Deirdre and Dan well and joined in the conversation. They introduced themselves as Andy and Bo. Andy then took over the conversation and Maddy noticed that Deirdre and Bo both rolled their eyes at each other. Andy told her immediately that he was a travel writer and had written several books on the local area.

Michael arrived and Dan introduced him, but Maddy and Michael nodded at each other acknowledging that they had already met.

Dan turned to him.

"How long ago did you leave? I have been here quite a few years and I don't remember seeing you before."

"It was a long time ago and I did not live in the village but out in the country between here and Bourg Madame."

"What made you come back?"

"Nostalgia I suppose. I had some family in the area, some of them died and then the younger ones moved away and I thought it might be a good idea to travel for a while."

Dan did not seem to want to let the matter drop and was about to ask further questions. Maddy who had been on the side lines of the conversation noted Michael becoming tense and stepped in and asked Dan what made him move to the area permanently. Dan then embarked on his own history and why he and Deirdre had sold up and moved to France.

Michael threw Maddy a grateful look which made her wonder why she had done what she had by saving him from more questions.

More people entered the room; one in particular took Maddy's interest. She was a widow who had moved with her husband to the village several years previously. Her husband had died recently and the group probably provided her with a way of maintaining a social life that had disappeared on his death.

All in all, it seemed, that was the group. Nobody else arrived so Dan welcomed everyone, gave out a few notices and then turned to Andy and introduced him as the speaker for the evening. The title of the talk was going to be 'The Cathars and their beliefs'.

This is going to be interesting, thought Maddy. She had heard of the Cathars and when driving down with Colin seen the road signs through the South of France indicating that drivers had arrived in the 'Pays du Cathars' but knew very little about them.

Andy's talk lasted about forty minutes and was mostly concerned with battles and skirmishes, rather than on the fundamental beliefs of the 'Cathars'. From his brief introduction, however, she did learn that they were a religious sect that flourished in the 12th century and that they became a threat to the Catholic Church. To counter the threat, the Church launched a crusade against them eventually wiping them out completely by the mid-13th century.

Interested in the social aspects of life, rather than the more aggressive masculine aspects, Maddy decided to do some reading about them.

After Andy had finished his presentation, everybody gravitated to a side table to get a glass of wine and take some of the savoury snacks. Everybody stood around chatting and Maddy said she would be interested to read some more about the Cathars. Sarah, the widow, said that if Maddy dropped by her house during the week she could let her have some books on the subject.

"Paul and I have collected so many books over the years. I could do with freeing up some shelf space, so you are very welcome to as many as you can carry."

Maddy thanked her and they ended up chatting for a while and she arranged to call on Friday when she came to the market to do her weekly shopping. Sarah seemed really pleased.

By now, the whole group were standing around in a circle. Dan asked Maddy how she was getting on with living at the Croft on her own. Maddy felt herself summing him up as 'nosy'; she had observed him asking questions of the others in the group but not actually revealing anything about himself or his personal life.

Maddy replied that she was enjoying it, especially for having the time to work on the garden. She mentioned that she had uncovered the strange building; saying that she called it 'strange' as it was the only way she could describe it. She said it had become a passion for her now to clear the whole of the garden as it might reveal more unusual features.

"You know that there is a legend attached to the place, don't you?" said Michael.

Everybody turned to him, and began to say that it was all just local hearsay.

Maddy was intrigued. "What legend?"

Michael said that the house she had renamed The Croft had always been known as 'la borda' by the locals; the very elderly locals knew the old man who had returned to the derelict building before the Second World War. The building and the land had been in his family for generations. He had tried to get his family back to run it but had not succeeded; they had moved away and eventually he had died.

"But the story attached to the house and land seems to go back far into the past and has given a mystical history to your property that the locals are very fond of. They always talk about it with affection."

Maddy prompted, "And…?"

The eyes of the whole group were now on Michael who asked,

"How many of you have heard the story?"

Many of them muttered that they had heard that there was a legend but had not really taken it seriously enough to find out . more, but Maddy said, "I would obviously like to hear it, as I am living there and if it has mystical associations, how wonderful!"

Sarah chipped in with, "Be careful, it depends what kind of magic."

Maddy turned to her and sensed that she quite probably knew a great deal about 'magic'.

Dismissing Sarah, Dan exclaimed, "Nonsense!" and Andy backed him up by quipping.

"For heaven's sake we have had the 'Enlightenment', surely no-one believes in that stuff anymore?"

Turning back to Michael, Maddy asked him to tell her the story as simply as possible.

"I am interested even if the others aren't."

The others wandered off and he took her aside.

"Obviously some people," and glancing towards the others, "just don't like talking about things that are slightly mystical or have the word magic attached to them.

The legend recounts that a Princess was brought to 'la borda', the Croft, probably in the Middle Ages, to hide her from the persecution imposed on any religious groups that were the offshoots of the mainstream of Catholicism. They were all seen as heretical threats to the Church and were wiped out as, for example, you have just heard about the Cathars.

Further it tells that a precious stone was brought with her and together she and the stone were bound together in an eternal bond called 'A Seal'. To cut the story short, the Seal was one of twelve Seals that one day would unlock the gates of heaven and fly the

Earth and its inhabitants to heaven. Only those of goodly heart will pass through. Until that time, all the Seals would remain hidden. It goes without saying, as with all legends, that there were some 'baddies' trying to find the Seal. That's a very short synopsis of the legend but perhaps you have the gist of it."

Maddy actually would have liked to hear more but noticed that people were tidying up the chairs in the room ready to leave and that she and Michael were being encouraged to follow everybody out. They gathered their coats and followed.

As they walked towards the door, Maddy wished to continue the conversation.

"So is the legend actually saying that there is something still buried at the Croft? Obviously 'the princess' probably does refer to a person who lived there. Most legends are based on some kind of truth. It does sound a bit far-fetched and the usual kind of story to attract tourists to the area, though perhaps it is not as well-known as the other histories, such as the Cathars."

"Perhaps so, there are many stories of things that have been hidden in this area, many more towards the heart of the Cathar region in the Languedoc, for example, around Rennes le Chateau. The priest there in the late 19th century was suspected of finding a hoard of treasure but nothing came of any of the speculation around the subject.

As for something still at the Croft, with all the digging and renovating that has changed the place, I would have thought anything would have been found by now."

Maddy and Michael were now outside the cafe and she sensed that he wished to end the conversation, so she thanked him for telling her the story. He was very gracious and took his leave.

As she drove back up the track to the Croft she dwelt on the story. It made her feel somehow comforted, that the Princess in the legend had been brought here to keep her safe. That was the feeling she had; that she felt safe here away from the world; that perhaps people would find it difficult to find her. She had noticed how well-hidden the Croft was behind its trees and the surrounding landscape.

***

Later that week, she ventured into the village to the Market to do her shopping and called on Sarah as was pre-arranged.

Over coffee they talked about the meeting. Sarah was not a great admirer of some of the others in the history group describing them as 'stuck up'. Maddy liked her, especially her down to earth take on life.

Sarah was small and rotund with a mop of hair dyed dark brown and a bit straggly. Maddy put her age at around the mid-60 area. She had a strong Liverpudlian accent and also, it seemed, a lack of self-confidence.

Sarah told her that she had heard about the Legend and had done some comprehensive reading on the Cathars. She told her that the legend probably had some basis of truth, as people in those times would have had to have hidden their beliefs or else been burnt at the stake. They would have had to cover their physical tracks with stories they shared amongst themselves.

Sarah also told her that she knew several people who thought they were reincarnated Cathars and had felt a compulsion to return to this area to live. She belonged to a group that met to meditate on a weekly basis and invited Maddy to go to a meeting.

It was something that Maddy had not thought about before, so she told Sarah she would consider it. Maddy took a pile of books on the Cathars and agreed to meet next week on market day. Maddy liked the idea of the regular get-together as she felt she had made an interesting friend.

***

Chapter 16
Old Uncle Simon

The following day Maddy had an unexpectedly early phone call from Colin. Madeleine, Maddy's mother, had called to see him the previous evening and told him that her cousin Simon had contacted her. This had been a complete surprise to her, as they had lost touch after both of them had left France just before the outbreak of the Second World War. Madeleine had come to England with Thomas, Maddy's father and had never found out where Simon went. However it seemed he had disappeared only to surface after the war ended. He had written to her just after Maddy was born to let her know that he had taken a house in the Lake District. She had only heard from him once again and that was when Maddy was twenty-one but then not again until yesterday!

He had told her that he was getting old and wanted to return to France, back to his roots. He asked her how the children were. Simon remarked on the fact that Maddy was currently in France and asked her mother her exact location in France. On being told that it was somewhere on the border between Spain and France in the Pyrenees, Simon had told her mother that it must be in the region where they were born and had grown up before the War. Simon was planning to return to Perpignan, but finding out that Maddy was in the area had asked Madeleine whether it would be an imposition if he went to see her.

"What do you think? Your mother told him that she would ring to make sure and as I ring every day she passed the message on to me to deliver. He told her that he would not expect to stay with you, but it would be nice to revisit some of the towns and villages of his youth and, if it was not too far out of the way, to see you. From her conversation with him it sounds as if it is very close to where they were brought up."

Maddy had heard very little of her Uncle Simon; the last time was on her twenty first birthday when her mother had given her the strange necklace, the Collar. She realised she had forgotten all about it. At the time Maddy had not known what to do with it and on her mother's advice had eventually put it back in the bank vault for safe-keeping.

"How interesting! Tell Mum to let you know when he is about to arrive, so that I can look out for him. In fact, give him my phone number and then he can ring me."

***

Simon was 85 years old and feeling his age. His limbs were stiff and curled with arthritis, too much time floundering around in ditches during the war ironically he thought to himself. He had diabetes and several other more minor complaints that most of the time left him feeling irritable and quite miserable.

The last time Simon had had a visit from Michael was in 1969 when his niece had reached 21 and he had been told to write to Madeleine and inveigle her into handing on the Collar. This he had done and Michael, satisfied, had left promising that he would return when necessary but would be keeping watch.

So on this damp and misty morning, when the lake below and hills were completely obscured by mountain mists and clouds, he somehow was not surprised to see Michael emerge from the gloomy atmosphere. For some unaccountable reason he had been expecting him.

"You look just the same as I remember you Michael, bet you can't say the same about me."

Malachi noted the changes but smiling said nothing other than, "Good to see you Simon, you know why I am here?"

"Not exactly, though obviously it is about Maddy. I have had no contact with the family since you last came, when I told Madeleine to pass on the Collar. I have no idea what has been happening to them since then."

"I have kept a watch on them. Maddy has had some problems which we had to take care of."

Malachi frowned, thinking about what Nammu had told him about how events had made them move one of her potential futures into a parallel dimension in order to keep things on the right track in this dimension. It still niggled him that he had not been told.

"Things are proceeding well on the timeline. However, currently we are having some difficulties. She has to become aware of who she is and her contract; she has to start remembering and realise what she has to do. We need your help. I am afraid you have to go back to France."

"Oh and there was I looking forward to dying peacefully here in the next few months." Simon replied, his face setting grimly, his eyes narrowing.

"Look I have not gotten the energy to travel back and I have nowhere to go."

"Maddy and her husband have bought 'la borda', the place your grandfather lived in just before he died. You remember the place. You used to visit him there many times, as did Madeleine. That's how you became so close."

"The exact place? What a coincidence! Although something makes me think you and your lot had something to do with it so, perhaps, not a coincidence."

Malachi averted his eyes and with a small smile around his lips said, "That could be true. She does need to be there which is why we guided things in a particular way."

"I don't know much about your world or from wherever you come from, but I thought it was against some universal law to intervene and change things."

"Yes, it is, but we did not change things, we just guided them in a particular direction. Since you seem to have been doing a great deal of reading, you might be interested to read some of the literature on the definitions of 'destiny' and 'fate'…"

Malachi had been walking around the room and was running his finger along some bookshelves which were crammed with books on physics, psychology, ancient civilisations, in particular Sumerian and Egyptian.

"That there are many potential futures in many parallel dimensions for us all. It is all a question of probabilities and free will and choice where predominantly the eventual pathway lies.

Anyway, back to our protégée and my role and yours in the events that are unfolding. They have already begun; you may have noticed when you watch the news that things are beginning to change," he concluded with emphasis.

Simon had noticed recently how communication technology, computers, mobile phones, becoming so readily available to everyone on a global scale, had resulted in considerable unrest throughout the world.

As if reading his thoughts, Malachi continued.

"This is only the beginning, the mood and move to equality will increase alongside some bad elements. Religious factions will begin to vie for superiority and holy crusades will again become major destructive issues for everyone. It will be a global realisation this time though because of the media, not like in the past where communication was limited.

Our concern, however, is to raise sufficient awareness in the population to overcome what could be a very negative outcome for the planet in general and its population.

Maddy holds a crucial role in this and we need to bring her into that awareness."

Malachi had been pacing about the room and stopped and looked very pointedly at Simon who felt compelled to say something.

"I am following what you say, some of it, however it is still unclear to me. I remember that I am sworn to help but it all seems such a long time ago when I was initiated and having reached my present age I somehow thought it was not going to happen in my lifetime.

What is happening to her? Why has she such a crucial role in what is happening. I have to ask you now to give me a much fuller explanation of what is going on here. I don't know where you come from, only I am sure that it is extra-terrestrial and that there is a far bigger picture to all of this. Probably you have only told me what you think I am capable of understanding. But believe me, I have done a lot of reading and have a good imagination so please, fill me in, I am not an idiot."

"Well, the time has arrived and it is in your life time. I will fill you in with the full picture and you will have to do the same with Maddy.

What I will tell you, so you have something to think about, is that Maddy is what we call an 'old soul'. Her soul has had many incarnations, probably about 500, to reach today. In incarnation, it is usual for the subject to have amnesia about all their previous lives; hence why, because needs must, we are talking about 'waking' her up, making her aware at the moment.

Way back in the beginning of the current, let's call it adventure, approximately 8000-10,000 years ago of your Earth time, Maddy's soul was an Ancestor Guardian; an ascended master. As such, she agreed to incarnate on Earth as a safety measure for Earth and its evolving population to this particular time because of what we call the 'Alignment'. The Alignment means the planet in symbiosis with its population will ascend to a higher dimension, that is, a higher level of spirituality in your present understanding.

It would mean, quite simply, peace on Earth. The population of the Earth has never risen above a very primitive level of existence, fighting and killing each other for millennia.

To achieve ascendancy, however, because of other factors, which I will explain to you and Maddy in the near future, a certain ritual has to take place in which she has to perform a crucial role. That is why the most important thing is that she remembers the contract she undertook long ago before her first incarnation here on Earth.

Certain actions have already been taken; people have been placed and are entering her life to assist her, although they are not consciously aware of their roles. It is going to take some time and effort for her to get her awareness back and also to understand how old she really is in universal time. I can assure you that she is capable of this understanding. We have seen this in the various probabilities of her future.

So, my old friend, all I ask of you at the moment is to trust me. You have to start packing, put your house in order and get in touch with your cousin to set our plan in motion. Maddy must know you are coming and you will have to build some kind of relationship with her. You have to impart the knowledge you have of the family situation from the past."

Simon sighed. He knew that, for whatever reason, it was he who had been chosen to do this. Satisfied with the knowledge that he was going to get an explanation soon, he shook hands with Michael, who bid Simon farewell, and disappeared down the lane leading from the chalet.

Simon, as usual, was fascinated with the way Michael seemingly disappeared. No car, bike, vehicle of any kind or noise. He noticed how still and quiet everything around him and the chalet had become, as if time had halted for a few seconds.

A large bird flew across the pathway in front of the house; it looked like an eagle or some kind of bird of prey. Low, almost touching the ground, it broke Simon's focus on Michael.

He recalled a story of how North American Indians held the belief that when a bird flew across your path you had to stop and consider as it was signalling something momentous was going to happen. They believed it changed the timeline of your existence and directed it onto a different pathway. This seemed to fit comfortably into his experience of when Michael visited him. Every time his life changed dramatically after his visits.

***

Chapter 17
Simon Goes to France

Almost immediately after having been initiated into the Order, war broke out in Europe and Simon found himself volunteering for the army. However, running away from the French collaboration with Germany in the south of France, he found himself in the North, disappearing underground helping the resistance forces. Surviving many dangerous tasks, after the war he gravitated across the Channel to England and eventually settled in Cumbria. Whether, perhaps, deep down inside, he remembered the commitment he had made reluctantly concerning Maddy had influenced his move to Cumbria in an attempt to be closer to her should she ever need him, he was not prepared to admit to himself. However, he found himself settling into the English way of country life and found it a relief after the turmoil of the previous years.

Simon was not poor, though he appeared as if he was. The chalet he had bought in Cumbria was modest and all the furniture and fittings likewise, though on closer inspection one could see that there were some expensive items such as his favourite armchair which was leather and commodious. You could imagine he spent much of his time sitting in it reading by the fire.

He did have at his disposal some incredible savings. For most of his life, in the earlier days of his young adulthood, he had travelled throughout Europe. He had read extensively many books that fell across his path by chance. As his library grew he had become fascinated with every aspect of the paranormal and theories on ancient civilisations and ancestors, particularly Sumerian history dating back some millennia before Christ.

Consequently, he had started writing and had earned a considerable amount of money. He wrote mainly about the war and his travels and the income from this had been deposited in a Bank in Switzerland. Currently, he had started writing a historical novel based on his interest in ancient civilisations. Mainly to order his thoughts on all the writings he had researched over the years, to get them and his imaginings into some logical framework.

"Now what should I do with all this stuff?" he muttered to himself.

"Oh, I can't be bothered."

So he quickly tidied through the small chalet, packed a suitcase with his few clothes, a book and writing note book which he always carried.

He then made a reservation for a flight to Perpignan in two days' time. Where he was going to stay he had no idea, he would cross that bridge when he got there.

***

Simon arrived in Perpignan courtesy of Ryanair from London two days later. Going to the information desk, he enquired about some hotels in the middle of Perpignan. He had decided to stay in the centre the first night and perhaps have a look around for a couple of days to see if any of his old haunts were still there. Flying in and seeing the Pyrenees and the Montagne Noir, he had felt nostalgic and memories came flooding back, especially in connection with Madeleine and Tom; they had spent many hours together frequenting the bars in the local area.

The courier at the airport gave him the name of a small but good hotel which took only 30 minutes to reach. Feeling weary but satisfied, he decided to have a light supper as it was now 7:00 in the evening. Leaving his unpacking for later he went straight down to the restaurant and ordered a simple meal, soup, followed by lamb cutlets. Again memories crept in of his family meals when he was a child. He had forgotten how the very simple cuisine of the local people was so good and so different from that of the English. His dinner increased his weariness so retiring he went straight to bed and slept one of the deepest sleeps he had had for a very long time.

The following day Simon went to a local car hire firm and hired a car. He worked out a deal with them as he was not sure how long he would be staying in France.

After taking out a large sum of money from a local Bank (he had transferred some from Switzerland before he left the UK) he put his suitcase in the car, checked out of the hotel and began the drive towards the mountains.

It was a perfect early summer morning and winding his way out of Perpignan, he looked towards the mountains and saw that there was still snow on the peaks and the air was sharp and fresh. He thought how good it was to breathe such clear air.

A couple of hours later, he arrived in Bourg Madame. It was lunchtime and the town closed down completely. He parked the car and wandered down the street and came across a small bar that served food. It looked clean and he entered and took a table by the window that looked out towards the mountains. The sun shone brilliantly and the mountains were crystal clear in the distance.

A waitress appeared at the table, he noticed that she was limping and seemed slightly hunched over to the side. He suspected that she had rheumatoid arthritis and felt sympathy for her. She was quite young and it was a crippling complaint.

He ordered a green salad and cabillaud (cod fillet) and a glass of the local red wine. As he had walked towards the bar, he had noticed that things had hardly changed at all. He supposed that a small rural town such as this would not have changed due to its remoteness. It was in a ski resort area, but probably because there was not a great deal to attract skiers in the way of night life it had remained relatively untouched.

He began remembering his trips up to his grandfather's before the war and wondered whether he would be able to remember the way to the house and also whether Maddy was aware of his arrival. Madeleine said that she had spoken to the husband who was going to speak to Maddy. How much Madeleine had told the husband he did not know or whether Maddy was aware by now that they had bought their great grandfather's house! He had never met Maddy in person or her husband so he wondered what she would be like.

The cabillaud was delicious, cooked in olive oil with black pepper and served with some vegetables and bread. He was not a man that liked sweet things so he declined the waitress's offer of dessert instead taking a black coffee.

He decided then to find a small Pension where he could stay while looking for somewhere to rent in the small village near La Borda.

By the time he had finished his lunch, it was mid-afternoon and he was left considering whether to go on with his journey or whether to leave it to the next day. Travelling over the past few days had left him drained and so he decided to go and find a guest house and rest, have supper, go to bed early and venture out early the next morning.

***

Simon arrived in the village at around 11:00 a.m. He parked in the centre of the village, in the market place. Getting out of the car he remarked how little the place had changed in his absence.

It was a sunny day and looking around the square, he noticed a café with quite a few people seated outside at its tables. He locked the car and made his way over to the café, sitting down on the outer row of tables. A waitress appeared and he ordered coffee. When he had visited his grandfather those many years ago, he had stopped frequently in the village and been to this bar. Then, it was just one room with a bar and stools and a couple of tables inside.

Looking around, eavesdropping on some conversations, he soon became aware that there were quite a few foreigners; mainly British and Dutch by the sound of it. When the waitress came out to tend another table, he beckoned to her and asked her if there were any houses to rent in the village. He told her that he was looking for somewhere to stay for a few months. She very quickly told him that her father was the bar owner and that his brother might be able to help. The bar owner directed him to a house just around the corner where his brother lived and then picked up the phone to tell him that Simon was coming.

The bar owner and his brother were the Alverez, well known in the area for having a finger in every pie. Jean Alverez, the brother, chatted away as he led Simon through narrow streets to the edge of the village. This was not far as the village was not that large. Taking a key out, M. Alvarez opened the door of a small house which appeared to be in the middle of what had once been, by its outside facade, part of an overall larger house. Inside, it smelled musty but as M. Alvarez opened the shutters and windows, letting in air and light, the rooms were lit up with a warm glow. Looking out of the window, Simon saw that he had a view out over the surrounding valleys that was breath-taking.

M. Alverez told him that the house was very old, one of the oldest in the village, and that it went back as far as the 13th century.

"Look at the beams and the way they are slanting off, one would think the whole place was going to collapse. Don't worry! We have made sure that it is structurally secure, we don't want any accidents. We think it was some kind of farm building or hostelry, it has what we think were stables on the side."

It was a small house that was being offered, one room downstairs that had a dining table, settee, armchair and bookcase. A small wood burning stove with a pile of logs stacked up the wall next to it.

Upstairs there was just one large bedroom and bathroom/toilet area. Despite the musty smell that had hit him on entering the house, he thought that once lived in, it would be very cosy and not unlike his chalet in Cumbria.

He was also picking up some strange sensations about the house and related it to the fact that he had spent his youth in the area and that it was not unlikely some of his family had occupied the house in the past. It was more than that, something he thought he would question Michael about in the future.

He agreed to take the house for three months and they settled on a rent. When both were satisfied, they walked back to the market place. M. Alverez asked him what he was doing for lunch and recommended his brothers café, he said his sister in law was a superb cook and recommended he had the local dish. He discovered M. Alvarez was right; his sister in law was indeed a very good cook. The meatballs were cooked in a rich piquant tomato sauce. It was rich and tasty and he washed it down with a rather rough and spicy red wine produced by a local vineyard.

Simon had forgotten how pleasurable it was to take the two hour lunch break that the French adhered to. He watched as he saw all the local workers pick up their things, kiss each other twice on the cheek and scurry back down the side streets to their jobs.

Taking out a cheroot, he ordered coffee and a cognac and sat soaking up the warmth of the sun. He noticed the swallows swooping and soaring above the square.

Out of the corner of his eye he saw Michael approaching, pretending not to know one another he noted him taking a table to his side. The waitress came out with his bill and as he drew out his wallet to pay her, he asked her if she knew of a house called La Borda. She replied that she had not heard of it but would ask her father. M. Alvarez, the bar owner, came out and said that he did know it and thought it had been renamed The Croft and it was out on the road that led further on up into the mountains. The road did not lead anywhere other than tracks that in the olden days used to be mule tracks for transporting goods over the border into Catalan.

"Is it an English lady you are looking for...?"

Simon replied, yes, she was his niece. M. Alvarez turned to Michael.

"You know her don't you? She belongs to the group that meet in the room above?"

He introduced Michael to Simon. After a short while, the bar owner returned inside and Michael said to Simon, "That was nicely done! I can now offer to show you the way up there. They know that I am a 'walker' often out in the countryside, so it will all look quite normal. So, how are you getting on and when did you arrive?"

"The day before yesterday, I stayed in a hotel in Perpignan and came up to Bourg Madame yesterday and stayed in a Pension for the night there. I have just found a small house here which I am taking for three months. I hope you are going to tell me that that is going to be sufficient time? I had forgotten how wonderful this area is, however something is disturbing me. The house I have rented, it makes me feel agitated, some kind of atmosphere. Don't suppose you could enlighten me a little? I am sure you could fill some gaps, either in my memory or the history of my family?"

"Yes I could and you will be informed over the coming days, as it is essential you know the full story as well as Maddy. You both are playing a part in a much larger drama that began a very long time ago. I have to add, as I told you when we met before, that it was something you both agreed to do but it was necessary for you to have no memory of until now."

"That sounds ominous. Okay, let me go back to Bourg Madame and collect my things. I will also need to do some shopping and settle in here. Give me a couple of days and then we will discuss going to visit Maddy, though isn't it going to appear strange to her if we turn up together?"

"Don't worry, she and I are quite well acquainted now and it won't surprise her to know that we met in the village. This is a small place and everybody knows everybody and very quickly gets drawn into the expat community as she has done herself."

***

Chapter 18
Simon and Michael Visit Maddy

The day following Simon's arrival, Maddy made her way down to the village market stopping en route to pick up Sarah. They had now gotten into the habit of going to the market together and then having coffee, sometimes lunch afterwards. It depended on funds as Sarah was not that well off, living off her pension on her own.

Although Maddy rang the doorbell, she was used to entering Sarah's house without waiting and was always fascinated by the atmosphere; it was a very old house. Sarah had obviously had a very interesting life and travelled widely. Every wall was covered with either paintings or sketches, photographs or hangings that looked probably as if they came from India, or somewhere else in Asia.

She also had two walls that were taken up with books. Maddy had browsed through them on a previous occasion after her first encounter with the History Group and while Sarah had been selecting some books on the Cathars. The subject range was extensive, covering psychology, ancient history, languages and many other subjects.

There were several mandala placed around the house, star shapes decorated in different ways and in different materials; painted, embroidered or collaged. They had obviously been placed for meditation purposes as there were comfortable chairs or cushions placed in front of them which indicated to Maddy that Sarah must spend a considerable amount of time meditating which probably accounted for her serene and calm demeanour.

Sarah was on the telephone and Maddy could not help over-hearing that she was arranging to go to a workshop the following week and that somebody interesting was coming to run it. Finishing the call she apologised.

"Sorry about that, I had to book a place on this course and I had left it to the last minute. There is a woman coming from the UK to run a workshop on meditation. She is a medium of some repute and is giving individual sessions and I wanted to book one of them. I belong to this group who meet regularly to meditate. We usually listen to a guided meditation; they are mainly about healing. Some of the group are Reiki Masters and practice as such. We share information, for example one of the groups has become particularly interested in crystal healing so we had a day sharing her experiences."

Sarah paused and looking at Maddy curiously.

"I don't suppose you are interested in anything like that?"

Maddy said, "Yes I am, though very superficially. I have never had the time to give it much attention."

"Would you like to come next week, if I ring now I am sure you can attend, though you might not be able to have an individual session?"

"I would love to!"

Sarah picked up the telephone and made the call and booked Maddy in for the session the following week. Having done that, they gathered their bags and went off to do their weekly shop as usual.

***

Walking back to the Croft, at midday, Maddy fell to thinking about the session next week.

As a teenager looking for something to read other than her school text books, she had resorted to scanning her parents' bookshelves. Her mother had been an avid reader of the classics, Dickens in particular. Her father though had had a more eclectic selection and amongst his books she had come across the writings of a number of authors whose work had been discredited; mainly the writings of Erich Von Daniken and Zecheria Sitchin. The theories of both authors though current reading in the 50 and 60s were debunked mainly by the scientific community who referred to their work as unfounded research, a view she thought that was still held today. Their work covered the authors' research into ancient civilisations and archaeological findings and linked these to extra-terrestrial visitation to the Earth. Maddy had at the time found it very interesting reading but whenever she had tried to talk to anyone about it found the reaction was the same, that all their theories had been debunked. Because of this she had been very wary about expressing any interest in the subject since then.

However, she had found that from time to time throughout her life, books had come to her attention, for example authors such as Graham Hancock. They all seemed to have a common principle concerning religion and the nature of God and many had linked in to that early reading.

Not a particularly religious person, growing up Maddy had found it confusing. Her mother was Catholic, her father Church of England and her grandparents on her father's side were agnostic though her grandmother had attended the local congregational church. She had no knowledge of the beliefs of her grandparents on her mother's side. Her brother was an atheist. He was a scientist and his education had led him to believe that this individual life was all there was. Maddy, however, had held an open mind because of all of these very individual influences and therefore recognised immediately her eagerness in responding to Sarah's invitation.

She had found herself excited with their conversation and the forthcoming meditation workshop. Finding herself in this part of France and having a lot of time to herself without Colin, she had become increasingly more contemplative. She thought the meditation might be useful. Since arriving at the Croft she had felt that somehow she belonged here and that in a strange way the workshop might answer some questions that had been percolating in her brain.

***

Approaching the Croft, she saw two walkers making their way up the path beside the Croft. She recognised Michael immediately in his walking boots, hat and body warmer and waved and shouted out to him.

"Hello, out for a walk, lovely day for it."

She noticed the elderly gentlemen with him, who looked a bit strained as if the walk up the incline had been a bit too much for him.

"Hello there, we actually came up to see you."

Michael turned to Simon

"Let me introduce you, I think you knew that your Uncle was coming? Well here he is. Simon, meet your niece Maddy. We met in the cafe in the village the other day."

"Oh, pleased to meet you. Colin, that's my husband, told me that you had spoken to Mum and that you might be visiting the area. Well you had better come in. Can I offer you a drink?"

Michael and Simon followed Maddy inside and accepted her offer of a drink. She put the kettle on to make some coffee.

"How long have you been here?"

"I arrived two days ago, I was staying in Bourg Madame but have now rented a small gite in the village. It's quite a walk uphill from there."

Simon seemed out of breath and a little pale, so Maddy pushed the bowl of sugar towards him.

"Perhaps you should take it easy; it is quite a stiff walk. I am used to it now and considerably fitter than when I arrived," she said laughingly.

"How nice to meet you! Actually I have to confess that I had forgotten about you. Mum has only spoken about you to me once and that was on my twenty-first birthday. She gave me a necklace or rather she called it a Collar, which she said belonged to her family, obviously your family too. Funny I had even forgotten about that too. I asked her to put it back into the bank vault where it had been since she arrived in England. It looked quite valuable and it was too bulky to wear, not really jewellery. It was interesting though, mmm."

She realised that she had been talking to herself and that the two men were looking at her with a slightly odd look on their faces and something else. She sensed something she could not put her finger on.

"Forgive me, but why have you come back to France? I can understand it, I suppose, as it is where you were brought up and there probably comes a time when we all want to return to our roots. I know I am speaking generally."

Simon, who had now recovered his composure said, "Yes, you're right, even though I lived mainly in Perpignan and your Mother lived way over near Castelnaudary, a long way off. However, the one thing we had in common was a need to escape our parents and when we came across each other at family gatherings, we always ended up talking together. However, that is another story but it is how we became close as part of our escape strategy was to come up here on an excuse to see our cousins who lived nearby and to visit our Grandfather.

What you probably don't know, and I have to say it came as an enormous surprise to me and your Mother, is that you and Colin have bought the very same house where your great-grand-parents lived and to which your great-grandfather returned in the latter years of his life and where we visited him regularly. I realised as soon as I arrived here."

Maddy felt a thrill rush through her body as if the cellular structure of her body was vibrating.

"This is it?" she asked incredulously.

"Well that may explain why I have been having these funny feelings about having been here before?"

At this point Simon got up and went over to the front door of the Croft and walked through the door onto the terrace and stood looking out over the valley.

"Madeleine and I used to visit our grandfather here, not always together but often our visits would coincide. As I mentioned it was an escape for both of us. Neither of us got on with our parents and after your great-grandmother's death—Madeleine was very close to her grandmother—she began to visit grandfather regularly."

Maddy began to absorb what Simon was telling her.

"I am amazed. You are telling me that this is where my great-grandparents lived, my mother's grand-parents. She has never talked about them to me. Obviously I know that she is French, as you are, though nowadays you would not know it, she has always seemed very English to me. But I know that she came here when she was only 18 years old, just before the Second World War. This is bizarre."

Simon continued, "Obviously when they lived here it was nothing like it is now. I remember my cousin renovated one of the outhouses of the building so that he could live here. A small chalet was also built to house grandfather when he got old and infirm, so that my father and his second wife could look after him. This upset grandmother who lived in the farm down the road. I noticed the ruins that are left of that place on the way up."

Maddy now totally absorbed in Simon's memories, interjected and offered them lunch as she did not want to let them go and thought it would prolong their stay.

"I have only just arrived back from the village myself and was about to make lunch. Would you like to share it with me?"

They seemed pleased and readily accepted. She set about preparing a salad and some charcuterie in bowls and on plates, cut some bread and brought over a bottle of the local red wine. Pouring a glass of wine out automatically for everybody she paused and said, "I hope this is alright, I did not ask, it seems the natural thing to do here."

Simon chuckled.

"It's in your genes; you seem to have picked it up easily."

"It does seem to be, only the other day I had a dream and the following day kept having what you could call 'déjà vu' experiences. It was as if I knew where I was, as if I had been here before; really quite unnerving at the time."

The conversation veered away from the family history and settled into an exchange of comments about the local area, the expats and the ease of travelling around the region compared to the UK. Finishing their coffee after lunch Simon asked Maddy if he could call in a couple of days' time. He said he had brought with him some photographs of the family dating back to the early 1900s that she might be interested to see.

Maddy was delighted and told him that she was reading about the history of the area and turning to Michael she inquired,

"I expect Michael has told you that I have joined the local expats history group?"

Settling on Monday to call again, the men took their leave and set off down the track back to the village.

Maddy while washing up was left thinking about the day. She felt excited to find out about her family on her mother's side. She had always wondered about the French connection and how her Mother had never returned to her homeland. Perhaps, the meeting with Simon would open some new avenues for her with prospective visits to long lost French cousins.

As the afternoon light began to fade, the sun was setting behind the mountains and leaving patches of gold on the valleys below, Maddy made a light supper for herself and decided to have an early night. The weekend was before her and she decided that she would continue with clearing the garden down below. The weather was forecasted to be hot and sunny and she thought she would make the most of it before the summer heat really set in.

Taking a book to bed she fell asleep reading it, only to wake up with a start. Everything was very black; it was the time of the month when the moon disappeared so there was no light coming in through the window. Turning on the bedside light, looking at her watch, she noted that it was 3 a.m. Unable to get back to sleep she made herself a cup of tea and lay in bed musing on her meeting with Uncle Simon. She dozed, and then some recollections came to her:

... I was feeling, almost sensing, rather than seeing, a man on horseback on a dark pass climbing a mountain. He looked back over his shoulder to see if his woman, also on horseback was secure. His look was of concern for her safety. The horse was turning and the woman's long hair was splayed out over her cloak. They were both wearing dark blue cloaks.

Laying there half asleep she felt so relaxed her body seemed to be dissolving down into the bed and she had the sense of an aching longing that was so intense and blissful. For what seemed like a fleeting moment, she felt as if she was floating above her body.

Then it was gone and she was awake but the memory remained and she was feeling a dreadful sense of loss of something she wanted to remember but could not grasp.

Maddy shook herself fully awake; shreds of memory gradually fading, leaving her to wonder if she would remember anything in the morning.

***

Feeling that the meeting with Simon and Maddy had been successful Malachi stepped up into the presence of Nammu and told him what had happened, stating that he felt the process of waking Maddy up had commenced.

Pleased, Nammu affirmed this.

"We haven't much time before the Alignment in which to do this. It's not going as quickly with her as we would have liked. However, one has to realise that waking someone up whose memories have been buried for thousands of years of incarnations is not a quick process and also very individual. We are not the only ones involved in Maddy's existential evolution. Remember she has had interventions made on her by the Halqu.

We are sending somebody to remove the block that has been placed on her and also introducing other elements into her life that will accelerate the process. These you will become aware of.

We should never forget Malachi that these planets have time lines and we don't. Aeons of earth years mean nothing but a figment of imagination to us. Return to the time and keep us informed. Also tell that cat of yours to behave herself; she could be more trouble than you think."

Malachi stepped down back to the village feeling uncomfortable. He had been up and down several times recently and he could feel his cellular structure on Earth suffering. Watching the humans he noticed when they drank too much, they sometimes had what they called hangovers and thought to himself that it might be that he was feeling, as a niggling headache attached itself to him as he returned to his house.

He wondered what Isolde had been up to for Nammu to comment. He remembered her teasing the Pyrenean dog on his visit to Maddy the previous week. He knew the Ancestors knew everything so they must have seen what she was doing. She had been playing, that was all. Was it something they understood?

The linear timeline of Earth, the Ancestors and Malachi had to realise, was something that had to be dealt with in their instantaneous existence. It was no good them dealing with situations within their experience as it had no relevance to existence on Earth. They had dealt with the situation the Halqu had imposed on Maddy by removing her temporarily from one dimension to another but it had been twenty-two years of earth time in that dimension before they had sent a healing angel to repair the damage to her. In that period, it had caused Maddy enormous difficulties in her emotional life and Malachi suspected that this was one of the reasons the block was difficult to remove.

How to be aware, though, and keeping track of timelines was not easy. The evolution of natural ascension however dealt with this by providing the necessary lessons, but acquiring knowledge of Universal Physics was another matter altogether as he was finding out in his own ascension process.

Dwelling on the process of ascension he realised he needed to go to bed and rest and recharge his cells, something very necessary in Earth time.

***

Chapter 19
Simon's Visit to Maddy

Simon walked up the track to La Borda. Without Michael he was able to take his time, so strolling he arrived at Maddy's door mid-morning and this time, not breathless. It had also given him time to think about how to begin the conversation he was going to have with her about her family history and beyond. It was not going to be easy and he expected her to think that he was probably off his head. However, it was something he knew he had to do.

Maddy came to the door and it hit Simon again how much she looked like her mother. She was quite beautiful as her mother had been, but there seemed to be something a little more, an aura emanating from her.

She welcomed him and they went to the kitchen where Maddy made coffee, which they then took out on to the terrace.

"I am really intrigued about the family history. It has left me feeling a bit puzzled as to why you have returned to France after so many years and found me. I don't want to sound unwelcoming as I am pleased to see you but it does seem to be a bit odd after all these years and also as if you have some kind of purpose."

Simon was not surprised by her comment, as knowing her history he realised that she would be very perceptive of reading other people's purpose and emotions. Probably not fully aware of it herself, he knew, that she would not be easily fooled by anything but the truth.

"Sorry if I have been a bit direct but I arrived at that conclusion after dwelling on mother, you and why the question of her family has never been discussed within our family life. Ever!" Maddy said with emphasis.

"In fact this was discussed only once, on my twenty-first birthday. I told you that was when Mother gave me a necklace which I placed in a safe box with the Bank."

Listening to her, Simon was quietly withdrawn for a moment.

"There is a purpose and there is also a story that you need to be told. Best I think to start with a little family history if that is alright for you."

"That sounds good to me," said Maddy as she settled back into her chair. The sun was throwing deep shadows across the mountains; it was so clear and bright this morning. She felt something like time and age passing over and through her and found herself looking forward to whatever Simon had to tell her.

Simon too, settled back in his chair. Having finished his coffee, he was gazing out like Maddy onto the mountains and valleys. Without looking at Maddy, concentrating on the landscape, he began recounting to her in measured tones.

"You are a descendant of a very old French family that goes back to the 13th Century and beyond. The family line, or the bloodline, goes back even further probably originating in the Middle East thousands of years ago.

I can only tell you what I know and what I learned from my grandfather—his knowledge was somewhat sketchy too. I can only relate to you what happened to me. I have decided to tell it in parts which I hope will make it easier for you to follow so I must ask and hope that I can return next week?"

Maddy nodded her agreement though wondered what he was going to tell her that might influence whether she would want him to come back or not the following week. Without comment she allowed Simon to continue.

"Just before the outbreak of the War my grandfather called me to see him. At the time I was only twenty years old. He showed me the necklace, though we call it a Collar, which was given to you on your twenty-first birthday, and told me he was going to give it to Madeleine, your mother, and that it had to be kept safe. It had been handed down to him and had always been in the keeping of a male in the family appointed by a society; an Order that called itself the *Cloitre de Lilith*, the Cloister of Lilith. This Order has overseen the guardianship of the Collar for centuries. There has always been a male member of our family nominated into the Order for his lifetime and so on, down through the generations. As I said this has been the case for centuries. There was however to come a time when the Collar instead of being in the guardianship of a male in our family would be handed to a female within the family and this time arrived and your great grandfather passed on the Collar to your mother. At the time, he appointed me a member of the Order and to take on guardianship of your mother. He told me that I had to look after Madeleine and had always to keep watch over her.

This all happened and it was the reason I eventually moved to England and although I have not been a very present person in Madeleine's or your life, I have always been aware of what has been going on in your life."

Maddy interrupted, "But how could you do that, I hardly knew you existed and Mother never mentioned anything about you until she gave me the Collar?"

"Well, I had the means; I think I can tell you now as I have been retired for a good number of years. I was part of the under-cover resistance operations during the war and afterwards worked in intelligence for the Ministry of Defence. As I held a very elevated position in the service I was able to access any information and keep a track on your mother and you. This continued even after I retired from the service; I had reports sent to me regularly and would have been alerted if anything happened to you.

There is a great deal to pass on to you and it may take more than our next session because you will need time to digest all of this. Anyway, to continue, this morning let's just deal with the French family of which you are part.

As you have had no knowledge of the family you belong to, you probably have not heard about the legend, in fact, the two go hand in hand."

"Oh but I have heard about it, I was invited to join the local history group and when they discovered I lived here they immediately told me about the magic that is said to be attached to this place and they told me, what they said was a simple version of the legend."

"Interesting, that's good as you have a base on which I can tell you the true origin. Although all the old customs and histories have begun to disappear, it is remarkable that the legend still seems to capture people's imagination.

However, it is not a legend. It is a true but slightly exaggerated history of the origins of the family going back to the 13th century. Originally, the site the Croft stands on was a Beguinage run by a group of women called *Beguines*."

"What an unusual word, I have never heard of it."

"Well, in those times they were women who banded together to survive and they set up communes on the edges of villages and towns and provided a service of care to the local poor.

It was in the 13th century when one of your ancestors, a young girl, was brought to the Beguinage here to live with the women for her safety. She was brought to them by her uncle, another of your relatives. Her father had been imprisoned and tortured at the hands of the Inquisition. It may be of interest to you that your family were relatives of the Count of Toulouse at the time."

Glancing at the book opened on the coffee table just inside the door, Simon remarked,

"I see you are reading about the Cathar genocide—it was not just the Cathars the Inquisition sought to exterminate, it was any groups that worshipped or had beliefs that they considered to be heretical and opposed to the Catholic Church. The girl's father was sympathetic to the Cathar cause and therefore considered to be a threat and was taken and imprisoned.

She would have been taken too but her Uncle was sent to rescue her—her name was Malena and she and one of her father's servants, who was the brother of her friend and servant, Helene, and his family came with her Uncle to this place. The servant Jean was set up with his family in the village nearby and was left to oversee Malena's life.

The Beguines, the woman in the commune, were able to leave the commune; they were not tied like nuns by vows. Eventually Malena married Jean, the brother of her friend. Jean, a freeman, was able to set up as a farmer, growing enough to support his expanding family—he and Malena had several children.

Eventually Malena and Jean passed away but their family evolved, growing and spreading over the surrounding region from the Mediterranean coast to the Pyrenees on both sides of the border between France and Spain. As the family spread, and it was prolific, the family carried a story; a history which was passed down through the centuries becoming the Legend you have heard about. However, you will see how the story of Malena transformed a memory of something important that needed to be remembered down through the generations to the present day."

Simon paused, having told the Legend as he had been instructed by Michael. Squinting he looked up at the sun which was now well overhead. He looked very tired and Maddy asked him if he should not stop now and offered to make something to eat and drink. As he followed Maddy into the kitchen she turned to him.

"The neck-chain you spoke about in the Legend, it's the Collar isn't it, that Mum gave me? It's been handed down. It's unbelievable that it has not gotten lost over the centuries."

"Yes that's right, it was meant to come to you eventually."

Simon remained quiet as he realised she needed time to assimilate it.

Maddy, in turn, was quiet as she prepared their meal. She immediately picked up on what he had just said.

"You just said eventually, as if it was pre-planned that I would be receiving it. That does not make sense, how could you or our relatives, way back then, know that it would be me? And what happened to the Beguinage where the Princess, my relative, was brought to?"

Simon replied, "The Beguinage, which you have now named The Croft, here, over time gradually fell derelict. The occupants, the women, either grew old and died or were absorbed into the neighbourhood, as wives or servants to the population if they were young as happened to Malena in the Legend. As with all things time passed, the country suffered depopulation due to the Black Death and other catastrophes. The property became derelict until your Grandfather came here. He remembered his inheritance and came searching up here and restored 'la borda' or 'la petite ferme' which was the name he knew it as.

He and your grandmother divorced and there was a great deal of family turmoil. Your mother and I suffered from this and both our parents divorced. We were thrown together in our unhappy family lives and that is how we came to build a relationship with your grandfather and possibly why he ended up passing on his knowledge of the family history and the Collar to us.

The memory of the original Madeleine, or Malena, became buried in the legend. The family survived and has always been aware of the legend, whether taking it seriously or as a joke. And, of course, there has always been a girl child called Madeleine, now you are as it were the eventual Madeleine."

Maddy now looking perplexed.

"So, what is it about now that the Collar has ended up with me? There seems to be more you have to tell me. "

By now they had finished their lunch and were taking coffee on the terrace again. Simon said that he felt he had told her enough today and asked if he could call again later in the week and continue. He was tired and felt that she needed to take in what he had said today before continuing. Maddy agreed, she was feeling a bit confused; there was something deeper that she was not grasping.

Simon said he understood and she was quite right there was much more to tell.

However, before he left, he asked her again about the Collar telling her that it belonged in France and asking whether she could bring it over as it might be needed. This further puzzled Maddy but she said she would get in touch with her mother and get her to give it to Colin who she was expecting to join her very soon.

Before he left, as he was going down the path, he turned.

"Maddy there is one thing I must add as when I come again it will help you understand further. I must bring Michael with me. Again I am asking you to bear with me as this must all seem so mysterious to you. He is part of this story, our story and I need him to explain certain things to you which, believe you me, even now I find difficult to believe."

Maddy felt herself relieved as she had felt this meeting with Simon intense and felt that Michael might give a lighter perspective to everything.

"Oh I am always pleased to see him, so no problem about bringing him up. Somehow I felt as if I have known him for a long time, that déjà vu I was telling you both about."

Waving he set off down the track and as he trekked back to the village, Simon smiled inwardly thinking how little Maddy knew about how they were connected.

***

That evening Maddy phoned Colin and her mother. The call to her mother was quite straight forward. They exchanged news, everything seemed to be quite normal and her parents were well and active. Her mother was a bit hesitant, though, when she mentioned Colin saying that she had not seen him for a while. When they spoke she had invited him to Sunday lunch the previous week but he could not come as he told them he was going off with a friend on some business trip to Scotland.

Her mother promised to retrieve the Collar and to phone her when she had it and then they could arrange to get it to Colin so he could take it out to France.

Putting the phone down, Maddy felt a little disquieted. When she had spoken to Colin the last time, which was a couple of evenings ago, he had not mentioned that he had been away. She was also unaware of the mention of the business associate he had been away with although she assumed that it was his friend, Chris.

It was unsettling as she had noticed increasingly, reluctance on his part to come out and join her even for a weekend or holiday which had been their plan. In fact apart from one weekend at the end of June, he had spent no time at all here with her.

She also had to admit grudgingly to herself that despite this she had settled into living here and occupied with the Croft, the building and the garden, she had not really missed him that much. At home in the UK they had lived quite independent lives.

Maddy picked up the phone again and dialled Colin. There was no answer and she left a message on his answering machine for him to ring her. Dissatisfied with having to wait, however, she then phoned his mobile and after a couple of rings he answered. She decided to keep the conversation light:

"Hi, how are you?"

"Fine! How about you?"

"I'm alright! I wondered when you would be coming out here? It would be good to see you. So much has happened here and it would be good to share it with you.

I have just spoken to Mum. I don't suppose you remember a necklace I was given years ago on my twenty-first birthday? Well her cousin, Simon, has turned up here. Anyway he is getting on a bit now and wanted to return to where he was born. You will never believe it, it seems the Croft is where my French great grandfather lived."

"What a coincidence! That's incredible isn't it?"

Maddy could tell by Colin's reaction that he was as surprised as she had been when she first heard it.

"However, to continue, he said he would like to see the necklace. I have asked Mum to get it out of the vault and hoping that you would be out here soon that you would be able to bring it out with you?"

Colin's response was a bit hesitant.

"Well, I was planning to but Chris is going on a business trip to Dubai and wants me to go with him. I have gotten rather involved with the project and though I would love to come down to see you, I need to go with him to see it through. You know how it is, so it would be in about three weeks' time the soonest I could come, I promise. Would that do?"

"Well, I suppose it will have to. I am a bit disappointed though, in fact I am beginning to feel cross that you can't come down. Buying the Croft was your idea but it seems I am the one who is here organising everything. After all we are retired and the idea was to enjoy ourselves, not go chasing off after more work."

Maddy could feel herself getting very angry and decided to stop as she knew this made Colin close down, she could already sense his withdrawal. As there was no reply, Maddy carried on.

"Alright, well let's say three weeks' time then, but you had better make sure you keep your promise. Helen did say she wanted to come down so I might give her a ring and see if she could bring it with her."

Colin replied more brightly.

"That's a good idea. I bumped into her the other day in town shopping."

After exchanging more news about the children and local affairs, Maddy put the phone down. She wasn't sure how she felt. On the one hand she was enjoying her life here but on the other hand she felt some resentment towards Colin. It was his idea to buy the Croft and come out here to live. She had been the one who was at first very reluctant to do so but had gone along with him as was her usual response to his excitement about the different projects he got involved in.

Hmm, she thought feeling uncomfortable, mainly about the direction of her thought processes, trying to deal rationally with her emotional response to the situation.

Later, she picked up the phone and rang Helen who, it turned out, had been on the verge of ringing her to ask if she could come out for a short break. Maddy told her about the Collar and said she would get her Mother to get it to her to bring out. Looking forward to Helen's visit made her feel happier and settling in for the evening, she began to rethink everything Simon had told her.

It pleased her that she was part of this old French family and it intrigued her that going back so far in the history, the Collar had not gotten lost. There also seemed to be something that so far was not evident and she was looking forward to her Uncle's next visit to see what might come to light.

***

Chapter 20
Maddy and Sarah Go to the Meditation Workshop

Simon's next visit had been fixed for the following Monday. Maddy spent the rest of the week gardening and doing various repairs on the Croft, so by the time Friday came she was looking forward to her trip to the weekly market.

This time she was going to have lunch with Sarah and they were then going on to the workshop Sarah had invited her to the previous week. She wondered who would be there, whether any of the other members of the history group would be present.

As she walked down the track she began thinking about the people she had met since being here. She felt a certain empathy with some of them in particular with Sarah and Michael. It had been a surprise to her too that Michael had turned up with Simon.

By now she had reached the village and headed for the market. Sarah was already there buying some vegetables. They finished looking round the stalls and finding a table at Les Guingettes, ordered a glass of wine and then lunch. Finishing just before 2 o'clock in the afternoon, they went back to Sarah's house to freshen up. Maddy left her shopping there.

"You can collect it on the way back, in fact I will drive you up to the Croft as by the time we get back it will be late. The session does not start until 3:30 p.m. and we have quite a way to drive. It's over the other side of Bourg Madame, way down in the valleys."

It was a wonderful drive through the mountains and valleys and took just over an hour, travelling from one region to the other, passing through different terrain and climate changes. They had just passed over the top of a perilous ridge and looking down they could see the circulade of the village they were going to. As they wound down to the village you could see for miles across to the horizon with more small villages perched on high points.

Arriving in the village, Sarah took a turning on the outskirts and began winding the car up a narrow track that led to what Maddy thought was open countryside. However in the middle of what seemed to her as nowhere, a house could be seen in a vast expanse of ploughed fields. It was in a small dip in the valley with woodland around it. Barely visible itself, there were no other houses to be seen. They wound their way up and down over the tracks and eventually turned into a small lane with a letter box standing isolated on the corner. After another five minutes' drive, they found themselves in front of a barn containing an old dilapidated car. There were also several other cars parked at various places in the yard. Making their way from the car on a narrow paved path, they came to two doors. Maddy, standing back, was wondering which one was the main door when a woman appeared and greeted Sarah with a kiss and they chattered away.

Quietly observing them, Maddy saw that this woman seemed completely the opposite to Sarah. Introduced to her, Arabella was a petite woman, blonde hair cut in an unusual style which looked rather striking. Her clothes were very classical and expensive, cashmere, designer trousers and gold jewellery. Maddy was fascinated also by her nails which were perfectly manicured and blood red. Inviting Maddy and Sarah in, she said that the others had all arrived including Pam, the workshop leader, and led the way to the back of the house into a large room. Walking through the house Maddy was slightly awestruck at what seemed to her the number of *objet d'art* scattered about, piles of books on low tables and beautiful lamps. It gave the house the feeling of a museum, the pieces having been collected over years of travelled experience.

The company gathered were all women, except for one man who looked a little uncomfortable and shy. Overall there were eight people sitting around in a circle, obviously waiting for them to arrive thought Maddy. Sitting down, Arabella handed over to Pam who said it would be a good idea to get things going if everybody introduced themselves and shared their intentions about what they hoped to gain from the day. As everybody took a turn Maddy felt increasingly comfortable noting everyone as friendly.

The gentle atmosphere made it easy to share a little of her own background. She realised that half of the group had been there in the morning and had had their individual sessions.

Pam said that she was going to lead the group with a short meditation and then take people in individual sessions. As one of the group had dropped out, she offered an individual session to Maddy to which Maddy readily accepted.

Maddy found the meditation session very relaxing, concentrating on breathing steadily and then relaxing the muscles throughout the body. Pam then moved on to in her terms, "Connect through their bodies to the Earth and then up into the universe." This was achieved by visualising a silver cord running from the region around the heart down into the Earth and then through and upward out into the universe.

Maddy found this even more relaxing and at the end of the session, she found herself feeling very peaceful and everything around her seemed more alive and colourful. She looked out and around the group and sensed an energy running around it.

Invited to express feelings on their individual experience some were saying that they had seen different colours and others smells and one girl said she had sensed an angel by her side.

After a few minutes, Arabella invited everyone to take coffee and Pam started taking people into another room for their individual sessions. Some people left as only a few had taken up on the individual sessions.

When it was her turn, Maddy followed Pam into a small room; it was like a mini library and she thought it must be Arabella's study. It was lined with bookshelves and there was a desk, filing cupboard and computer in the corner and two armchairs which they both sank into.

Pam asked Maddy whether she had had any previous consultations and what she hoped to get from their session together. Maddy said she was just curious, that she had had a Tarot reading in London several years ago. She recounted how her Uncle had turned up recently and that she had discovered that Colin and she had bought the exact house that her Mother and Uncle knew of as their grandfather's house way back in the 1930s. She told her that she had several déjà vu experiences during which she felt that she was returning and the question was, to what? It had begun to feel increasingly strange to her and that she had been dreaming more and more recently which seemed to exacerbate her feelings of strangeness.

She told Pam that she thought perhaps this session might help reveal something that was relevant.

Pam had been staring at her quite intensely which had slightly unnerved Maddy. Pam said,

"Don't worry about my looking at you. I have been looking past you at your aura to see if I can sense anything before we begin."

Maddy asked, "And have you, I mean, sensed anything?"

Pam said, "Something, but it's not clear. Shall we get started?"

Pam led Maddy through a relaxing process asking her to breathe deeply and visualise herself being led down a staircase and into a vast library. She asked her to take an imaginary book off the shelf and open it. A quietness ensued between them.

Maddy felt something change in the ambience of the room around her; like a temperature change in the air. Pam was speaking, taking her through visualisation out of the library and up the stairs and brought her back to the room and, counting, three, two, one, told her to open her eyes. Maddy started and became aware of where she was. She felt disorientated and she thought she had not been asleep, she had been 'away', it felt very strange. Pam asked her if she was alright and whether she wanted to talk about anything. She said it was not necessary to do so but Maddy could if she wanted to.

Maddy said she was not sure what she was imagining but thought she had seen, or felt the presence of a woman dressed in gold; in fact everything was gold and seemed to shimmer. The woman in gold had held out her hand, her palm open and took something. Then things faded and she disappeared.

She was aware that Pam had reacted instinctively in response to something she had sensed.

Pam said that she too had the experience of somebody appearing and that they had come to remove a block and had done so.

"I don't understand, a block? What do you mean?"

"I don't know how much you know about the beliefs of reincarnation. In some trains of thought we all have a soul that reincarnates through time. Each time we incarnate we are set lessons that our soul needs to learn in order to ascend spiritually.

Just before we are born, we agree on a contract with our spiritual family about how we are going to go about learning our lessons. However sometimes a block is put on certain people when they incarnate and it seems a block was put on you at the time of your present incarnation."

"What do you mean a block? I don't really understand what you are talking about. That I made a contract before I was born to live a certain kind of life, is that what you mean?"

"Yes, a soul contract."

"So everything that has happened or is happening to me is a kind of predestined plan that I agreed to?"

"Kind of, though you still have what all human beings have, the choice of free will that can override the contract."

"But would I be aware to do that, I mean override it?"

"Normally, the unconscious part of your psyche would rise up and enable you to do so. However, the block placed on you was so intense that it had to be removed by a spiritual presence, in fact quite a high spiritual presence, what we would call an Ascended Master."

"But why, I am not aware or can't remember anything; previous lives, contracts, whatever."

"Perhaps not, but the block has been removed. As I understand blocks are placed because the person would not be able to cope with the information of their past life, or lives, or experiences that may have been so terrible. It seems however that what is happening is that you are now needed to wake up and remember and that is why the block has been removed."

"Wake up. I don't understand. I am sorry, I keep repeating myself but I don't understand!"

Maddy shook her herself and went quiet, she thought perhaps she needed to listen to Pam.

"At this present time no, but it has been removed and you will begin to become, let's say, more aware and remember."

"Remember what, here I go again, it seems like a riddle to me and I am beginning to feel very odd, in fact even a little frightened. It seems as if we are venturing into things that are rather supernatural."

"I think the best thing to do now is for you to give yourself time to think about what happened today and what is going on in your life generally. It seems you have had too much information over the last few days so perhaps you need to take a break. However, I am not prepared to let you go now unless you promise to see me next week so that we can talk further. I am sure I can help you begin to unravel what's happening. Will you promise to meet me next week?"

"Yes, definitely, I am feeling confused, it would help."

They arranged to meet the following week. Pam told her that she was staying in the area and would visit Maddy at the Croft as it seemed that it seemed to be the centre of what might be going on.

Maddy returned to the rest of the remaining group and, after a short while, left with Sarah to go home. She was very quiet on the way home, Sarah asked if she was troubled but did not push her to disclose what had happened during the session sensing that something had touched Maddy deeply and disturbed her.

***

Having collected her shopping from early in the day and as Sarah drove up the track to the Croft Maddy was going through, over and over, in her mind what Pam had said about the block that had been placed on her before she was born. Maddy had done some reading about alternative religions and so could relate to some extent to the idea of being born into a certain family and the ideas about lessons one needs to learn, karma and reincarnation.

She also mulled over everything she had learned about her family history from Simon and about the Cathars. Now with Pam saying that a block had been removed she began thinking about how she had felt several times about returning to this region and that Pam was perhaps right; that whatever was going on was deeply rooted in the history of the local community.

By the time she reached the Croft she felt an overwhelming tiredness overtaking her. Pam had told her that she must drink some water and that the effect of their session together might result in some after effects, memories, and that things could change.

Having had a good lunch with Sarah in the market square earlier in the day, she made herself a very light supper and decided not to have any wine. Taking a mug of warmed milk and honey she went to bed early.

***

Chapter 21
Attending the Second History Group Meeting

Maddy woke with a start. Something had woken her and she sensed a presence in the room. She turned the bedside lamp on and saw the clock registering 3:15 a.m. Hearing footsteps, she peered over the side of the bed and saw the black cat, the stray, walking across the room. She had left the window wide open as it had been a very warm day and the bedroom had been quite stuffy when she went to bed. She always left a crack for air but not fully open.

Maddy put the cat, wriggling and purring under her caress, outside the window onto the ledge. Getting back into bed Maddy realised that she must have been dreaming as fragments of the dream were coming into her head.

I *remember that I was with Colin's parents and they seemed to be preparing for something and I was helping them. Then there were two 'gyroscopes'. Funny that the word and image of them came into my head and dream as gyroscopes were something my father used to talk about a great deal when I was a child. The gyroscopes were spinning in the dream and I sensed that I was in one of them and it was going faster and faster. I thought I must have been scared of losing control and tried to stop it... It must have been then that I woke up...*

The next thing Maddy knew was waking up with sun streaming through the window. Looking at the clock she saw it was 9:00 a.m. and thought she had never slept in so late, she must have been tired. She remembered the cat waking her up and that she had been dreaming but could not grasp at any details.

Whilst making breakfast she felt very lethargic and said to herself, *No wonder*. What with Simon and Pam, her week had been full of revelations; a great deal of which did not make sense but it was all coming at her at once. In addition, there was another meeting of the History Group tomorrow, Sunday afternoon.

Trying to rationalise things as was her way, she decided to try and not think too much about what had happened and get ready for Helen's arrival on Monday. Though she did not have to pick her up until the evening she decided that she would cancel Simon coming up. She felt she needed to give herself time before seeing him again.

She rang Simon and cancelled their meeting. He seemed perfectly comfortable about this and said he understood.

Maddy decided to spend the day leisurely, reading some of the books Sarah had loaned her. She had browsed through them previously and one in particular had caught her attention. It was by an author who was a psychiatrist relating his experience with one of his clients. It was unusual because before the experience, he had no knowledge of the Cathars or the region in which they existed. His client, he concluded, was a reincarnated Cathar from the 13th century.

As Pam had raised the question of reincarnation she thought it might give her some insight into the subject. Settling down she thought she would give it a go and try and read it before the meeting tomorrow.

As the previous meeting had been about the Cathars and she had not gleaned very much about them from Andy's lecture she had googled a couple of history sites to get a synopsis of who they were so that she could at least be a bit informed.

The Cathars, she discovered, were people whose beliefs differed very much from the Catholic Church and because of this they were seen as a threat and called heretics. In the 13th century it had resulted in the Catholic Church creating an Inquisition into their practice and the complete genocide of the Cathars; in fact the largest case of genocide in Europe up until the First and Second World Wars.

They believed that God was within everyone, not a separate entity and that the physical body was the vehicle for the soul for its earthly duration. They led a very simple life without the need for churches or permanent places for worship and were sympathetic to women unlike the Catholic Church.

As she was reading the psychiatrist's story she began to feel strange relating more and more to the psychiatrist's client who from childhood seemed to have had, as it were a 'tap on the shoulder', dreams, visions and memories surfacing of a life she had lived back in the 13th century.

Her case was researched profoundly by the author and many of the facts she recalled from her dreams or visions were confirmed by him and verified by several leading French experts on the Cathars.

Maddy became enthralled and wondered if one of her reincarnations, according to Pam's theory, was in the 13th Century.

***

Sunday afternoon arrived and Maddy set off for the History Group meeting. She met Sarah in the cafe for a drink before the meeting started and chatted generally to her about enjoying the books she was borrowing. Maddy told her about the book by the psychiatrist and said how it had triggered some memories of her own. She told her how when she had first come out to visit the Croft she had been struck by a feeling that she had been here before. Also that the feeling was not just one of her lifetime, it had somehow touched a deeper chord within her. She also shared the fact that she was feeling a bit disorientated by the information her uncle had imparted the previous Monday and then by the session with Pam, that it had left her feeling unsettled and something unresolved. She felt she was now looking for answers but not sure what the questions were.

"It's not the first time since I have been here that I have felt a bit deranged as if I am going mad," Maddy laughed and they both ended up laughing.

Other members of the group had begun to arrive and everybody gravitated to the upstairs room. This time it was Dan's turn to talk and he had paired up with George, a man from a neighbouring village who had not been at the previous meeting. Their talk was about the Catholic Church and St Dominic who had lived in Fanjeaux a village in the Aude region of France.

Maddy found St. Dominic interesting as he had set up homes for fallen women including Cathar women for example who had reverted back to Catholicism. There was a monastery at Prouilhe nearby to Fanjeaux which was one of the founding homes for these women. However, it seemed that at the time many similar kinds of establishments had been set up for women, not just ex Cathar but for elderly noble women, or women discarded by their husbands. Eleanor of Aquitaine seemed to be an example, who after a tumultuous life as Henry II's wife ended her days at Fontvroid Abbey in the Loire region.

Having drinks afterwards George bore down on Maddy wanting to talk about the Croft and its history and the legend. Talking to him she began to feel really uncomfortable and was trying to understand why. As he was talking she realised that he was a devout Catholic and when she mentioned the Cathars sympathetically he turned on her almost violently saying that they were heretics and that the stories about the Cathars had been made popular but nobody heard about the other side, that of the Catholic Faith. She had a really bad feeling and at the first opportunity when other members of the group joined in she made her escape.

***

That evening feeling really tired and even more overwhelmed with information she thought some physical activity would do her good, so set about tidying the house and making up the bed for Helen. She was really looking forward to seeing her. They had been friends since they were 11 years old. Though they had had a break of about 20 years due to Helen divorcing and moving away, they had resumed their friendship at a recent school reunion and picked up as if it were yesterday. By 11.00 p.m., satisfyingly exhausted, she took herself to bed and fell immediately into a deep sleep.

Dreaming...

I was at the top of a large marble staircase, marble floor, on my knees, crying and screaming, my mouth wide open and no sound coming out. There were huge men in armour around me, holding me. I heard my voice saying... my father, my father, where is my father...

The scene moved to a small dark room, a dungeon, I was held down and a small man in a dark robe was pacing up and down beside the plinth on which I was lying, ranting at me to tell the truth... I was screaming... 'I don't understand, I don't understand.

The scene moved to a hillside... looking across I saw my father tied to a post. I realised I was also tied to a post. They lit the faggotts below and the flames shot up and began to engulf my father...

Maddy shuddered and realised she was awake and had been dreaming, her whole body was shaking and she felt terrified. Looking at the clock she saw it was 3.45 a.m. and so shaken she went out and made herself a cup of tea. Sitting out on the terrace she began to feel calmer. Fragments of the dream kept coming back to her and as it did she felt waves of fear wash over her. She felt she had been somewhere else and come back as it were into herself and it was frightening. She had felt something similar in her session with Pam but certainly not the terror of this latest experience.

She decided she would get Sarah to ring Pam and arrange to see her as soon as possible. I need help she thought to herself realising that she was not able to deal with such experiences and would need somebody to guide her or at least give her advice.

Having calmed down somewhat she returned to bed and fell into a fitful sleep.

***

Chapter 22
Helen's Revelation

Early on Monday morning, after breakfast, she rang Sarah and asked if she would arrange for Pam to visit the Croft and give her another session.

Maddy told her that she was going to pick up Helen from the airport so would not be back until mid-afternoon. Sarah said that she would give her a ring that evening.

Helen's flight was due in at midday but despite this Maddy thought she would set off and give herself plenty of time. She arrived at the airport at about 11.00 a.m. and bought herself a cup of coffee. Looking at the notice board she saw that the plane was on time. Sipping her coffee she found herself feeling close to tears, unusual for her, and she sat wondering why she was feeling so emotional.

Maddy saw Helen come through the gate and waved to catch her attention. They embraced, and she thought how good it was to see a familiar face. Helen had a very maternal feel about her and Maddy found herself drawing on this for comfort.

They drove away from the airport chatting mainly about Helen's children and the effort it was to organise everything to escape for a few days.

Helen told Maddy that she had seen Maddy's mother and had brought the necklace with her safely packaged in her hand luggage. She had also brought with her other things that she knew Maddy could not get in France which were typically English most notably strong tea.

"Colin told me he bumped into you the other day?"

As soon as she said it Maddy sensed a reluctance in Helen when she said that yes, she had bumped into him but had not had a chance to talk to him.

Arriving at the Croft, Maddy prepared lunch for them both while Helen unpacked and freshened up. She had been up very early to catch the plane that morning. Helen came out onto the balcony and said to Maddy.

"It's lovely Maddy, you seem to have really made it into a second home. Are you enjoying living out here? I mean I know it is only for the summer, but you seem to be very content."

"I am, or let's say I was until recently, last week in fact. I love the slower way of life here. I have discovered I love gardening and cooking, everything is so seasonal, it makes you very aware of how close we all are to the earth and how detached we may have become from it. I wonder how I am going to feel when I go back to the UK in the autumn."

Helen frowned, "You say until recently, why?"

"Well, just that certain things have happened in the last week and it has made me wonder about coincidences in life, and almost, as if I was meant to come here."

Maddy then told her all about the things she had learned, the arrival of her Uncle, the visit to Sarah and Pam.

"Wow, that is a coincidence, that the place is actually part of your family history. I remember when we came out on that first visit together you saying that you felt as if you had been here before."

"So you can see, I am feeling a little unsettled. Also…"

Looking intently at Helen.

"Can I ask you something, Helen? When I mentioned Colin on the way back from the airport you seemed a bit, well, as if you did not want to say anything. I sensed that you were holding something back, so I am asking you as we are close friends, please tell me if there is something I should know."

"Maddy, this is really awful, you have put me on the spot, I feel very uncomfortable about this. I don't know where to begin, but you are right, we are old friends and you deserve my loyalty. You do need to know what I have become aware of, I don't want our friendship to be spoilt, which it could be otherwise."

"What is going on…?" queried Maddy

"Well, when I bumped into Colin as I told you, he was with a woman, quite an attractive one, about our age, perhaps a bit younger. I don't know who she is. He introduced her as a colleague, a friend of Chris's, you know the person he has been working with on that project you told me about. Colin seemed a bit awkward about my bumping into them, but I don't know what he was thinking, we were in the middle of Denton High Street where I regularly go to meet our friends. You know, the coffee shop where we meet once a week."

"Yes, I know it. So…?"

"Well, it's just that some of our mutual friends have been hinting about Colin and this woman. You know what it's like. I had coffee with Janice and Mike, you know them, and it came up in our conversation that Colin had been seen with this woman on several occasions, in the local pub, restaurants and in his car. Other people had mentioned it to them as well."

"Mother did say that he had been away to Scotland on a project with a colleague but he has not mentioned this woman to me at all. He has seemed a bit preoccupied and I have not spoken to him much recently."

Maddy herself began to look somewhat preoccupied, thinking over recent weeks and how the telephone calls had become less frequent between her and Colin. Being honest, she had noticed a change in their conversations which she had denied to herself.

"Do you think there is something going on between them…?"

"Well rumour would have it that there is, but you know what people are like, two and two make five. Also about the fact that you are away in France, while the cat's away, nasty stuff but, you know what it's like."

Feeling a bit unnerved by the information, Maddy said,

"I have to say if I am honest that I have noticed a change in Colin over recent weeks, but have been reassuring myself that it's just my imagination. The thing that has been troubling me is that he seems reluctant to make any commitment about coming out here as we had planned.

I'm now feeling really strung up, and to be truthful, resentful. This house here was all his idea, I went along with it to please him. I admit that a change has come over me and I love it here, but it's not the point. It was his idea not mine and it seems I am running it for him while he is in the UK, doing what now, working, having an affair, what? I am beginning to feel really angry."

"Maddy, why don't you come back to the UK and see him and find out what is going on. It is no good getting wound up, it could all be above board and just rumours. You need to see him and spend some time together and see what's happening."

"Yes, you are right…trouble is I want to do it now as quickly as possible."

"Well how about seeing if you can come back on the same flight as me on Friday. You could spend a long weekend if not more until you have sorted things out. As you said, it was his idea about the house here so in a way why should you be the one to be stranded out here if he has no intention of joining you."

"That's a good idea, I'll see if I can get a flight. Can you give me the details and I will go and do it now. I can phone Colin this evening and let him know that I am coming back."

Maddy left Helen so that she could have a 'siesta' on the terrace and went off to get her passport and make the flight booking. She also phoned Sarah telling her of the change in plan. Luckily Sarah had not been able to get in touch with Pam so had not made an appointment for a further session yet.

She phoned Simon and told him that she had to go back to the UK for a visit. She did not tell him why but just said that she needed to see her Mother. She also told him that she had the Collar, which seemed to please him. Maddy told him that as soon as she got back she would make arrangements for him to come up to the Croft with Michael.

Her last call, late into the evening after supper with Helen, who had now gone to bed early, was to Colin. Maddy did not mention anything about what Helen had told her. She merely told him that Helen had arrived and that they had spent the day catching up. She then told him that Helen had persuaded her to come back for a short visit as she had seen Maddy's Mother who did not look well. Maddy thought that it was a good excuse as she did not want him to be prepared for what she thought he might consider a confrontation. Best to catch him off guard when he could not close down on her.

Though feeling unsettled she went to bed and fell asleep quickly.

∗∗∗

Chapter 23
Maddy Returns to the UK

Maddy and Helen spent an enjoyable week, going to the coast and mountains, eating out and just generally relaxing together as only old friends can.

They did not talk about the situation Maddy was in regarding Colin as they both found to do so put them in a negative mood and took away their enjoyment of having a short holiday break together. However, as the day of departure to the UK loomed and Maddy prepared she felt a certain foreboding descend over her. She did not know how much to take and decided in the end to take only hand luggage, packing a few items of clothing that matched and some underwear, her thoughts were that if she needed anything else she would go out and buy it. Somehow, she was feeling a bit defiant and wondering why she had to do this and what was in store for her.

On Friday, Maddy locked the Croft. They packed the luggage into the car and set off for the airport.

"I am feeling sick with apprehension," Maddy told Helen.

"Well, I can understand that but try to look on the positive side and that it may all be a storm in a teacup. You can't speculate on the situation as you have no idea what is going on in Colin's life at the moment or what is going on in his head. Best wait until you see him and let him explain. Just put some tentative questions to him and see how he reacts, let him do the talking. However, I know you; for once hold back and give him the room to explain and don't react and jump in with accusations."

"Mmm…" said Maddy ironically. "You do know me don't you?"

"Well since we met when we were 11, I suppose apart from Colin I am the only person who knows you that well and can say it as it is!"

They both burst out laughing and the rest of the journey to the airport was fun with banter between them.

***

The aircraft circled Stansted Airport and then made its descent through thick cloud. Looking through the window, Maddy saw that it was pouring with rain and very overcast. She thought to herself of the wonderful weather and landscape she had left and the contrast of her life there and what it would still be when she returned to the UK.

Colin was standing at the gate and greeted her with open arms, kissing her on the cheek and then turning to greet Helen. Maddy thought to herself that he seemed his usual self as they made their way to the car park, chatting to Helen about her stay with Maddy, about the weather and general chitchat about getting out of the car park.

After they dropped Helen off, a silence fell between them until they reached their house. Colin parked the car and carried Maddy's holdall into the house.

"Shall I make some tea?"

"That would be lovely thank you. Nothing like a cup of real English tea, the stuff we get in France is rubbish, weak and tasteless."

"I was going to bring some out to you."

"Helen brought out some with her so I am stocked up for a while."

Over tea they chatted generally about France and family and having got their news up to date there was a pause. Maddy looked quite intently at Colin and he caught her eye and returned her look.

"What made you decide to come back with Helen?" Colin asked. Maddy thought he looked a little apprehensive.

"Oh a couple of things really! One was Mother; she did not seem very well when I spoke to her and you know what it's like between mothers and daughters. The main thing though was about the Croft. I have been out there since the spring and I had

181

hoped you would have come out to see me. In fact, you have only been out once. I thought you had intended to come out for an extended holiday during the summer but it never happened. I missed you and was beginning to wonder if there was something stopping you from coming?"

Maddy looked Colin directly into his eyes and held his gaze, giving him a chance to respond. She found herself holding her breath and remembering what Helen had said about not jumping in.

"I'm really sorry. I got very involved with work and then it seemed to take over. Contracts built up and then I had to travel to Scotland quite a few times. In fact, it has become a full time job which of course I had never intended it too."

"So what do you plan to do, are you going to continue working? And if so what am I supposed to do, stay in France or return?"

"Well for the time being I have to carry on as I have got myself in too deeply."

"Helen said she bumped into you in town with one of your colleagues, not Chris, but a woman. Has the project expanded so that you have taken on other employees?"

"Yes, that was Diana. We brought her in to look after the office and PR. As the marketing side grew so quickly, we had so much to do on top of the main project we needed somebody to deal with the admin."

"Who is she?"

Maddy sensed Colin was beginning to feel a bit uncomfortable.

"She is a friend of Ellie, Chris' wife. She was in a difficult situation; her husband died last year and she needed a job. Ellie thought as the project was growing it would be an ideal situation for her. Also she was not expecting to be paid a great deal salary-wise which at the time was helpful."

Maddy was beginning to feel angry, she felt Colin was keeping something from her and she did not know how to probe the matter further without an outright confrontation. At that moment the telephone rang. As it was in the same room Colin got up and answered it. She could see that he was speaking to whoever was on the other end of the line in a guarded way.

"Hello there, no I can't come in this morning as Maddy has arrived and we are just about to go out for lunch."

Whoever was on the other end was making Colin listen intently.

"Okay, I understand. I'll see you at the office towards the end of the afternoon."

Colin put the receiver down and sat down again opposite Maddy.

"Where would you like to go for lunch? I thought as we have not seen each other for quite a time it would be good to go out and relax. You can unpack later while I go into the office and deal with today's post."

"Who was that on the line?" Maddy asked.

"It was Diana." Colin looked rather sheepish. "She has a few things that need dealing with."

"Why can't Chris deal with it? It is his project too. After all, as you said we have not been together for quite a while, a day off surely would not be a problem."

"He's in Scotland and I am dealing with the operation here on my own at the moment."

"I see."

***

They went to a restaurant nearby, one which they had visited often in the past. Having finished their lunch and lingering over coffee, an uncomfortable silence fell over them both. Maddy, as ever straightforward, wanted to clear the air.

"This is not like us, I sense there is something between us and I can't put my finger on it. Is there something you are not telling me? I am feeling a bit vulnerable at the moment. We haven't seen each other for quite a while and I feel we are not sharing any of the anticipation or excitement about being together. I feel you are holding something back.

Helen told me that all our friends are talking about you and this woman. Diana, you said her name was? Perhaps it would be a good idea for me to come to the office with you this afternoon and meet her?"

"I would rather you did not do that."

183

"Why not, what are you not telling me and why can't I meet her? Is there something going on? For heaven's sake Colin! We have known each other all our lives, can't you just tell me yes or no—are you having an affair with her?"

"No—well, I am not sure that I know what qualifies as an affair."

Colin blustered then turning white he went quiet and then after a few minutes, continued, "We have been seeing a great deal of each other, due to work in the beginning, then we had to go to Scotland together and things just got out of hand. Initially, I found her good company and amusing and then things developed. It all happened so quickly. I tried to stop it…"

His voice faltered and fell silent, his eyes down and head turned to the side.

While he had been talking, Maddy had felt her blood pressure drop and was feeling faint. She felt she had been kicked in the stomach and was beginning to feel sick.

"I…don't say anymore for a minute… I need to get things clear. You have been having an affair. Is it still going on or have you ended it?"

"When you said you were coming back it pulled me up as to what I was doing, I talked to Diana about it and asked for some space to sort my feelings out. She understood but obviously…"

"Yes, obviously, your cosy little arrangement was going to be upset."

Maddy retorted sarcastically, which was unlike her.

"Oh God… I don't know what to do…"

"Well, I tell you what, I am going home now to unpack and then I am going to see my mother, probably Helen too. In the meantime you can go and see Diana and sort yourselves out. This evening we can talk about the situation again. In the meantime think about this—I feel I have been deliberately dumped in France in order that you can have some freedom, probably to re-visit your adolescence. Anyway, see you later."

Angry, Maddy got up from the table, grabbed her bag and went to the front of the restaurant and got the Manager to call a taxi for her and went home. She was fuming and near to tears and making an exhibition of herself.

***

As she had only arrived a few hours before, Maddy decided not to see her mother until the next day. In the state she was in at the moment, she did not want to burden her mother with her emotions. She knew her mother would not want to see her and Colin at odds with the possibility of separating and therefore she felt it best to leave it until she knew herself what the future held. She asked herself how had it got to this point so quickly, from what she considered a happy marriage to what seemed a bleak future that might mean her being on her own.

Instead, after unpacking her few things and deciding to move into the spare bedroom instead of the marital bed, she rang Helen, told her what had happened and asked to meet her. Helen immediately drove over and picked her up and took her back with her to her own house.

Seeing Maddy, white, shaken and holding back tears, Helen poured her a small brandy while she made some tea.

"Drink this, I know you don't like alcohol, but I think you need this. You have had a shock and it will make you feel better, even if only temporarily."

"I feel like an absolute idiot. I know you told me what you had heard but something in me was stopping me believing it. Now I am questioning everything; our whole marriage. Has he been unfaithful before? It feels crazy. How could he let me go to France and then do this without thinking?"

"Perhaps it was not quite like that," said Helen.

"First of all buying the place in France he probably was totally enthusiastic about it and saw everything in it that you shared. Then the opportunity through his friend to start a new business he could not resist. You know what he is like, he has always been totally consumed by his job and the idea that he was going to retire peacefully, go fishing or play golf once or twice a week was never going to do it for him."

"Whose side are you on?" Maddy interrupted crossly.

"Let me go on! Then on top of everything else, with you out of the way, an attractive woman appears on the scene, probably batting her eyelids at him and making him feel like some kind of 'god'. He is not the only man of his age to succumb. I am not excusing him, just pointing out that there are many men in their later years that go through this mid-life crisis."

"She's attractive then is she?" Maddy interrupted again rather cynically.

Helen coloured slightly, "Well, in a rather mature way."

"I suppose the bottom line is that I was probably a bit stupid in going out there alone. Also I am not the needy type so coping well on my own was not a problem for him, he could just get on with what he wanted to do. In fact we have always been a bit like that, only I never expected this to happen. It makes me wonder though whether he has done anything like this before.

I'm devastated. I feel I just want to walk away from him, let him get on with it. I feel so angry."

"Leave it for this evening, sleep on it and see what tomorrow morning brings. You say he has gone to see this woman, what's her name, Diana, now. Probably they will be sorting things out so you will know more this evening. It's all been so sudden for you. Remember it is not like that for them. You coming back so suddenly has probably brought them to their senses.

You need to take some time, try not to make any rash moves. My advice would be to let him make the suggestions, you need to find out what is going on before you make any decisions."

"Yes, you are right, however much I love him, loved him, not sure I do now. In fact I have never really had to think about that, I have always taken it for granted. There is no point being with him if he is unsure or wants something different. I just feel used and deceived. Why keep me out in France, it just feels unfair and rather callous. I feel he should have told me as soon as he decided to play the field. Perhaps if I had known I could have done the same!"

Maddy began to feel she was sinking into a resentful rage and pulled herself up. Not given to wallowing in negativity she turned the conversation to Helen, asking how her family were getting on.

After more brandy and tea, Helen took Maddy home. It was now early evening and there was no sign of Colin. He still had not returned by 10:00 p.m., and having been up early to catch the flight that morning, Maddy, tired and slightly drunk, decided to go to bed. The bed in the spare room was not very comfortable but within minutes she had fallen into a deep sleep.

Colin did not return until just before midnight, looking for Maddy and not finding her in their bedroom, he thought she had gone to stay with her mother. Tired also he went straight to bed. He knew the following morning was going to be difficult.

***

Both Maddy and Colin woke up in their different rooms with the sun streaming through the window. Going to the bathroom they bumped into each other, rather awkwardly, not looking into each other's eyes and avoiding contact, passing like strangers on the landing. Later, down in the kitchen, Maddy made some coffee and sat at the table, neither had felt like having breakfast.

"Well…?" said Maddy, "What's the picture now…?"

"I saw Diana last night and, well this is really difficult."

"Oh for God's sake… get on with it…"

"I think it would be best if you—well I am not sure about my feelings. Diana suggested I stop seeing her, she said she could not go on seeing me if I was not sure about her… or you…she asked me to choose."

"Are you expecting me to do the same, ask you to choose?"

"I have not been fair to you, I know that's why I think I should take some time to sort my feelings out. It's not about choosing. I love you, I always have and will."

"Or would, if you go off with her?" questioned Maddy.

"Well, after what has happened I have to know that if we were to carry on together that I really want to be with you. Whether you would do the same again, whether it is just something you need to get out of your system or whether our whole life has been a sham."

"I am sorry, I love you, but this just happened and made me think about my life in a different way. In one way, logically it does not make sense."

"I think you are going through a mid-life crisis, revisiting your adolescence or something. However, I am not standing by watching you go through it to end up with you eventually. Somehow, I feel this is all over between us."

"Oh don't say that, I could not bear to think that I might not see you again."

"Didn't that cross your mind when you started your affair with her or did you just go into it blindly, you must have known what you were doing, putting your whole life on the line? You have ruined everything. We had a lovely marriage, or that's what I thought, lovely children, lovely life and in just a few months you have blown the whole thing away. Not only that but there is the financial aspect too, where are we going to live while you are sorting yourself out! Are you expecting me to continue living in France, or come back here? Where are you going to live, move in with Diana?"

"I just did not think."

"That's just it then isn't it, your brains descended to your balls!" Maddy said vehemently.

"I have spent my whole life working and looking after the family and I am not saying that you have not done the same. But doing nine to five and commuting every day of my working life the freedom actually of not thinking came over me like a breath of fresh air. So please don't go on."

"Well, thanks for putting in that perspective. For me enough is enough! I'm done for the time being."

With that Maddy got up and went up to pack her things. She decided to ask Helen if she could stay with her until she had made up her mind what she was going to do while this was being sorted out. Later on, Helen picked her up and took her back to her house.

Now she felt really depressed and confused, having confided to Helen her discussion with Colin.

"What a mess. I think I must go and see Mother today and then later on meet up with Colin. I have to decide what I am going to do."

***

Maddy spent another three days in the UK. Having seen her Mother and given her a brief explanation of what was going on and talking things through with Helen, she decided to return to France, put the house on the market and stay there until it was sold.

Colin was agreeable to all of this though reluctant, as he had hoped to have more time to sort his feelings out. Had he decided eventually to stay with Maddy and if she was agreeable to it, he thought the Croft in France might have been a good place for them to reconcile together. However, as it was all his fault he felt, he had no alternative but to go along with her train of thought for the time being. He did not think the house would be sold that quickly in France anyway as the housing market in Europe was very slow at the moment.

Maddy sat at the airport waiting for the departure gate to come up on the overhead display. Looking out over the runways, seeing the aircraft come in and take off, she felt desolate and more alone than she had ever felt in her entire life.

***

Chapter 24
Desolate, Maddy Returns to France
Malachi Visits Nammu and Simon to Review the Situation

Having received the phone call cancelling his visit to Maddy, Simon was rather bemused about what was going on. Maddy had not given any reason for rushing off to the UK other than that she needed to see her mother.

Simon knew that Helen, Maddy's old school friend, had been visiting, so he had not had a chance to see Maddy before she went back.

He decided he needed to see Michael to find out if he could throw any light on what was going on.

Simon met Michael at the local cafe; they had been making it a rendezvous once a week so that each other was kept in the picture as to what was happening.

"Did you know that Maddy has gone back to the UK? She seemed to have made a rather impulsive decision and dashed off with her friend last Friday. I was supposed to meet her today to carry on with the family history, but it's been postponed now until she gets back, and I don't know when that will be."

"Yes, I knew she had gone. Isolde told me and I saw the Overseer to find out what was happening. It seems that the guardians decided that they needed her husband out of the scene while all of this is going on. They felt that she would probably confide in him if he came out here and that he would influence her away from what she needs to do. Therefore they created, let's call it, an artificial experience."

"What do you mean? Nothing drastic I hope?"

"Well, no, just unpleasant for her but she will get over it when she comes to understand her destiny. They have created a situation taking him out of her life for the time being."

"And...?"

"He is having an affair with a woman he has been working with. Returning to the UK Maddy has now found out. They are separating so that he can, as you say, 'sort himself out', I think that's how you humans refer to situations like this."

"Isn't there a danger that in the circumstances Maddy might just say it was Colin's project in France and he could get on with it while she returned to the UK?"

"Well, we are hoping not. She has become attached to the place and you have made her aware of her heritage. She has to come back anyway because she has agreed to remain here until it is sold; which they won't do by the way as it will be her real home and she will come to realise that."

"You seem so sure as to what is going to happen. You say she will remain here, how do you know?"

"You know, Simon, about time, it's written, seen, done..."

"Oh if only I could see through your eyes..."

"You could if you meditated regularly," Michael retorted.

"Anyway the guardians told me that the block has been re-moved and Maddy is now beginning to remember, though I don't expect she would describe it like that."

"You mean she is dreaming and having déjà vu experiences."

"Yes, exactly. She is also seeing a medium who is assisting. The medium is what we call a light worker and we have enrolled her to speed up the process. Maddy will see her next week."

"How do you know?"

"You are exasperating me Simon! How many times have I explained to you about the illusion of time that you humans have?"

"So everything is now, and you can see everything all at once, it confuses me. I get caught up in speculating on probabilities, this could happen instead of that but there is only the present, this moment now!"

"It's a waiting game now until she settles down?"

"That's it!" exclaimed Simon.

***

Maddy arrived back in France feeling battered. Helen's visit, the confrontation with Colin and previously the visits of Simon and all the information she was absorbing, completely overwhelmed her.

So, tired, she took a sedative and went straight to bed crying almost wishing she was not going to wake up.

It was Thursday before she surfaced. Looking in the mirror she felt as if she had aged and her body felt strung up like an over-tuned violin. Always pragmatic and positive she began thinking about the situation. What was clear was that she would probably have to stay in France until the house was sold.

On top of everything Colin had said that financially it was not going to be easy but, if it came to separation eventually, it would probably mean that she could have the proceeds of the sale of the Croft. This had made her even sadder. She had become attached to the property and the way of life, even in the short time she had spent there over the summer. Now that had all disappeared. It had been obvious to her that he had not even thought of coming out to France. She wondered how long the affair had been going on and what other unpleasant surprises were going to appear out of the blue. Anyway, in the meantime, she had to get her life back on track to survive. She rang Sarah and arranged to meet her in the market the following day.

***

Meeting her the next day, Maddy recounted the whole sad affair while Sarah listened attentively.

"That's a real bombshell, you poor thing."

"You can say that again. I felt totally stunned. It all seems unreal and I can't understand how I could have been so blind to what Colin was so obviously up to. There were no clues, well until recently; his never coming out to France. I just feel I have been a complete idiot!"

"What are you going to do now?"

"Quite honestly I haven't a clue, other than having to put the Croft on the market and sit it out until it's sold. It's the only positive thing that I can do at the moment. I just need time to think. Apart from that I have been feeling numb with shock but now I am beginning to get angry."

"Selling the house could take some while, my friend is an estate agent and she was only saying the other day that the market is very slow now."

"I am just going to have to live day to day. Money isn't a problem at the moment, I have my own state pension so I can manage on that and there is no mortgage on the Croft. I just have to pay for the utilities. Our tax is dealt with in the UK, so Colin can deal with that side of things."

"How about coming to see my friend and put the Croft on her books, that's a start."

"Yes, that would get things going. Who knows it might sell quickly."

Sarah and Maddy crossed the square to the estate agent's office and after half an hour the property was on the books. Maddy went back to Sarah's afterwards having bought something from the delicatessen to share for lunch.

Mid-afternoon Maddy left to walk back to the Croft. Sarah had phoned Pam and arranged for her to come to the Croft on Sunday.

***

Chapter 25
Pam Visits the Croft

Sarah arrived with Pam on Sunday afternoon. After a cup of tea Pam asked Maddy, "Shall we go in and see whether we can find out anything more?"

They left Sarah on the terrace, saying that she was going to walk around the garden as she wanted to see what Maddy had been doing.

As before Pam led Maddy into a light trance state. Maddy felt she was aware and present but also somewhere else. This time, she did not feel or think anything.

Afterwards Pam, who had also seemed to have gone into a trance like state, asked her if she had any comments. They sat for some minutes and after a while Maddy said,

"Really nothing. Maybe because I am totally immersed in what has been happening in my marriage over the past week. I can't concentrate on anything else."

Pam was thoughtful and said, "Probably!"

"You seemed preoccupied, did you get anything?"

"Well, yes and actually I am a bit stunned."

"Why?"

"Well, as you know I do see things, I am clairvoyant. What I saw was that you are surrounded by a golden army—it's immense. It is all around you and stretches everywhere, to the horizon and beyond. It seems you are heavily protected by, well let's call them guardians. By the way they are Ancients, I have never encountered them before; usually my encounters are in the more immediate spirit world, when people pass away. There is one presence in particular, I think female, in a totally golden aura. Do you remember I sensed her in our previous session?"

"Yes, I think I remember sensing her too."

"Well, she will be coming to collect something."

"Perhaps it's the Collar…?"

"What Collar?" Pam countered, startled.

"I thought I mentioned it to you before."

Maddy told her about the Collar and its history and how she had had it brought back recently. She herself had forgotten it temporarily due to the upset with Colin.

"Well, perhaps it is that, but I sensed it was not something so solid. It seemed more ethereal, an abstract thing that had been hidden here a long time ago.

Look, you must understand I cannot interpret what is going on exactly. You have to view it as if it was a giant jigsaw puzzle without a clear picture on the face. We are putting the pieces into place, piece by piece. Eventually it will make sense.

The other thing is that I can't give a time limit—this kind of thing occurs within Earth time and space constricts. The guardians, angels, spirits, whatever you like to call them, who are communicating with us at this time don't operate within our Earth's three-dimensional boundaries. Ten years to them can just be a blink of the eye within their universal concept. That's why when I see things or get visions and can talk to them I say that I would appreciate it if they considered our time line. No good asking for help now when in their understanding now could be any time past or future."

Pam was being very ironic and Maddy laughed.

"Good to see you a bit lighter. What has been happening to you in the last week has obviously dragged your energy down; I can see that in your aura."

Looking to the side of Maddy Pam saw her aura as a nondescript grey hovering and flashing, obviously struggling to raise energy.

Maddy was beginning to relax a bit. "I get the jigsaw puzzle comparison and I feel somewhat relieved all of a sudden. It has given me a way of looking at my life and what's happening, rather than expecting answers immediately."

"Exactly! I am around for quite some time so shall we get together again soon. I seem somehow to be involved in your story too. I can feel it and it seems to go back a long time, perhaps through many incarnations."

"You mean, that we shared the same life time in the past."

"Yes, but not one…it feels to me quite a few."

"Well, if you are willing it would be a great help to me and thanks. Somehow it feels right, as if you have been sent to help me through this. It's difficult to understand what is going on and then with the added break up of my marriage so totally unexpected."

They went outside and found Sarah sitting on the terrace gazing up at the sky.

"Look up there," she pointed across the valley.

There were two eagles circling high up in the sky. It was a perfect day, the air clear and very hot. All of a sudden the eagles swooped and flew close across in front of the Croft. They were enormous and had an amazingly intricate colouring.

Maddy ran in to get her camera and took some photos. Later that evening, having downloaded the photos onto her computer, examining their colouring and googling them, she discovered they were short toed eagles and could often be seen with snakes in their beaks as it seemed to be their preferred diet.

The close ups of their colouring revealed an orb in the sky behind them. Wondering what it was she enlarged and sharpened the image but got no further in finding out what it was, perhaps a star, or the moon she thought. Puzzled however, she looked up moon phases and saw that it could not be the moon, so perhaps it was a planet?

Having the session with Pam had relaxed Maddy. She was feeling sad because it was the first time since returning that she was able to go over in her mind some of the things that had happened. She realised that her stay at the Croft had given her a different perspective on her life. She liked the climate and the slower way of life and felt healthier and mentally more herself. All she had to do was to accept that she had changed and that perhaps the break up with Colin was going to happen anyway. Something she was reluctant to admit to herself just yet.

***

Chapter 26
Maddy Is Told Her 'Soul Contract'

On Monday morning, Maddy rang Simon and arranged for him to visit that afternoon.

"May I bring Michael? You know I told you that it would be of interest for him to come along."

"Yes, perfectly alright."

As she put the phone down Maddy wondered again what Michael had to do with her family history. They arrived just after lunch.

Simon began with,

"Not sure where I left off with the family history Maddy, I am getting old and the memory is going."

He laughed, rather nervously she thought.

"It seems a while ago so much has happened since I last saw you. You don't know but I had to go back to the UK and while there, for a number of reasons, Colin and I have agreed to separate for the time being, it may mean we will be getting divorced in the future. I have to sell the Croft which I am a bit sad about as it has grown on me and I like it here very much. So, you see, things have been a bit difficult."

"Oh I am sorry to hear that," Simon murmured in sympathy glancing at Michael quickly.

"Well it certainly wasn't something I had anticipated; it came right out of the blue. Anyway, that aside, you said where had we got to with the family history. You told me that our family originates back to the 13th century and the legend about my ancestor Malena and her escape from the Inquisition.

Also, that this house is where Malena was brought to back in the 13th century and that my great grandfather restored it in the

1930s. That was the most amazing coincidence. That Colin and I should have bought it."

Simon caught Michael's eye.

"That seems to be the gist of it. Basically I am the descendent of an ancient family that carries some kind of secret?"

Maddy shrugged and looked at Simon seeking his agreement that she had understood the story correctly.

"Oh and of course the Collar!"

Maddy turned and went to the cupboard in the corner of the room and took out a box and brought it back to the table.

"I got Mother to get it out of the bank vault and Helen brought it over with her. I did not know at that time that I was going to the UK or I would have brought it back myself. Anyway, it got here safely. It's really unusual.

You said Michael should come along with you this time and I wondered why? What have you got to do with my family?"

She said turning to Michael. Michael looked at Simon, who nodded his agreement for him to continue.

"Simon has told you about your family and that it has a long history back to the 13th Century. I am here to tell you about your family history that goes back even further and why I am connected with it. However what I have to tell you may test your beliefs somewhat but I must ask you to bear with us in the meantime."

Michael looked to Simon, asking for his silent approval to what he was about to say.

"Perhaps today I will tell you about your ancient family, it will be enough for this session. There is much more to tell but I think you will need time to digest it and it will be easier if you have the information in smaller amounts. There is another perspective to the history that you will need to learn as well."

"Well I am intrigued."

"The story of your family goes far back in the history of Earth. I am sure you had a religious upbringing so you will be acquainted with the bible stories about Jesus, Moses, Egypt and further back Adam and Eve and the flood. Those stories you heard at Sunday School have similarities with all religions. They originate from a civilisation that existed in Sumeria long ago which was very highly advanced.

Some 450,000 years Earth was visited by extra-terrestrials who had an interest in the resources of Earth, in particular extracting gold. Their species experienced difficulties mining underground, their bodies were not accustomed to the gravitational demands of the atmosphere which were different to those of their own planet.

As I said, they were a highly advanced race capable of many scientific achievements not even comprehensible to the most clever scientists here on Earth at the present time. To help themselves overcome the problems they were experiencing they genetically engineered the indigenous race on Earth at that time with their own species and created a race of 'earthlings' to do the mining for them. It is those 'earthlings' that the present day population of Earth is descended from."

Michael paused as he noticed that Maddy looked puzzled. She interrupted him.

"So what you are saying is that all of us are descended from these visitors, presumably from space, that we are partly aliens?"

"Yes, shall I continue? The next bit I have to tell you will perhaps test your beliefs as I told you it might."

Maddy nodded in agreement.

"Maddy I know from our meetings and the history group that you are quite a sensitive soul and are interested in quite a broad perspective regarding various religions, that's so isn't it?"

"Yes, but it is only since I have been here that I have been able to read more. Sarah, the friend I have made in the village, has an amazing library of books on a variety of subjects which I have borrowed from her. See for yourself."

Maddy pointed to the piles of books on the kitchen table.

"So what would you say your belief is about reincarnation; the theory of having had a previous life, or lives, going back in history?"

Maddy thought of the recent sessions with Pam and the workshop at Arabella's.

"At one time I was rather sceptical about it but some of the stories I have heard and read about recently have been convincing. Added to which I have been having some really unusual dreams, which seem more like actual happenings than 'dreams' if that makes sense."

"So, what would you say is the thing that gets reincarnated?"

"Well your soul, it can't be your body as when you die that deteriorates or disappears if you are cremated. It has to be something apart, ethereal, perhaps an energy that separates away."

"Sorry but you were telling me that we are all descended from these alien visitors and you are now talking about reincarnation. I can't get the connection, and why you are telling me this, and why you are here."

"Well Simon needs me to be here as he understands to a point but he is a player in a larger drama, let's call it that, which has been going on for a very long time."

"How long…?"

"Well, if I were to tell you 8,500 years ago would you believe me? I am here because I was appointed to watch over your soul back in the early days of the civilisation I have described to you. I have been watching you over the centuries; following you, shall we say, through your many incarnations."

Incredulous now Maddy could only ask

"Why? What has it got to do with me today and surely through the many births and deaths in families I can't have any connection to that time."

"You can and do. Your lineage, let's say your bloodline and family history, has been kept pure. I don't want to test your credulity too far at the moment but actually the species that was evolving on Earth originated from even more ancient visitors to the planet, not the visitors who created the 'earthlings' that I talked about.

I am not sure whether you have had any blood tests through health problems, but if you have you will know that your blood group is very rare. It does not carry the elements of DNA that were engineered into the indigenous population by the more recent Visitors. Your blood carries DNA from the ancient visitors.

The actual history of human beings originates from much further back and out in the Universe. The beings who exist there, I have already referred to them as the Ancients, are even more highly advanced then the Visitors who came to do the mining. It is their DNA that originally created the indigenous population on Earth that the Visitors genetically interfered with and, of interest, they created the genetic strain of the Visitors. They are concerned with the evolution of the Universe and the part that Earth and its current population are part of."

The sun was beginning to go down. Maddy was gazing out of the window seemingly lost in thought.

Simon said to Malachi, "I think that's enough for now. I don't think it's fair to Maddy to carry on, she needs to take this in."

"But there is more to tell her and she needs to know."

"Maddy, are you alright…"

"I don't know what to say and to be honest it seems a bit far-fetched, for example the bit about my blood group being rare. I have had no reason to know that as I have been very healthy."

"How about tomorrow, can you come back? I am not doing much this week, so perhaps we could do another session tomorrow."

"Yes, that's a good idea."

Maddy made some tea, and Simon and Michael were talking rather heatedly.

"You are going too fast, if you are not careful she will throw you out as talking a load of rubbish."

"Yes, I do realise, I keep on forgetting the capacity of the human brain. She would have been given an upload on my planet…"

"What do you mean?"

"It is just a meditation technique which our children learn in school to help them take in huge amounts of data and the technique also teaches them how to access it quickly."

"I wonder sometimes, I would be interested to know where you come from."

"I may take you there sometime, not soon, but your imagination may be questioned when I do."

Laughing, Malachi muttered to himself…

"And what I look like might give you a fright too when you see me outside of this human framework."

***

After tea Simon and Michael disappeared after reassuring Maddy they would be back early in the morning to continue the story. She was left feeling overloaded but it had taken her mind off the predicament she was in with Colin.

***

Chapter 27
Maddy's Awakening

Simon and Michael turned up the next day and said they would stay longer if she was agreeable, swinging some carrier bags which they said contained lunch.

After settling Michael picked up the story from the previous day.

"Just to recap, yesterday I told you that I had been appointed to watch over your incarnations from that early time in your civilisation.

If you remember the legend, it talks of a 'song' and a 'stone'. Well the 'song' is carried in your bloodline, more specifically your DNA. As I said your bloodline has been kept pure down from that time, it has been my job and the Ancients' to ensure that.

I have to get a little more scientific here to try to make it clearer for you. Everything that exists, literally everything in existence is a combination of energy and matter, in a constant exchange of energy causing change and then change again. This exchange occurs by frequencies.

Just for example you know that radios tune into certain frequencies to pick up particular radio programmes, say Radio 1, 2 or 4. You tune in to receive those programmes. Do you follow Maddy?"

"Yes, radio waves that are picked up to transmit television or radio, telephone etc."

"That's right."

"Well, we can take that further. When I say everything that exists operates on different frequencies, I also include us; people, animals, trees, everything and the vehicle from which the frequencies operate or transmit or pick up messages is in everything, everybody's individual DNA. The DNA acts like an antenna that picks up the codes that come in on different frequencies and like language get translated.

Currently your scientists are researching this, but to get back to your DNA specifically, it carries special frequencies.

My appointment as your soul guardian was made at a time when the Sumerian civilisation was created but then began to disintegrate due to wars between the Visitors to the planet. If you remember I told you they were the ones who genetically interfered with the indigenous population.

The myths and legends as they have been handed down by the Egyptians, Greeks and Romans all refer to these Visitors and it is from them that the word God originated. It literally means if you take the translation back through Egyptian, Babylonian, Assyrian and Sumerian cuneiform texts—'those that from heaven came.' The text actually describes these wars and the vying for power between the brothers and sisters of the Visitor dynasty.

Returning to you however, your bloodline was kept pure. Although it comes from the Visitors' genetic interference, it retained the predominant characteristics of the original ancient bloodlines that respond to certain frequencies and when activated give you special powers.

I can see that you are looking puzzled?"

"Yes I am, I am trying to clarify what you are saying, basically that I am of a special bloodline that has been kept pure through thousands of years and that it carries special powers?"

"Simply put, but yes."

"I am totally unaware of these powers, I am just your average middle class housewife and can't imagine anything else…?"

"Up until now. You are quite right, you are unaware because to become aware necessitates some special training to activate the frequencies in your DNA."

"To what end?" said Maddy frowning.

"You have a role to play."

"I do?"

"Yes, not only does it concern you, but the whole population of the planet and the planet, Earth, itself."

"You have just referred to Earth as something you see part of something else. Obviously it is part of a solar system, galaxy. But you seem to be viewing it far more objectively?"

"I am, Earth is part of a huge, let's call it, mechanism that is reliant on all its parts working together cooperatively. Rather like a car engine, it has to be fuelled and oiled to run smoothly.

Likewise Earth rotates around the sun with the other satellites, you call them planets, in a solar system which in turn rotates within a constellation and so on out into the depths of the universe. Everything is rotating and moving in connectivity.

However, it gets more complex. Earth is three-dimensional, that is, it exists within a time/space restriction. Its three-dimensionality is defined by a specific frequency. If this frequency were to change, then perception of existence on the planet would change.

Frequencies define dimensions, the higher dimension the more ethereal the matter becomes the matter less dense.

It is called ascension, the goal of all spiritual teachings. Life, existence of all things begins one-dimensionality and then ascends until it reaches a point when it becomes absorbed back into the original Source from which all frequencies, all dimensions emanate. However, ascension depends on the state of the evolution of the planet and its population together; not on the individual person.

As the planet and its population ascends, its whole molecular structure changes to a higher frequency, the interaction of matter with the higher frequency changes everything."

"So, you talked of my having a role; what has this to do with it?"

"Going back to my description of the Universe as a mechanism there is an Alignment due to occur soon of planets, constellations, galaxies, even further out that ripples into other universes and across dimensions.

Linear time on this planet is a way of making sense of existence for people in the early stages of their evolution as it is for any population bound to any planet. For example on a planet much larger than Earth the time frame would be different, measured by Earth years it could be that one year there would be 3600 Earth years.

This coming Alignment gives Earth the potential possibility of ascending out of its three-dimensionality to higher dimensions. It is a period in Earth's history described as the coming of the age of Aquarius, the golden age when everything and all peoples live in a state of harmony and peace.

Currently it is in doubt whether this is possible. There are forces at work trying to stop it because of other things. But, that aside, we need to focus on you at the moment and your role."

"Yes. What are you expecting of me because I am increasingly beginning to think I am not going to be of much help. It sounds absolutely unfeasible, especially the emphasis you seem to be putting on me as having a key role!"

Michael glanced at Simon who was signalling with some stern facial expressions that it was enough for today.

Simon intervened.

"Let's have lunch, we can continue afterwards if you feel like it Maddy."

"That's a good idea. What I don't understand is you say that our scientists haven't reached an understanding of this, yet you are expecting me to believe you and you will expect me to act on what you are saying with no proof. Why hasn't the media or the government told us all about this."

"That's another story, for another time. However, the song of the universe is going to change. That is the Universe has the opportunity to ascend and Earth is the key to it entering that process. You are part of the key, you are what we call a 'Sentient Seal'."

"A Sentient Seal?" Maddy said.

"Yes, dormant for millennia, waiting for the appropriate time, when you wake up and remember your soul contract."

"This waking up you refer to, does it have anything to do with the dreams and visions I have been having."

"Yes, you are gradually remembering certain things from your soul life."

"I have been seeing a medium and we have been trying to make sense of my dreams but I can't quite grasp it."

"Yes, just so, in fact Pam was sent to you. We sent her."

"We?"

"The Ancients and others."

"Others?"

"Time for lunch!" Simon intervened, seeing Maddy glaring at Michael with utter amazement.

"Good idea," said Maddy needing the break.

Simon and Michael had brought along a variety of cheese, pate, breads and salad and also some local red wine. Maddy also took the opportunity to stroll out into the immediate garden for some fresh air.

She was finding it difficult to take in what they were telling her. It was all beginning to sound too serious and she thought, scientific. In a way she preferred that to some of the other concepts she had heard coming from religious sources. Somehow she found it easier to understand frequencies in relation to tuning into a radio station. However she was having difficulty trying to relate that to ascending or changing dimensions. The concept of dimensions was eluding her somewhat.

Going back in she made coffee, filling the coffee filter, she heard Simon again telling Michael that he maybe was going too fast and perhaps they should leave it for a day or so.

Michael however did not seem to be being very receptive to what Simon was saying. He seemed to give the impression that he felt she was perfectly capable of coping with more information today, and that it was necessary to press on.

***

Having relaxed a little over lunch Maddy felt ready for Michael to continue.

"Before we go any further I think we must tell you more about your family history, about the Cloitre de Lilith. The Cloister of Lilith.

Going back to that very early time in Sumeria when civilisation was becoming corrupted by wars the ancestors saw that the natural evolution of the planet and its inhabitants would be destroyed if they did not do something.

A young priestess named Lilith was selected at that time to carry the DNA down through time so that it would be in place for the coming Alignment."

"But how could it be carried down without being dissipated through the generations of families without being tainted by intermarrying. You only have to look at family trees going back to see the multitude of people concerned. To keep one bloodline pure is an impossibility. And how would the knowledge of that be preserved over time, knowing that the Alignment was going to occur?"

"Well that's just it, it's done, it has been preserved or you would not be here today listening to your story.

The Cloister of Lilith was created to preserve the knowledge and to protect the lineage. The ancestors intervened and created it to hold the secret of your lineage and the role you have to play with your sisters."

"Sisters? What sisters?"

"Lilith was the daughter of a noble family within a tribe, she was made a priestess. At that time twelve tribes were selected to have the equivalent of a Lilith within their tribe, all with the same role as Lilith to play. All twelve carried the 'song' with the same goal which would be their unification on the Alignment. You along with them are all Sentient Seals and collectively are the Sentient Shield of the Planet.

Remember the legend of the Princess, Malena, and how it describes her as carrying a song and that with the 'stone' she would one day open the gates of heaven?

You carry the song."

"So what about the stone, what is that?"

"The stone was placed beneath the Croft back in the thirteenth century. It had to be taken from its original safe place as its whereabouts was discovered by certain people who had been seeking it for centuries. If they had got hold of the stone they would have obtained a powerful instrument for their own designs."

"Who are they, and is the stone still buried there, anyway what is it?"

"No it has been retrieved, I think you had a dream or vision where you saw somebody take something?"

"Yes, a golden lady…"

"It's safe now. It is like a CD but smaller, made of a mineral that has special qualities.

But more importantly I must keep this on track. You are probably not safe now. You are the component part to the stone, it can't be activated without the frequencies that you can generate."

"Oh, that's fantastic now you are saying my life is in danger…are you?"

"Not to worry too much. Ever since the Cloister was formed you have had the ancestors and myself watching over you. In addition, a male member of each family you were incarnated into has been designated into the Cloister to protect you on the Earthly plane. Currently that is Simon."

Michael nodded towards Simon.

"The male knew only to pass the Collar on to the next designated person. Your great grandfather in France however was told to hand the emblem on to your Mother, your mother however knows nothing of the role. She was just the carrier of the DNA that passed on to you along with the Collar.

The Collar has certain powerful properties, basically recognition of membership of the Cloister but it can open doors and do other quite magical things."

"But this Cloister, Collar, song and Seal sounds totally unbelievable, like a novel. And you are expecting me to believe all this?"

"Yes, it is a serious society founded for a specific purpose, your protection and that of the role you will play soon in the ascension of this planet. You were Lilith in your initial incarnation and you have had many physical Earth lives since then. Mostly uneventful other than the usual lessons one learns in their spiritual ascension. I think psychotherapists now call it individuation. Generally the civilising and aspiring to spiritual values.

You were Malena in the 13th Century which was particularly traumatic for you. Pam at that time was your maidservant and stayed with you through your life then. Actually you married her brother and your family is descended from then."

Maddy gasped, she felt her head spin. However, Michael carried on, feeling he had to get the last points across to her. He thought to himself that he would then leave her for some time to take it all in.

"You and the eleven other 'souls' hold key positions, all connected by your unique DNA and in the coming Alignment you will link up and open doorways to other frequencies and dimensions.

Now it is important for you to do only one thing, and that is to learn how to raise your frequency, that is your bodily vibration. You will learn to do this by meditation practices.

Not only are you important to the ascension of the planet but there has also to be a certain percentage of the planet able to meditate and raise their vibration to a higher level. We are not sure that there are enough enlightened people at this level, they are called light workers and to a certain extent understand what is happening. Pam is one of them.

I have to impress on you that what is happening is a scientific fact, those concerning planetary alignments can be checked out on the internet if you want further clarification."

Maddy stopped him.

"What am I supposed to remember? You mentioned early on about a contract and a role I have to play. You said I chose to do this…?"

"Where you are now is towards the end of your journey, that is, your soul's journey. You have travelled or your soul has, through the linear time of Earth but what you are about to experience is outside the restrictions of this dimension.

Pam has been with you through most of your incarnations and now has been sent to help you, or rather remember all of what we have spoken about. Perhaps it would be good for you to see her and talk to her. She herself is not fully aware, she knows of her previous lives but not yet the ones she has shared with you.

When we come next time we will tell you why you have been guarded and protected over the centuries. What we have told you so far is the most straight forward explanation we can of your destiny and the coming Alignment.

However, there are other forces at work which you must become aware of. I can see that you have had enough for today."

"Yes, I must ask you to leave as I am beginning to get a headache and need to rest. Also I am feeling rather angry and resentful. I have enough to cope with at the moment and this on top of everything is beginning to make me feel ill.

And, from the sound of it the question of choice on my part in this doesn't seem to be an option?"

"No, sorry about that, but the situation is becoming urgent and we need you to understand and co-operate. You will begin to remember and then it won't be a problem. I hope, however, at the moment we have not worked against ourselves and the purpose."

"No. It's alright, just I need time to think things over. When were you thinking of coming again."

"Perhaps in a couple of days? If you can get hold of Pam and talk to her then let us know how you feel and we will come up."

After Michael and Simon had left, Maddy felt wrecked. Her head was beginning to throb and she needed to take a sedative and go to bed. However, she immediately rang Sarah and told her she needed to see Pam urgently.

Sarah said, "You sound panicky."

"I am, I can explain but I would like Pam to come along as she can help me. I have just had my Uncle and Michael up here for the day and found what they have told me has thrown me somewhat."

"I'll ring Pam now and see if she can come up tomorrow and I'll come too."

Luckily Pam was free and they arranged to meet the following day.

***

Chapter 28
Quandary

Sarah arrived with Pam early the following morning and they were immediately concerned for Maddy who looked very pale and drawn as she had not slept much, going over everything Michael and Simon had told her.

Over coffee she related to them everything she had been told by Simon and Michael, her family history and the extended one back into the past. Then she told them of the later revelations about her destiny, the contract she had made and the coming Alignment.

"They told me that you are part of it Pam, that you are a light-worker, whatever that means, and were enrolled in the process of waking me up. Is that true?"

"Well now you have explained things to me I can only say that it makes sense, perhaps I needed waking up too. All I knew was that I would meet someone and that that person was special and needed to be reconnected with the light, that there was something coming, or rather happening and that she, or he, would be needed. That is all I was aware of.

When you turned up and we had our sessions together I had come to the conclusion that you were that person but it was not clear to me exactly what was coming or why you were important. It is clearer now though what will actually happen we still don't know do we?

It looks as though we have had many incarnations together, how do you feel about that, as it obviously may be quite a new concept to you."

"Well it is not. I have always, I suppose, believed in reincarnation though I had not taken on board that it could be more than one. The idea of having had several, if not more, lives before my present one is difficult to take in. I still think I need some time to think about all this."

"Yes, you are right it's not easy to understand. On my part, although I remember some of my incarnations and I can now see that you were there in some of them, I can only remember one in particular and now I can see that you were there too. It was way back in ancient times. I can't remember the place but I know that there was a ceremony and you were there dressed in white. You were very young and from what I could take in, you had special qualities. I would describe myself as a priestess at that ceremony, it was not clear exactly what the ceremony was about. I do remember however there being something given to a male member of the audience, it was some kind of jewellery, on a chain, no not a chain a kind of Collar."

"Hang on a minute."

Maddy dashed off to the office and returned with the box containing the Collar.

"Is this it?"

"Oh…" Pam looked stricken as if something had hit her.

"That's it. Where did you get it?"

"I mentioned it the last time we met. It has been handed down in my family that is on the French side of it, according to Simon and Michael, through the male members of the family. It seems it is needed now by the female, which happens to be me, as part of the coming, what would you call it, happening? What sense I could make was that I am going to play an important part in some kind of ritual about the planet ascending."

"Yes, in psychic circles there has been talk of what we are all going to go through on the spiritual level. It seems that we have the chance to ascend to a higher plane, where there is harmony. Hunger, wars, disharmony amongst people is going to disappear and the world will be a different peaceful place. You have heard of the age of Aquarius. The Golden Age is dawning. One of the main issues that will be confronted is the unification of all religions and an understanding of religion itself."

"What do you mean?"

"Well if you look at what is going on in the world today, the wars and disharmony, the majority are caused by different religions fighting one another for what they believe to be the one and only religion, or the true god.

When Jesus appeared 2000 years ago his main message was that God is within all of us. That was his message. Because of its simplicity and the fact that he drew crowds of followers he antagonised many of the powerful leaders at that time in the Middle East resulting in his crucifixion and then the suppression of his followers. His teachings were also suppressed and distorted, eventually not for so called religious purposes but for power and control."

"Why, to what end?"

"Power, in the main, was in the hands of what eventually became the Roman Catholic Church and defined by the Council of Nicaea in 362 AD. It was basically about retaining an Empire and not about the spiritual aspects of the concept of God. Hence the world has been at war ever since."

"You still have not explained why the word was distorted."

"Think about it. If we all knew that we had God like powers within us; let's say we could have free energy, heal ourselves, didn't have to rely on money, what effect do you think it would have on the world?"

"It would be a totally different world. We are so tied up in our day to day existence and its reliance on money that to change would be such a difficult thing to do."

"Exactly, in addition it would also entail a major re-education of our beliefs, about how we came to be here on this planet and our true history. We have been taught history, share a history and that would all have to be rewritten. Think of the impossibility of doing that overnight."

"I see what they mean about waking up, I feel my eyes are opening wider and wider as if I have another eye within my head."

"Well," Pam laughed, "actually you have but we will leave it there for today. I think you have enough to think about for the time being. You said that they are coming back, when?"

"They said later in the week to explain more. I wondered if you could be here too. It would really help."

"Well I was going to go back to the UK as my contract for being here has been fulfilled with my contacts. However I have nothing planned in the immediate future so yes, I could be there."

"Where are you going to stay?"

"Well at the moment I am staying in Carcassonne, quite a long way away and was going to check out tomorrow. I can stay in a Chambre d'Hote nearby though which would be better."

"Well how about a better idea and come and stay with me. It would be good to have some company in the circumstances."

Pam looked from Maddy to Sarah and back again and nodded in agreement with a smile.

Happier, Maddy said, "Well that's settled, I will make up a bed for you. When will you be back?"

"I can come up on Thursday. However, would it be possible for you to pick me up as I am returning my hire car, it would save some expense and I don't expect I will be needing a car for the next week or so."

"Of course. Thank you. I am feeling a lot happier knowing that you will be here. They keep on about my waking up, not sure what that is going to entail."

"Well actually, I can only glimpse at that. As I said I think I am waking up too, you are not the only one. All I feel is that there has been this struggle between good and evil which has perpetuated and distorted history but I feel it has been used to control people in general. The real question is who is doing the controlling, and why. Perhaps Michael and Simon are going to let us into the secret when we see them.

Let's meet on Thursday at the cafe in the village, I will bring my luggage."

Kissing and hugging her, Pam and Sarah left leaving Maddy feeling a little more relaxed. She felt relieved that Pam was going to be with her as she seemed to have a deeper insight into what Michael and Simon were hinting at.

She settled down for the night running through the events of the day, falling into a deep sleep.

Waking in the night she came to, gasping; it was the dream she had had previously about burning at the stake. Having difficulty in shaking off the frightened feeling it left her with she went downstairs, made a cup of tea and sat out on the terrace. It was light, it was nearing full moon and the air was sharp and clear, the stars bright and twinkling. She felt overloaded and uncomfortable. It was as if her world was changing dramatically and she was trying to cling to some kind of the normality her life had been up to this point.

***

Chapter 29
The Halqu

As planned, Maddy picked up Pam and her luggage from in front of Les Guingettes in the middle of the village. Expecting Simon and Michael to turn up later in the morning Maddy was feeling weary and wondered if she could take much more. As they drove up the hill to the Croft Pam chatted lightly to her trying to keep the rising panic she could feel in Maddy under control. Somehow there was a feeling of foreboding hanging in the air between them and she was not too sure herself what might happen, what they might hear today.

As they approached the Croft, they saw Michael and Simon entering the garden and waved to them to come up to the house. Maddy went in and put the kettle on to make some coffee as she did not want to plunge straight into more information without some stimulant. While she was doing that, Simon and Michael helped Pam in with her luggage. Maddy had noticed that Pam travelled quite lightly as there was only one largish case and a small travel bag on wheels. She found herself feeling slightly envious, it must be a good feeling to have few material belongings and from what she had sensed Pam did not carry baggage around in her head either.

Settling around the kitchen table Michael started with the next instalment. Maddy sat sipping her coffee slowly her eyes going from one to the other of those present.

"Today we have to tell you why you have been protected.

Previously we told you about the lineage which descended from ancient Sumeria and that your bloodline has been kept pure. We also have to tell you that the people we refer to as the Ancients go back much further in Earth's history in fact many millennia before that. They have been guardians of Earth and watching its evolution. They also watch over the Universe in this quadrant.

There are other species who have visited Earth, in fact many. They have come for a variety of reasons, some of them not good. Like the ancient visitors they have technological abilities far beyond the comprehension of the most advanced scientists on Earth today.

However, it is important to point out that all of the visitors, and I say all, originate from what we mostly call the Source, the essence of existence from which all things have evolved, the Creator of All. Their reasons for visiting are many, some good like the Ancients who are guarding and watching evolution here, others self-serving, taking resources from the planet such as the Visitors we told you about."

"Can I interrupt you…" broke in Maddy.

"Hasn't this all been debunked though. You know the idea of ETs, Aliens and spacecraft. When anybody talks about that kind of thing they generally get laughed at."

"You are right. It has purposely been kept out of the media and debunked, your governments know more than they want the general population to know. They have their reasons, whether right or wrong. However, extra-terrestrial visitors do exist and they do pose a threat which is why we need you to become aware of one group of visitors who are particularly hostile at this time. They are the reason I was appointed as your guardian and why we, the Ancients, have followed you through time to safeguard you and keep you on a particular course.

This group of visitors are named the Halqu which in Sumerian means the 'Lost Ones'. We named them this because this is how the Ancients view them. As I said earlier we all, everything that exists, come from the Source, and we all have the potential to evolve and ascend back to Source which created everything. You can if you wish give this the name 'God'. However it would be a limiting term for something that is extremely complex. It just 'is' and we are all part of it and evolve back into that state of existence.

The Halqu, therefore, have the same potential of evolving back to Source as we all have as that is where they originate from too. However they have been operating against the Source for

217

their own self-serving purposes. The Ancients have been helping some of the Halqu who have agreed to reform but they are a renegade group and the majority have rejected this help."

"This is getting a bit deep and I am not following, what do they want and why are they a threat?"

"I am just getting to that, sorry for going off course but I felt you needed the input of that information as it will make things clearer to you as to how we will do what we have to.

Anyway, the Halqu are a species who come from a planet far out in this universe, and I stress this universe as there are many universes. The Halqu come from within this universe in a parallel dimension.

On their planet within a certain linear timeline they developed technology which is currently far advanced to that of Earth's today. In particular two areas, genetic engineering and time travel.

With genetic engineering they had been manipulating their DNA and reproducing themselves artificially instead of biologically. However each time they engineered reproduction their species became weaker, gradually they saw themselves dying out as a race. In addition one point to make about the inherited factors of their reproductive experiments is that although technologically superior they regressed spiritually and socially."

"So why are they threatening us?"

"Their aim, very simply put, because they are able to travel in time and space is to find a way back to their planet before they began genetic engineering and correct the mistakes they made in order for their species not to die out."

"So, why are we implicated in their plans? Do they want to live here, wipe us out and take over Earth?"

"No it is a more elaborate scheme than that. What they want to do is not to transpose or transfer themselves here. They want to find the way back through time and space to their planet."

"But if they can time-and-space travel, why don't they just do that?"

"It is not that easy. To travel in time and space it is necessary to be able to access certain portals. These portals are located throughout the Universe. Similar to your railway junctions, they have to be opened and closed and you have to know the sequences to enable them to do so. The portals are operated by sound frequencies. Frequencies open and close the doors and there are millions of these. Think of a railway system with all its junctions, all interwoven. It is where the lines cross over that you can travel through and down different routes.

Earth is in a time zone; that is you experience it in linear time, past, present and future. There are many planets in your universe and all have their own time zones.

This is where it may get complicated and confusing for you.

There are also multiple dimensions of each time zone. For example Earth has many dimensions, all different, all with their own time zones and all with potential probabilities for their futures."

"You are confusing me, potential probabilities?"

"Yes, time is constant, now, the potential probabilities are how things might turn out and that is dependent on the state of the planet and the interaction of its inhabitants with the planet.

Humans for example have free will. They can determine the outcome of their actions. Currently the planet is experiencing severe climate change due to the way its inhabitants have interacted with it. It could have been different. Does that make sense?"

"You mean if we had been more aware of the resources of planet and misusing them?"

"Yes, in fact that is what the forthcoming Alignment is about, Earth's future is dependent on what its present inhabitants are doing and whether they can become aware quickly enough to change one of its potential futures."

"You mean we could be on self-destruct, perhaps being wiped out?"

"Exactly, the planet will survive but the human species may not."

Eyeing Michael quizzically she responded,

"I take it that you are not Human?"

"No not Human but I share a great deal of your DNA heritage, we are still connected. However, we have gone off track. Maybe it would be time to take a break and restart in half an hour, what do you think?"

"Good idea," piped up Simon who was looking tired.

Pam and Maddy went to the kitchen to make a tray of coffee. Michael and Simon stepped outside and were stretching their legs by walking down into the garden.

"What do you think? Is she getting tired, is it too much… or what?" Michael asked Simon.

"No, I don't think so, but it is an enormous concept to take in. All of a sudden you are telling her that she is descended from some extra-terrestrials who can fly around the universe at will. Added to which she is now being asked to do something, of which she has no idea about."

Simon stressed looking hard at Michael.

"Obviously she is feeling apprehensive, who would not?"

"Well I have to continue. Luckily Pam will help out. I feel she understands or if she does not know what it has been about up to now she will be able to put things together."

Simon murmured assent.

Pam was trying to calm down Maddy who had suddenly flipped and was threatening to throw Michael and Simon out.

"I am not sure whether I am angry, frightened or what…!" Maddy blustered.

"I think there are too many coincidences in the story and you must stick it out. I know it's difficult but you have come so far, best to hear the rest of the story, don't you think?"

"Perhaps you are right, though I am losing patience. I wish they would get to the bit as to what I am supposed to be doing. It's all this long explanation."

"I think they are trying to help you remember, because if you do you will understand that what happened in the beginning, thousands of years ago is what you contracted to do, what you committed to."

Pam looked at Maddy and raised her eyebrows questioningly.

"Alright, I have to say I am getting a glimmering of things. I will go along with it for today but they had better get it over with soon. I don't think I can stand much more."

They took the coffee out onto the terrace. It was a lovely sunny day and all four sat and basked in the sunshine. Sipping their coffee they turned their faces to the sun, closing their eyes.

Maddy began to revive, the sun always had that effect on her, it seemed to inject an enthusiasm into her body.

And boy, do I need it! she thought.

***

"Just to recap, where were we?"

Before he launched into more information Maddy interjected.

"I think you were trying to explain space and time travel. You said we exist in linear time, past present and future and that there are many time zones within our Universe. You also mentioned that each time zone, and I take it you meant each planets time zone such as Earth's, had multiple dimensions all with differing futures. You used the word potential, so I take it that those futures may or may not be the actual future but that it was dependent on how the inhabitants interacted with the planet. Oh, also who the Halqu are and why they are interested in Earth.

You talk about the planets as if they are living, breathing entities. Is that right, am I understanding you correctly?"

"Yes, but you have to understand that it is full of complexities. Do you follow?"

Maddy nodded.

"I think so."

"Though the time zones and multiple dimensions are intertwined they involve two separate systems.

There is a Time Portal System which is a series of gateways that enable movement back and forth in time within linear time within any given time zone.

And there is a Dimensional Locking System which differs from the Time Portal System.

Dimensions are maintained on specific frequency bands. For example, Earth operates on a three-dimensional frequency and everything that exists on the planet is subject to its frequency and manifests according to that frequency.

The Dimensional Locking System has mechanics that maintain the frequency bands of dimensions and enable safe passageways inter-dimensionally and further out to other multi-dimensional universes. Again, like the Time Portal System there are gateways and portals that can open and close.

At present on Earth, time and inter-dimensional travel has yet to be discovered, and mastered. But it will be in one of Earth's potential futures."

"It's like Star Trek and Star Wars," murmured Maddy.

"I know that this may be stretching your imagination but you need to understand the reality you exist in. I am trying to give you a framework that you can understand.

There are countless other species out in your universe and beyond and they all possess technology and operational knowledge of reality systems far superior to that of the human race."

Michael, serious, paused giving Maddy time to absorb his last statement. He continued…

"The Halqu use the Time Portal System and have an understanding of the dimensional locking system but it was with their experiments trying to learn how to get through the portals of inter-dimensional travel that things went wrong for them and their planet.

Their experiments destabilised the time portals and dimensional bands of their own system. This in conjunction with their genetic experimentation set in train the death of their planet, its dimensional counterparts and their species.

These events, from the perspective of Earth's time continuum, are occurring in what you would perceive as your future.

To find a solution to their problems they have travelled back in time trying to find a way to access the past of their planet to correct the genetic mutation and its destabilisation. Because of the proximity of Earth they entered its time continuum with the purpose of accessing other time and dimensional versions of their own planet through Earth's time portals.

Theoretically their plan was good, they had sufficient knowledge of how the time portals worked in a three-dimensional system but not of the time portals in other dimensions. They were able to enter Earth's three-dimensional system moving backward in time and access other versions of your time continuum but were not able to leap from there into their own other dimensional time frames. They became a dying race trapped between dimensions in Earth's time/space continuum far from home.

They began to look for other alternatives about which I will not go into in detail other than to say that their attempt to create a hybrid species ultimately failed. A takeover bid for Earth was never an answer to their problems as certain environmental elements were poisonous to them and they found themselves in accelerated states of deterioration. They had not planned to interact with you for any period of time.

They were also experimenting in other systems along the same lines.

The Alignment that is coming up is an opportunity for the Halqu but a threat to Earth as at the time of Alignment all of the Time Portals and Dimensional Locking Systems would be accessible and enable them to make their way back through time within a given period."

"Isn't that a good thing though, why would it be a threat?"

"Because their aim is total self-interest. They can't think beyond their own survival. Their aim is to get back to their planet so they can take a different developmental route but they don't care what damage they might do to the universe and everybody living in it by doing so.

They have not mastered the technology for inter-dimensional travel. By doing so they might de-stabilise the Time Portal Systems and Dimensional Locking Systems of the whole Universe. As everything is dependent on specific frequencies this could cause the destruction of this Universe and send out shock waves further affecting other Universes."

"But I thought you said the Ancients were involved and watching the course of events. Aren't they able to intervene and stop them? Isn't there the question of evolution? If what is happening is about us ascending to a higher frequency, higher dimension, would they not be included in this too?"

"The Ancients have tried to help them but they have not responded. They don't think individually but collectively and they don't have the same capacity for emotional empathy that humans do. They view other species quite objectively; for how they can use them. These renegades see the Earth as a platform from which they can relaunch their species, therefore they have to take over the coming benefits of the Alignment. They have the misguided idea probably that they can then develop programmes for time and inter-dimensional travel as they did before, but this time, with the knowledge they have, not take the development of their species and planet and destroy it."

"But why are they a threat to me from what you have told me?" asked Maddy.

"Because you are part of the key to the ascension of the planet, it is part of your initial soul contract.

Do you want to carry on or is it enough for today."

"Are you getting near to the end of this because if you are then I would like to finish it today?"

"Well, I think it best. We could have some lunch now as it is very late."

Looking at his watch he saw that it was 2.00 p.m.

"Let's stop for lunch and a rest and then start again say at 4.00 p.m. Does that suit everyone?"

Everybody agreed.

***

Maddy had retreated to her bedroom with a sandwich and cup of tea feeling she needed to be alone and think. She found herself in a quandary, most of what they had told her over the previous week and the morning she was beginning to think was bizarre, as if somewhere somebody was filming the exchange and would pop out and say that it was some kind of elaborate joke.

But then, on the other hand her thinking was that if half of what they were talking about were true and she had some key part in it left her with a hard knot that was forming in her chest, a sign for her of anxiety. She did not understand what powers she might have or how she could use them to save the planet. And also there was the dangerous side where it seemed there were a band of renegade extra-terrestrials pursuing her to do... what? Capture and torture her to get the key... and, exactly what was the key.

Joining the others at 4.00 Maddy sat down, noting that everybody was looking as jaded as she felt.

Resuming Michael said he needed to answer Maddy's question that she had made earlier about the threat to her.

"The Halqu became aware of the coming Alignment and that it would give them a path back to their planet before it was corrupted. Aware of their intentions the Ancients realised that they had to protect Earth so they placed a grid over the planet, basically a grid of frequencies that would prevent anybody interfering with the Time Portals or Dimensional Locks. The Halqu set on their purpose of taking these over quickly realised that they would not be able to get anywhere near them at the time of Alignment without some kind of key.

Unfortunately the knowledge that you, and the part you would play in unlocking the grid at the time of the Alignment, was passed to the Halqu by a member of your family who betrayed you. The Halqu have been travelling through time in order to track you down and use you as a means to access the grid.

It was then that the Cloister of Lilith was created to protect your soul and the disc.

The Ancients and the Stewards, those are the appointed servers in the Cloister of Lilith, were and have been present from the beginning when you made the contract. They were part of the decision to keep your 'soul' clear through the centuries. You were protected originally by an order of priests. To them you are the 'song' and as you are now aware it is a very specific frequency which is emitted from your DNA and triggers the 'stone'. The 'stone' was also kept in a specially prepared place.

All went well in the early days and through several generations, your soul coming through, incarnating all the time. Then civilisation at that time began to disintegrate and tribal wars began to destroy the temples and cities. The temple where you lived along with the 'stone' came under threat so you and it were removed to a safe place

At that time the Egyptian dynasties and their kingdom were the safest place and you were absorbed into their Priest cults. However, the knowledge of your commitment and that of the 'stone' were kept secret. You became a handmaiden to the Pharaonic court. The Cloister of Lilith that was created fundamentally to protect you followed you to Egypt. It kept its cult secret from the Priest temples and again for several generations existed peacefully without anyone finding out.

Whilst in Egypt the Cloister was betrayed again to the Halqu by the same member who had reincarnated into your family and the Ancients had to remove you from the situation and place you in safer circumstances. This is when your then family took you and the 'stone' to France.

The Halqu had lost track of you until the 13th Century when the reincarnated person in your family who betrayed you in Egypt betrayed you again and they tracked you down to this area. Because they had a huge influence through the traitor in your family, predominantly in the Church and the Royal House at the time, they were able to create a search for you under the premise of condemning heretical practices.

However, luckily the Ancients watching out for you were able to prevent the Halqu and instructed the Cloister to take you to a safe place with the disc. That is the story behind the legend that you have heard about."

"So, everything has been secure since then up until now? Are the Halqu still searching for me?"

"Unfortunately, yes. Only just recently it has come to our attention that the reincarnated traitor in your family has been reincarnated again in this area and we know that he has been watching events closely in the surrounding region. So far he has not found out that you are the Seal, but he has been getting suspicious, we know who he is?"

"Who?"

"George Bottomley, I think you talked to him at the last History Group meeting."

"Yes, I remember. I had a bad feeling about him. He was going on about the Catholic Church and how the story about the Cathars had been exaggerated. I felt something was wrong the way he was getting more and more worked up about it. Because I know so little about the Cathars I could not talk to him about them and somehow that seemed to incense him further."

"I think somehow he has picked up something about you; perhaps he was trying to trick you to come out with something. We know that he has people working for the Halqu close to him. I would stress you must be careful whenever you meet him, in fact try not to be at any functions, including the History Group Meetings where he might be present. That way we can keep his suspicions in check."

"It's funny, but after the last Meeting I had a very bad dream and it seemed to be in some kind of medieval scenario and there was a black priest ranting on at me in it. It may have been him. Am I in danger then?"

"Let's say we just have to be careful."

Maddy was beginning to feel apprehensive and Michael, sensing this, was not surprised when after a pause she said,

"Well, I suppose the best thing would be for you to explain what my role is and, when is it going to happen because I feel that the sooner it is over and done with perhaps things could resume a little more sanely."

"Well, you now know that you carry a frequency within your DNA that is special. It is an activation device which is the best way to describe it. The stone, or the disc, is triggered by the activation device, you, in certain circumstances. That is at the Alignment. It all happens simultaneously with you and the other Seals. What it does is release the grid from protecting the Portals and Locks so that the Alignment can activate and allow the Planet to ascend along with the rest of the Universe. The resonance of the planet will increase and it will go to the Fifth Dimension."

"The stone, the disc, where is it?"

"It was placed in the grounds of the Croft in the 13th Century, under what was then the chapel which I think you discovered recently. However it has been removed. I think you had a session with Pam and a guardian appeared to you and took it. It has special properties. It can disappear and appear at the will of the guardians."

"So what happens now?"

"The Ancestors and I have arrived at this time to see that the necessary ritual takes place."

"But what does that mean, you keep talking about waking up, me waking up and Pam and now it seems the whole population are involved. To wake up to what? What do I do now, I expect you have something planned?"

Maddy enquired.

Michael paused and looked around to Simon, Pam and then to Maddy, giving time for them to absorb what he had just said.

"To get you ready for your role in the coming Alignment you have to activate your DNA and raise you vibration. We explained to you, you are a Sentient Seal—your vibration, coming from your DNA emits a signal, like a language, a code that operates as a communication tool, rather like the binary code of computer technology."

"So how do we, or rather I, do that, raise my vibration?"

"Very simply, meditation. Over the next weeks Pam and I will work with you to teach you meditation techniques. That is if Pam is agreeable?"

Michael sought Pam's agreement and she nodded.

"Your counterparts are doing exactly the same and are probably ahead of you with this as we have not really started. Can we all get together early next week to make a start?"

Looking around the room everybody agreed silently by nodding their assent.

"Have we finished for the time being?" Maddy asked wearily.

Michael nodded in assent.

Maddy looked at Michael, her eyes opening and questioning.

"It is a very profound story and forgive my scepticism, has extremely high aspirations which seem a bit, well unrealistic on the face of it. And also a bit wacky, you know, as if we are going to save the world, the universe!"

Ignoring her comment he cut across any further conversation.

"The most important thing now is to get you ready for the ritual on ascension. Just remember should you be faced with any kind of danger the one fundamental truth about existence is love, that is, to love all things, all people equally without condition or judgement. It is your greatest protection."

By this time they were all silent, tired and thinking about what lay ahead.

It was now well into the evening and after sharing a light supper and arranging to meet the following day Michael and Simon disappeared down the track to the village leaving Maddy and Pam to mull over the day.

***

Chapter 30
Maddy Prepares

Pam had now become part of the events that were unfolding and sat with Michael, Simon and Maddy the following morning while Michael explained to Maddy what was going to happen.

"Your counterparts Maddy are all moving towards their designated places. I told you that there were eleven other females like you."

Michael searched Maddy's face for acknowledgement that she had remembered.

"Designated places? I take it that I have a designated place then too?"

"Yes, yours is not that far from here. The others are located at specific points around the planet chosen so that the whole of the planet is covered. For example they are located at the ancient sites that have become heritage protected such as Stone Henge, Angt Wat in Cambodia, the Sphinx in Egypt.

Yours is not actually a heritage site though it is protected because of the nature of the Earth there. It is special because of the minerals in the rocks that form it. It is in a valley composed mainly of sandstone which has been eroded over time and created a rather mythical landscape. The name given to it by the older generations there is the Valley of the Fairy Chimneys. If you look hard enough you can see all sorts of creatures and persons that nature has sculpted not man.

Within the valley there is a chamber, within a natural formation. You enter it via a cave. The chamber contains, I am not sure how to describe it to you. In your current knowledge of Egyptian history it would have been called a sarcophagus. Your archaeologists call these the equivalent of today's coffins in which you bury your dead. But it is not, and they were only coffins in one sense. From your language the word derives from Greek, *sarx* meaning flesh, and *phagein,* to eat, thereby fleshing eating stone.

They used to be the outer container for a series of coffins within and were generally made of alabaster which has special qualities. The word alabaster originates from an Ancient Egyptian Goddess named Bast, a warrior god who became associated with spiritual powers providing protection.

The sarcophagus in the cave however is made of a rock called 'metamorphised quartzite', a special mineral which resonates to certain frequencies. The original sarcophagi were vehicles, not only in Egypt but before, to travel on to the spiritual plane. They are activated for this by a certain sound frequency which allows the soul to transcend the physical plane onto the astral plane.

Why I am telling you this is that you have to learn to meditate so that you can raise your bodily vibration, your frequency, in order for you to step onto the astral plane."

"Weirder and weirder, why and how?"

"On the astral plane you can link with your counterparts and together emit a frequency that will open portals and locks throughout the universe. It will also unlock the grid that was placed by the Ancients in order to protect the planet."

"Can you explain more about vibration?"

"Yes, everything in the universe, including your body, resonates to sound and light wave frequencies. 70% of your body is water and it is the water molecules that vibrate your cells and carry a special coded language which provides you with a way to perceive your surroundings and your existence in general. If the frequency is changed your perception would change. Basically you and your fellow humans have been trapped in a specific wave band that is the frequencies of three-dimensional existence. Therefore your ability to perceive what the true reality is has not been possible."

"Now you are losing me, I don't get this, you say true reality?"

"As we explained to you the Visitors interfered with the evolution of the indigenous race on Earth genetically engineering your species. This has meant that they and the Halqu have kept your species in a state of amnesia to maintain their control of the planet.

Access to the 90 percent of so far deactivated DNA would allow your human bodies to travel inter-dimensionally and through time without causing bodily deterioration. The aim for humans after the Alignment is that this will be corrected. Your species have been deprived of knowledge that would open up to them a totally different world.

That is why we're going to introduce you to breathing and meditation techniques that will enable you to develop toleration to the higher frequencies.

Without these techniques you would not be able to do what you are intended to do, also your body would suffer irreparable damage. Some people can withstand higher frequencies due to certain elements they have in their DNA, others won't be able to.

The element is called silicate; you have it in your DNA so you already have an advantage. The silicate is important as where we will take you for the Alignment is a valley made of silicate sandstone, the metamorphosed quartzite that I described earlier.

It is a special element that connects you to the frequencies of the Universe directly, the harmonics of the universe. You may have already felt this from time to time. It is like a trill running through you; a tremulous vibration."

"Funny you should mention that, since I have been here I have felt something like that more and more?"

Pam interceded.

"I must have it too as I feel it almost constantly. I have always interpreted it as signalling to me that something significant is happening or going to happen."

"Do you have any more questions, I am sorry to hurry things up but time is running out. The Alignment is approaching and we have to be prepared."

Maddy and Pam murmured that they had none and were ready to continue.

Maddy's wondered how she came to be in this position. The last months had been a whirlwind, a complete turning upside down of her life. It was also peculiar that instead of feeling down and overwhelmed she was beginning to feel vibrant, alive, almost excited with anticipation. It was all very odd. She thought the best thing to do was to keep any apprehensions to herself for the time being. She obviously had a key position in what was going to happen and if that was her destiny so be it. Her life had collapsed recently and she felt herself giving in to the inevitability of her situation rather than fighting it.

Musing on whether she could, if necessary, make a run for it if it got out of hand she looked across at Michael and caught his eye. It twinkled and she knew in a flash he had read her mind.

"I know you are probably feeling frightened or apprehensive as you don't understand fully what is happening. But you have to trust in your destiny, you may be able to feel this deep inside that what is happening is right.

You have very powerful Ancients looking after you and they will not allow anything harmful to come to you. They have enormous powers and the Halqu are frightened of them. So you see, whatever happens they will be there to protect you should you need them."

"If the Halqu are frightened of them, how come the Ancients allowed the situation to get to this stage, couldn't they have stopped it before now?"

"You make a good point. Remember what I said about time and space, it's now, no past or future. Certain things have to evolve in a way in order that the end result is consolidated, right where it should be with no conditions. The Halqu had to be allowed to engineer this in the way it has unfolded in that they learn the lesson that they set for themselves in their soul journeys as well as that of everything and everybody else in the Universe. It had to happen this way.

The Halqu set the situation up in such a way as to wait for this coming Alignment. In the meantime the Ancients were negotiating with them in the hope that they could appeal to their original journey which we all share, the aim to return to Source.

But it has not worked and that is why this safeguard was set up in conjunction with the Alignment when if all else failed with negotiations to this point then the situation could be set right."

"Could anything go wrong?"

"No, the only thing would have been if we had not found you or if you refused to co-operate. Luckily we knew that this was improbable but we always have to bear in mind that humankind has 'free will'. You could have chosen, or choose now not to help us."

Michael looked at Maddy and raised his eyebrows questioningly.

"Well, put like that, I don't really think there is a choice after the case you have put to me. Anyway I am not doing anything else as my whole life has turned upside down, it might be the adventure I need."

"That is a good way of looking at things," Michael responded.

Maddy decided she had to be careful what she thought in his company as he obviously could read her mind.

"We will leave now. Pam, you are staying with Maddy you can begin teaching her the breathing and meditation techniques we have talked about."

"Sure. We will get started on it straight away."

Michael and Simon left arranging to meet the women in the village the following week to take them to the Valley of the Fairy Chimneys so that Maddy could familiarise herself with the setting.

***

Chapter 31
The Valley of the Fairy Chimneys

As they drove towards the valley Michael was talking about the Halqu, while Maddy was staring out of the car window. The countryside they were travelling through was vibrant, the sun shining and the air seemed to be like crystal.

"You have to understand…" Michael was reiterating, or rather ranting Maddy thought.

"…the Halqu want to stop humans from waking up to their real inheritance as powerful individuals. That way they can control the Alignment and get back to their own planet but also have Earth as a resource they can use. In the meantime, humans would become increasingly trapped in a fake world which would eventually lead to them destroying their species.

They see the human species as biological mind computers that they can programme for their own purposes, they have no empathic consciousness. Owing to them humans perceive the world in a very restricted way. The Alignment, if successful, will open a doorway and dissolve the illusion human beings have been living in since their creation and see the world as it really is."

"But there are so many of us now. The population of the planet is so great it can barely sustain us as it is. How can the whole population be made to see this, or more likely, believe this. It would not get past the media without being debunked. We would be called '*kranks*', or 'new agers'."

"That is again part of their covert plan which they have inserted into your race memory of the past century along with a lot of other things. They are called holograms. Because of the intricate genetic technology they are converse with they are able to change the perceptions of people in general."

"But how?"

"I keep on about frequency, that's how. They are so clever they are able to get into the DNA coding of, say a section of the population, and apply a certain frequency. That section then see the illusion and not the real world."

"But that sounds unbelievable."

"Only because you humans have not discovered the actual scientific mechanics of DNA processing yet; if all humankind meditated, raised their vibration, the illusion, amnesia would disintegrate and humanity will return to where it should be."

"But how does that link into the science, you said we have been genetically tampered with."

"Yes, but don't you see, by meditating, raising your frequency, you access a higher source. Compare it to the battery in your car. When it fails you can place clamps on your battery and attach them to the clamps on the battery of the other car, that way your battery can recharge.

By meditating, raising your frequency, you recharge your body with universal energy from the source that originally created you. By altering your perception the Halqu are keeping you on a limited supply and creating a thirst for the energy they are providing and thus under their control."

"Well I am beginning to understand. My brain is feeling punished but I suppose that fits in with what you say. I have lived my life understanding the world as I have perceived it, or how they have wanted me and everyone to perceive it. To wake up to a totally different reality, well, isn't that going to cause problems world-wide. I am thinking of all of the things that could happen—civil unrest, health problems, especially mental health problems."

"That is what they want, it keeps you in their power. The average person would find it too difficult to comprehend. They have manipulated the thoughts of your population to the point that it is virtually impossible to get it to wake up. The silliness of it is that it is so easy. By meditating regularly, let's say on a daily basis, even for 10 minutes, would gradually raise an individual's frequency and continue to increase it. You must have already noticed a difference in yourself meditating with Pam each day?"

Michael fell silent and Maddy began remembering the meditation practice that she had been following with Pam since the last visit of Michael and Simon to the Croft.

She had been taught breathing exercises initially to relax her whole body and then physical exercises based on several esoteric practices, mainly yoga. Maddy had attended yoga classes at one time in her life but was surprised to learn that the physical positions that were part of the practice were to put the body into the correct position in order for the mind meditation to work accurately.

As the lessons progressed eventually Pam had led Maddy through guided meditations to access different levels of frequencies. During these session images appeared and she found herself meeting with a variety of entities, Pam called them guides, or ascended masters.

She also learned from Pam that what she visualised in these excursions was given to her in the language she could understand from her education. Entities appearing in the form of characters derived from fairy tales, myths, history and literature enacting small performances in her dreams and visualisations which carried underlying messages.

Pam told her that there was a wider range of languages in the universe that at the moment she would not be able to interpret, that is, decode.

Michael on one of his visits confirmed this to her. He told her that it was a language in a symbolic code, not words. That it was the language of the universe. He told her to think of herself as a computer, that her DNA was writing the picture on the screen but the universe, the source creator, was the mother board of the computer, the overall organiser of the data. The language it transmitted was understood by symbols through sentience.

He had told her.

"You originate from the Pleiades, your DNA comes from them, you are a Sentient-being primarily, and have not been subjected to the tampering by the Visitors or the Halqu."

The landscape they were travelling through suddenly became shadowy, passing through valleys with high cliffs either side. The colour of the earth had turned to a reddish gold and was sand. They turned off the main road and wound their way across the valley, through small villages and then came to an entrance with a sign saying that the road beyond was closed. There was a small building on the side. Maddy assumed that probably they had reached a tourist site that was closed at certain times and that the building was an information point.

It was obviously closed today as the place was dark and seemed to be deserted. Michael got out of the car and was able to raise the pole and let Simon drive their car through. He replaced the pole which would deter anyone following them.

The road they were on narrowed gradually and turned into a grassy track. They wove their way through vegetation and overhanging trees for some distance and she began wondering exactly where they were going. With all the sand around she wondered if they were anywhere near the sea as she began to pick up a peculiar smell.

"What is that funny smell," she asked.

"Sulphur, it is coming from deep in the earth, there are fissures all around us. Also this area and for miles around is well known for its thermal springs. It's quite an attraction for health purposes. People come from all over to go to the spas."

Maddy was beginning to think she was seeing things as she thought she saw figures darting in and out of the trees but could not really get a good glimpse of them.

"Am I imagining it or are there people hiding in the trees and undergrowth, watching us?" Maddy asked.

"Yes, the fact that you can see them shows that your vibration has risen considerably, so all your hard work has paid off.

The entities you see are, to give the closest description I can, a fairy like people who live here, they can't be seen unless you have a particular attunement with their vibration. They are perfectly harmless, they live merged with their surroundings so they can pass through the vegetation quite easily and hide themselves. They are called the 'Igigi' which you may find interesting to know is Sumerian for those who see and observe. They have a purpose, to watch and protect the vegetation and minerals of the Earth and guard the entrance to the Valley and all it contains.

They are harmless though they can present as threatening— they are only harmful if you give way to fear, that is what empowers them to act sometimes, especially if they think you are going to damage the environment. They are in commune with the spirits of plants and have a special language with every plant."

The car drew up at what looked like a huge natural archway. Maddy could see however that part of it had been hewn out, probably to stabilise it. Behind the archway was a dark cavernous space.

Michael opened the boot and took out a brown paper package which he gave to Maddy.

"It is a present but something that you will need on the day. Perhaps you would like to take a look at it, and try it on just to get the feel of it."

"Are we going in there?"

"Yes, this is where we are going to be on the day of the Alignment and the ritual will take place deep inside this cave."

"I have to tell you that I have never been very happy about going underground, it makes me claustrophobic. I might have a panic attack."

"That's why you have been given the cloak, see what you think."

Maddy by this time was shaking out what was a cloak made of a very unusual fabric. She saw that it was deep purple in colour but woven with a metallic looking thread.

"Try it on," Michael invited her.

She swung the cloak around her and immediately felt a lightness pass over her body, her head cleared and what had been a rising panic in her about entering the cave disappeared. It was also warm, a comfortable temperature around her. It made her feel invisible.

"Have I disappeared or something?"

"No, but it is possible that people less attuned would not be able to see you. You are feeling and seeing things through a different window on the world."

"Wow."

Maddy began to feel different, almost enjoying herself, the task and its complexities seemed to dissolve and she found herself feeling excited about the prospect of what was going to happen.

"Well I feel ready now."

"Good, but we have to wait for the gatekeeper before we enter. It is not possible to pass through the entrance without him releasing the barrier and also he will ensure that the lights are powered for us to make our way inside."

Maddy was looking around.

"I don't see any barrier or cables or anything that would provide energy."

"The caverns we are going into are lit by crystal energy that comes from deep in the planet and links with the universal energy grid, a connecting line. The Ancients used this energy and it is free once you know how to link with it."

At that point a person appeared out of the darkness of the entrance. Maddy found it difficult to describe him to herself. He was small and curled up, his head tipping to the side seemed too big for his body and also bald, although looking closer she saw that it was covered with a fine layer of wispy grey hair. His body seemed awkward and he walked with a stick, hobbling from side to side as if one leg was longer than the other. His body seemed twisted and his clothes looked as if they were far too big for him. He had piercing blue eyes and a large mouth with lips that seemed to have spread out over his face.

He greeted Michael with an inclination of his head and a gruff hello, putting his hand out to shake. Michael took his hand in his right hand and then covered it with his left and shook it. They seemed to have some kind of bond that transcended words.

"Well my friend, here we are with the day drawing close and your job will soon be over."

"Can't say I will be sorry, it would be good to return home after all this time."

"Are we all set?"

"Yes, it's lit. I will stay here just in case you have been followed. I doubt it as I have not picked up any interferences."

"Good, well we have only come for a preview so that Maddy can be more at ease on the day. This is her."

He turned to Maddy and beckoned for her to step forward.

"This is Joab, he has been the gatekeeper here for many years."

"Pleased to meet you, how many years?"

"Ever since Malena, your ancestor, came to the area."

"But that's back in the 13th Century which means you have been here for 800 years, that's not possible."

Maddy, astounded, stepped back, her mouth dropping open.

"Let's go!" Turning to Pam and Simon who had hung back while these exchanges had taken place, Michael beckoned to them to follow. The party advanced towards the cave entrance, Maddy with them. She was looking back at the gatekeeper somewhat in awe and he held her stare.

They entered the cave and towards the back a narrow passage appeared, its walls glowing iridescent, changing colour as they walked through. They went deeper and deeper into the earth and eventually came to another cave.

This time, however, it was not dark, the walls ceiling and floor glowed by what Maddy could only think was a pink translucent crystal. The whole cave seemed to have been hewn out of the crystal which made up the rock, or earth of the whole area.

Michael said, "Here we are, this is where it is going to take place, in this chamber."

In the middle of the chamber was a sarcophagus, a huge structure made of pink stone. Michael explained to her that it was made of alabaster.

"As I told you alabaster was always known to have special properties. It was thought to aid the decomposing of flesh after somebody had died. However its most important quality is that it can hold and transmit frequencies.

Perhaps you are not going to like what I am going to say next. You will lie in it. Your presence in it and the frequency of your DNA will enable you to transcend and meet your co-workers, your sisters on the day of ascension. Together you will be able to open the doors and portals and at the same time break through the net the Halqu placed on the Ancients grid. That way Ascension will take place, the planet will ascend along with its inhabitants and in turn Earths position in the universal grid will enable the universe and its counterparts to ascend also.

Think of it, it will start a trend where there are no wars, there will be amity, healing. The Halqu will remove themselves from the Planet as they will have no control and they will also have to answer to the Ancients. It will be a complete restoration of the natural evolution of Earth and emanating from this a healing frequency to the whole universe."

Maddy pulled the cloak around her closely as she felt a tremor go through her. She could not understand why she felt a sense of foreboding as if something terrible was going to happen.

"Do you want me to try the casket out now," she asked Michael.

"No I don't think that will be necessary. I just wanted you to have the experience of the place before the actual day."

"Well, perhaps that is as well, I am feeling a bit apprehensive."

"You still have work to do on the meditation techniques, but you are nearly there."

"Shall we go back then?"

Maddy took off the cloak and handed it back to Michael. As she did so the feeling of apprehension engulfed her and driving back she was very quiet as were the others. She was beginning to understand what they meant when they talked about waking up. In the previous weeks she had experienced many glimpses of her past lives. Some were terrifying, involving torture, burning, drowning but others were wonderful. Once she had felt her very being torn away from her when dying at the end of a lifetime that had involved a relationship that had been with what she could only describe must have been her soul mate and which made her think about Colin. That experience had left her depressed and thinking deeply about what it meant to be alive and that the pain of grieving was of such intensity to make her want not to live again.

One dream, however, had made itself especially prominent. It was a dream once she grasped it in her memory that she realised she had had many times throughout her life. It was that of what she called a white world, where everything was white.

Dreaming …

Dressed from head to foot in white I met a group of people on the platform of a white station. Everybody was dressed in white and they were chatting amicably to each other and we boarded a white train. The train travelled at high speed to a white station and we were greeted individually by Stewardesses dressed in white who took us to white rooms. In my room was a young female…

It was at this point when Maddy woke up and was left wondering whether the person she met in the room was her mother, or her daughter.

***

Malachi and Isolde stood in front of Nammu and some Mareschal. They also noted that there were other beings hovering in and out of sight at the perimeters of the chamber. *Obviously Ancients*, Malachi thought.

Nammu had assumed the appearance of a Roman Senator with a wreath of laurels around his head and a white toga.

"You have done well Malachi, and you too Isolde."

Malachi bowed his head in acknowledgement.

"We can see the potential outcome and it is promising, however you still have to put this key in place."

"It is going to plan," Malachi responded.

"Maddy is remembering and there is now no barrier in her understanding her role. She has had some apprehension but we have devised a means to overcome her fears and that is working well."

"Excellent, then go and re-energise, the time is on us."

Nammu disappeared, melting into the atmosphere. Looking around Malachi sensed the Ancients having left already. Turning to Isolde he indicated that they should leave and do as Nammu had told them.

***

Chapter 32
The Alignment

All the events of the past months, and thought Maddy her life, seemed to come to a climax today. She went to make her usual early morning cup of tea and was surprised to find Pam in the kitchen.

"I woke early thinking about what might happen today. It's only 6 o'clock, I don't usually wake up much before 9.00 a.m. these days."

"I was always awake at that time until I came out here. It must be losing the hour or something."

"How are you feeling, it's a big day for you?"

"I'm alright, surprisingly though I am apprehensive about what might happen when I am in that casket. I am hoping it can be nothing but good. I am trying to remain positive."

They both took their tea and went and stood on the terrace. The air was lovely and fresh at that time of early morning and the mist over the valley was completely obscuring the landscape, swirling in swathes around the mountain peaks and lower hills.

Later on as they descended the mountain they stopped in the village to pick up some croissants and coffee. Maddy brought them back to the car. Michael did not take any so Maddy, Pam and Simon ate and drank as they continued with the journey. It all seemed very tranquil.

It was about an hour before they began to climb again towards Prades then out towards the mountains, winding their way up the narrow roads and then finally reaching the entrance to the valley. The mist had disappeared by now and the sun was breaking through. Maddy thought there was an ominous feeling in the air, even though the sun was warming up and the sky cleared to a brilliant blue.

As they entered the valley black clouds started forming on the horizon and with gathering speed were getting close very quickly. As they got near to the entrance to the cave it started to rain torrentially, the road behind them became completely flooded and it looked as if a small river was rising along the base of the valley.

Keeping it to himself Michael thought, *we must hurry, the Halqu are summoning energy*. However, he did not say anything to the others as he did not want to alarm Maddy.

Reaching the cave they got out of the car looking at the river that was now running down the valley.

Simon remarked that if it kept raining like this the river was going to be up to the entrance of the cave.

"Is it me or is there a funny atmosphere in the air?"

Maddy asked. It was silent she thought, that was what it was. She could not hear any birds, anything at all, it was completely silent and still.

"You are right," Simon said glancing around. "It's very quiet, no birds, nothing."

Michael confirmed their thoughts.

"When something happens as big as the Alignment, in fact anything to do with the planet, energy mounts, the frequency increases and the birds and animals all sense it and go to find safety until the event passes. You know when things are settled again because they will reappear."

The party filed into the cave passing the gatekeeper and various entities that Maddy could see quite clearly. Strange beings. All of a sudden there was the sound of falling debris and Maddy looked back to see that the entrance of the cave had fallen in and turning to Michael asked what had happened.

"Don't be scared, I closed the entrance because of the Halqu. I can open it again as easily. I was warned by the Ancients that they are nearby."

"How," said Maddy, "and where are they, the Ancients?" Maddy asked, nervously looking around.

"All around us. They are here to make sure this goes well," Michael said as he took her arm and started to propel her towards the back of the cave.

When they reached the chamber Michael took off his overcoat, as did Simon, to reveal robes underneath which were loose fitting and the kind that priests wore, with wide sleeves and high collars that turned out. Michael had a Collar similar to the one that Maddy had been given. She had brought it along as she had been told to. Michael told her to give it to Simon as it was his by right for the ceremony.

Pam helped Maddy into the robe they had given her previously. It was light and as before she was fascinated by the weave which was the same material as the robes of Malachi and Simon. In the crystal light of the cave it shone and sparkled as the light hit it.

Michael and the others helped her to climb into and lie down in the sarcophagus on its raised dais. Settling into the space Maddy immediately felt claustrophobic and her breathing and heart beat increased rapidly. They can say what they like she thought about it being some kind of vehicle for time and inter-dimensional travel this feels to me like a coffin. She wondered whether she should start praying or meditating but did not say anything but just tried to hold it together.

Michael came to the edge of the sarcophagus and leant over, near her head.

"Are you comfortable, good. We are going to start to perform an incantation required to raise the frequency. You will find that you will relax into a meditative state and then that something else will take over. You won't need to worry as your instincts and memory will take over and you will know what to do."

Maddy felt her mouth go dry, but nodded assent.

A calm descended in the chamber, Michael began to chant and was joined by Pam and Simon. Maddy began to relax into the meditative state she had been taught and found her body responding. The chanting changed in nature becoming more rhythmic, pulsing, and having learned something about frequencies she began to notice a change coming over her body which was tingling all over. Then 'zap' she felt her consciousness lifting out of her body and was able to look down and see herself lying in the sarcophagus. But she turned and felt pure light flooding through her, she was floating and free. She became just thought, a 'heavenly' feeling came into her mind, a release.

There was language but no language, just understanding, universal knowledge and understanding, awareness of all things.

Her consciousness, her soul, rose above the chamber and continued out above the planet and she was looking down on and around the whole planet. Her life flashed before her and all her other lives and way back to the beginning, the contract she took. She saw herself with the Ancients, Michael, Pam and others she had encountered through her journey in Earthly time. She remembered everything, all and before, her existence outside of time.

She came back into the 'now', seeing a complex grid woven over the planet, buzzing with connections and complete containment but at the same time the connections going out to the rest of the universe through the moon and then to the planets in the solar system and then further out into the galaxies and constellations. All the time flashing and pulsing. Everything was connected in one immense grid, network, order, no chaos, all held within. At the same instant, she saw another network cast around the grid of the Earth; this was not light or flashing and pulsing. It somehow seemed to be restricting the energy coming to the Earth.

Another 'zap' and Maddy's awareness was taken to her 'sisters', her co-workers; all wearing the same robe as herself. The threads of their robes issuing forks of electricity like lightning, growing in strength and connecting her to them.

Moving to the grid she positioned her consciousness on to what she could only describe as a platform above a crossroad and saw her sisters moving into place in the same way at similar positions all around the planet. A sensation passed through her, quizzically, wondering how she could see around the planet. It seemed a sensation of perception not of sight.

As thy all moved into place she began to see a grid, created by them, forming between them and it began to glow and strengthen.

She knew her 'sisters' remembering them in the beginning when they were all novitiate priestesses in the temple a long time ago. She remembered at the time being renewed, her soul given a freshness to start the journey into the future. She knew also that she was a very old soul prior to that and was one of the Ancients sent to guard Earth and that she had chosen this contract.

Maddy also remembered the 'Cloister of Lilith', that it had been created to protect her soul through to this point of time. And too, that Lilith was the name she had been given at the time of the contract but that before she was '*Ishtar*' otherwise known as '*Inana*' and that she was also a space scientific officer of the universe, just one of her duties.

Seeing her sisters she knew that they were the same and had made the same contract and pacts with corresponding Cloisters. How she loved them, how beautiful they were and her memories of before when there was just love.

Her consciousness prompted her and she was joined to her sisters, she knew that the time before the race of which she was part, and her sisters, thought collectively and that now they were thinking as one. Feelings shot through her ethereal mind as she was linked in with her sisters and they became one pulse.

As one they sensed, Maddy for the first time, the presence of the Halqu, dark, black and saw their net, the restrictive clamps set on to the planet's grid. The pulse was intensifying and reverberating around the planet, the collective resonance of the sisters grew and grew and she found herself shot through again and again with the pulse, tingling and euphoric.

The pitch grew and then reached a point when she saw the Halqu clamps and net explode, shattering like particles of soot, dissipating and dissolving into the blackness of space. As one with the others she found herself generating love and compassion, empathy towards the Halqu and to the negative energies as they dissolved.

Then she felt the Earth shudder as if it had received a shock and its energy turned off then as if it had taken a giant gulp of air she felt it shake off a cloak of grey mist, it was like a shroud exploding off into the universe and like the Halqu's net it dissolved into space. It felt as if the Earth was peeling off layers that had been clogging its function, like an orange shedding its skin, light and colour beginning to resonate vibrantly, predominantly blue and green like jewels that she had never seen before.

Like a layer of light coming away she sensed a loving departure from the sisters and dissolving away down and down and then her consciousness finding herself in the sarcophagus. Then struggling and panicking aware that she was trying to get back into her body. Job done the thought flashed through her as she was gulping for breath and began to scream.

Michael and Simon rushed over to her.

"Stop struggling, let your energy relocate by itself. It is always the way when you have been on a higher frequency. The more you struggle the longer it will take.

It's the same for me and is one of the things I find difficult when I have to come down into your three-dimensional world."

Maddy started to calm down and tried to regulate her breathing. Pam was there and led her into a simple meditation and she found herself gradually slipping back into her body and to some normality.

After a while, white and drawn she attempted to sit up and with Pam's help climbed out of the sarcophagus. Pam took her to a narrow ledge on the side of the cave and wrapped a blanket around her and sat with her. Maddy began to cry uncontrollably, Pam was reassuring with soft words and holding a cup of sweet tea nearby that she could sip.

"I saw everything, I saw everything…" Maddy was sobbing and repeating the same phrase.

Coming back into herself more, Maddy began to gulp and look around her, dazed.

Simon and Michael were walking towards the tunnel, standing talking and looking concerned. They then came over to her. Michael said,

"I am sorry but I have to hurry you, we must get away. The structures and the chamber will begin to crumble now we have done what we had to do. It has all been planned as we do not want the Halqu to access this space in case they are able to manipulate into it time wise and try and reverse what we have just done. We must get back to the Croft."

Feeling that she was recovering, Maddy, helped by Pam, made her way towards the tunnel. Reaching the point that Michael had blocked which led to the entrance they saw him make a symbol with his right hand and at the same time heard him make a small humming sound. The next thing she saw a gap appear amongst the fallen rocks and debris. They all managed to squeeze through and Michael turned and again making the symbol and tone closed it.

In the car on their way back to the Croft, Maddy found herself crying uncontrollably again, utterly physically exhausted. Pam had her arm around her. Malachi asked if she was feeling better.

"Exhausted, but what's more difficult is that I did not want to come back, I have got this awful feeling, it's sad, a sense of loss. I don't have words to explain or express it. Where I went was indescribable."

Michael raised his eyebrows but did not respond.

When they got back to the Croft, Pam helped Maddy into bed as she felt too exhausted to eat or drink. Michael came and sat with her.

"Why do I feel this? I feel sad, this sense of enormous loss, I can't find words to describe the experience."

"It is why we called you the Sentient Seal. Though you sense and communicate by the cells in your body when you are there, you are out of body, spirit.

You experienced what every human could and is capable of; the sense of release from their physical body. They would then not be frightened of dying and see it as passing back into their natural state, for that was your natural state of being."

"I remember who I was, my soul, my journey and where I came from but most of all I felt overpowering love encompassing me."

"Love is all there is," Michael murmured as he passed his hand over Maddy's head and she drifted into sleep.

Michael returned to the sitting room to join Simon and Pam.

"She is asleep. Only time will tell now whether it was successful or not, we must wait and see. There will be a few years to pass before the Alignment passes and the portals close."

Pam was feeling concerned about Maddy as she had never seen any reaction before like the one she had observed with Maddy that day.

"What about Maddy now. I know she contracted to do this but you have used her, or the universal source has. Has her job finished now?"

"Theoretically yes, her total life, physically, reincarnated and soul, has been about today."

"So what happens for her now?"

"She has choices, those will come to her and it is for her to choose."

"What do you mean?"

"She is a very old soul, one of the Ancients. I can't tell you what might happen, only she will know and she will choose."

"And me?" Pam said.

"You have your own destiny which you know of yourself and in the same way it is for you to make the choice you most desire. You have already chosen the path of spiritual awareness so it will come to you what you will choose next."

Michael turned to Simon.

"Well my old friend, how are you. What about you?"

Simon had collapsed into an armchair and had no intention of getting up for some while. He felt very old and exhausted.

"At this precise moment all I want is a stiff drink, if you could oblige? I bought it for Maddy so that I could have it whenever I came. She doesn't drink much but it might do her some good if she had some now." He nodded towards a bottle of whisky on the sideboard.

"Too much excitement for the moment for an old man like me. As for choices. The universe chose my path a long time ago so it can choose again. I am past making decisions or choices."

Michael poured Simon a large whisky and handing it to him said, "I think we might stay here over night as I want to keep an eye on Maddy. Have we got some blankets we could throw over us?" he asked Pam.

"I am sure Maddy has some in the cupboard, I will fetch them. I think it's a good idea. We need to have some rest and I for one don't feel like doing anything and I suppose you are not up to going down the mountain just yet," she directed at Simon.

Michael found himself wondering what to do. Whether he should go and report to Nammu or wait. He decided it could wait for a day or so to let things settle then he would sort things out.

Simon and Michael left Pam and Maddy the next morning and said they would be back to check up later in the week. Maddy was still sleeping but Pam said she would look after her.

***

Chapter 33
Job Fulfilled

Life after that day seemed to settle into an awful restlessness for Maddy; she could not settle to do anything. She had said good bye to Pam who had decided to return to the UK and her projects there, but said she would ring Maddy often to make sure she was getting on all right.

Michael and Simon had said they would be coming up to see her, but the way she was feeling she hoped it would not be too soon as she was still processing all that had happened.

The whole situation, including her break up with Colin had left her now not knowing what she wanted in the future. Her past in the present incarnation seemed to have dissolved and looking back she could not point to a time in it when she had been truly happy. This was, she realised, due to remembering who she was in time and the soul contract she had committed to.

The feelings she had experienced on the day had left her with a longing she could not explain but mainly to exit this present incarnation as soon as possible which surely meant to die. She questioned herself on whether there was more to do in this incarnation and, after some deliberation, she contacted Michael and asked him to come up to the Croft.

***

Michael, or Malachi, as was his real name, had been to see Nammu immediately he had left Maddy and Simon.

He and the guardians were satisfied with what had happened. The portals and locks had been released from the Halqu's net and opened. The planet was now resonating as it should to ascend. There was only one thing that could hold it back and that was if the vibration of the population of the planet was not high enough. This could pull it back.

The Halqu in the meantime, their net having been destroyed and having lost control of the planet, had retreated. For the moment the guardians did not know where but were searching for them; Nammu thought probably to some other planet where they had been carrying out parallel tactics to the ones they had been playing out on Earth.

However, Earth had been freed.

"What about Maddy now?" Malachi asked Nammu.

"Well, that is a question we have to look at. She has had the kind of experience that often leaves a sense of loss, a wish to return to her soul. I know that you have already spoken to her and she has told you that."

"Yes."

"She is not going to be content now and the rest of her life in this incarnation could be difficult because of it. She will always be seeking some kind of experiences to emulate it."

"What do we do then?"

"I will recall the dreams that she has had about going on a journey in a white world to meet someone, she has been worrying that it is to meet her mother or a daughter she lost. She has not lost a daughter in this dimension but in another, so that has created some void in her."

"In another dimension?"

"Yes, remember we had to place a parallel Maddy in another dimension to make sure that in this she kept on track with her contract.

The dreams about the white world and a journey are really about her visits to this daughter. That part of her was needed for the daughter in the other dimension. She needed her mother for nurturing."

"So are we going to take her there?"

"As I said I will recall the dreams and she will begin to remember them and that she has had the same dream since she was in her early twenties."

"It is up to you now to offer her some choices and let her make a decision about which one to take."

"What choices?"

"Well, she can return to the normal course of her life in France, sell the Croft perhaps and return to the husband. Perhaps take some study course on spiritual matters. Perhaps even become a minister in their so called churches. There are many options. The one that you can offer is the opportunity to meet us the Ancients. You realise that she is one of us and it would be as natural for her to resolve to return to us. How we arrange that we will discuss with you once you have had the conversation with her. However, what must be emphasised is free will; she will choose her own path."

"I see. Well, I will get back to you."

Returning to the Croft, Malachi did all that Nammu had instructed him. Maddy, weighing up the possibilities and comparing it with her feelings of loss and the experience she had, decided she wanted to meet the Ancients but before that she felt first she needed to deal with the dreams that she had been experiencing; those of the journeys to the white world.

**

Everything was shining white and sparkling. Maddy stood on the fringe of a group of people. Everybody, including herself, was dressed in white with white luggage and tickets.

A stewardess arrived, all in white with a white hat and uniform, and smiling led them to a white train. It looked supersonic, streamlined. Everyone climbed aboard.

The train moved noiselessly out of the station and the next thing she was conscious of was being greeted by ushers dressed in white on a platform. There were many ushers and they each took a person, one came to Maddy and led her to an individual white room with white furnishings.

Maddy was shown into the room and approached a chair by the window where someone was sitting.

The person stood up and turned around. Maddy felt a sudden rush of completion, as she merged into the surroundings.

**